VISITANTS

Also by Randolph Stow

Novels

A HAUNTED LAND
THE BYSTANDER
TO THE ISLANDS
TOURMALINE
THE MERRY-GO-ROUND IN THE SEA
THE GIRL GREEN AS ELDERFLOWER

Poetry

ACT ONE
OUTRIDER
A COUNTERFEIT SILENCE

For Children

M I D N I T E

Music Theatre

(with Peter Maxwell Davies)

EIGHT SONGS FOR A MAD KING
MISS DONNITHORNE'S MAGGOT

VISITANTS

★ A NOVEL BY ★

RANDOLPH STOW

Taplinger Publishing Company / New York

First American Edition

First published in the United States in 1981 by
TAPLINGER PUBLISHING CO., INC.
New York, New York

Copyright © 1979 by Randolph Stow
All rights reserved
Printed in the United States of America

Library of Congress Cataloging in Publication Data

Stow, Randolph, 1935-
    Visitants.

    I. Title.
PR9619.3.S84V5   1981   823   80-53710
ISBN 0–8008–8018–8

Tispela buk mi laik salim long
wantok bilong mi

T. A. G. HUNGERFORD

AUTHOR'S NOTE

The incident described in the prologue is not fictitious, but was widely reported in the press in 1959. It is discussed by Jacques Vallee in his *Anatomy of a Phenomenon* (New York: Henry Regnery, 1965; London: Neville Spearman, 1966). As I was then out of any sort of contact with the world beyond my own sub-district, I was in no position to connect that phenomenon with the one described to me at the time by the inhabitants of the island of Kitava, nor with the disappearance, a few weeks earlier, of three men from the island of Tuma. Both incidents are incorporated in the novel without comment. Like William of Newburgh, recording a strange aerial apparition over Dunstable in 1189, "I design to be the simple narrator, not the prophetic interpreter; for what the Divinity wished to signify by this I do not know."

It is a pleasure to thank the Literature Board of the Australia Council for a grant held in 1973–4, during the heady early days of the Whitlam government.

R.S.

Be not afeard; the isle is full of noises...
The Tempest

    Oh, my lords,
I but deceived your eyes with antic gesture,
When one news straight came huddling on another
Of death, and death, and death. Still I danced forward;
But it struck home, and here, and in an instant.
...They are the silent griefs which cut the heart-strings...

John Ford: The Broken Heart

PROLOGUE

On June 26th, 1959, at Boianai in Papua, visitants appeared to the Reverend William Booth Gill, himself a visitant of thirteen years standing, and to thirty-seven witnesses of another colour. At 6.45 p.m. Mr Gill, an Anglican missionary, glanced at the sky to locate the planet Venus. He saw instead a sparkling object, "very, very bright," which descended to an altitude of around four hundred feet. The craft was shaped like a disc, perhaps thirty to forty feet across, with smaller round superstructures, and had on the underside four legs pointing diagonally downwards. Uppermost on the disc was a circular bridge, like the bridge of a ship, perhaps twenty feet in diameter.

Behind this bridge, and visible from the waist up, human figures emerged and proceeded to busy themselves with some operation on deck. They bent and straightened from time to time, occasionally turning in the direction of the onlookers, but showed on the whole no interest in anything but their machine. The focus of activity appeared to be a thin blue spotlight directed at the sky. This was switched on at irregular intervals, each time for the space of a few seconds. The figures, seemingly four in all, continued preoccupied with this work for the rest of the night.

On impulse, as one of the figures leaned forward over the bridge, the clergyman saluted him by waving a hand over his head. The figure replied in kind, like a skipper on a boat (said Mr Gill) waving to someone on the wharf. Then a Papuan teacher called Ananias waved with both arms, and two other figures returned the greeting. Encouraged, Mr Gill and Ananias began to wave a good deal, and

1

were acknowledged by all four visitants. The watching Papuans were "surprised and delighted". Small boys called out, everyone beckoned the "beings" to come down. But there was no audible response, and the faces and expressions of the figures remained obscure: "rather like," as Mr Gill said, "players on a football field at night."

The tenuous contact ended with a display of technology by the groundlings, and wistfully on their part. They signalled to the disc with a flashlight. "The object swung like a pendulum, presumably in recognition. When we flashed the torchlight towards it, it hovered, and came quite close towards the ground . . . and we actually thought it was going to land, but it did not. We were all," said Mr Gill, speaking for the thirty-seven witnesses to his testimony, "very disappointed about that."

The craft, after floating above Boianai for two nights, ascended to a great altitude and vanished.

WITNESSES AT THE INQUIRY

held 28–30 November, 1959
before Mr J. G. Browne,
Assistant District Officer, Osiwa Sub-district,
Territory of Papua

MR K. M. MACDONNELL	Planter, of Kailuana Island
SALIBA	A domestic in Mr MacDonnell's household
MR T. A. DALWOOD	Cadet Patrol Officer, Osiwa Sub-district
OSANA	Government Interpreter, Osiwa Sub-district
BENONI	Heir to Dipapa, Chief of Kailuana

I

SINABADA

SALIBA

And he screamed: The house is bleeding. There is nobody inside, he said. But I said: No, *des'*, it could not be like that. A house is strong, I said, and has its own time. You will see, I said; you will see how a house endures.

Thinking of this house, and the far rooms, that voices go into and then you hear nothing, but still they are there.

When first I came from Wayouyo I said to Naibusi: This house is too hollow, too loud. Because a house among palms is like a house at sea, and the leaves are in it all around you, night and day. A house should be like a cave, I said, closed and dark. But Naibusi said: No, that is not the Dimdim custom. They like the wind in their houses, she said, and to look out on the sea, and I think he listens to the palms, because he planted them in the time when he was strong and young.

My house is a conch, he said. By and by it will ring in the wind.

When he spoke to me he was sad. The rain is eating my house, he said. We were outside, in front of the house, and we looked to see what the rain had done, and Misa Makadoneli was shaking his head, a sad man. The wooden walls were the black of rain and the red of rust and green of slime. In the rainy wind the palms were being blown all one way, and were soft like feathers, coloured by the sky.

Grey, he said. See, Salib', my trees are grey.

And your hair is grey, I said, and he moved his head.

All those palms are good for nothing now, he said to himself.

The light falls through the shutters green with leaves. His paths on the matting shine. If you knew nothing of the house, you would

7

know of him from the shine. You would say: There is someone here who walks and walks between the shutters. Someone who leans with his arms on the window-sills to watch the sea.

A house is a conch, he said; and I thought of the sound.

And of other shells, that roar inside like the sea or like palms, but lie in your hand so small and closed and still.

MACDONNELL

Well, I said, let's take a stab with a pin, and let that be where it started. You guess Osiwa three months ago, he guesses Guadalcanal twenty-seven years ago. Plenty of room in between.

Futility. Am I the only one who sees, the only bystander?

If anyone wants to know what I think, I think some people could spend their time more profitably than in humbugging around the islands in a boat paid for by the tax-payer. The *Eagle* they're calling it today. That shows the seriousness of the occasion. I said to the ADO: "Is that your tub from Osiwa, old man, that you're talking about, because we don't know her here by that name. She's the *Igau*," I said, "the *By-and-by*, and very appropriate, too. The only thing that's keeping that crate afloat," I said, "is the magic of an old fellow in Vaimuna, but you wouldn't know about that. Take my advice," I said, "stay at home with your sinabada on dry land as long as you can, and if you can't, then wear your Jesus boots, that's what I think."

The futility. The thing is ended. That was the point.

Why bother at my age with appearances? I know what I feel. Very little, to tell the truth: no shock, no loss, like the young ones. But still something, and what I feel is not curiosity. I'd tell some of them that, if they wanted to know, I'd tell them straight.

The futility.

But they must know, they say, where it began, for the sake of their files. Just a formality, to have it in black and white. And then it will be there forever, lying on a shelf, turning grey.

It is ended. That was the point.

Never did care for the sight of strangers in this room. The starched white clothes, the pink shining kneecaps. Now I notice the dust on everything, smell the rot. The books are dog-eared, I'd forgotten, and things are living in the horsehair that spills from the sofa. It was they who pointed out the cockroaches in the wireless.

8

Naibusi doesn't think of these things, they're not part of her life; but I must keep in touch. Shall I really have to get a new wireless, because of cockroaches?

It's late, late to be thinking of that sort of thing. Yet I must keep in touch.

I'll give you a word of wisdom, I said. If you twist my arm, I'll tell you a lie. That's translated from the Latin, I said. Oh well, then, if you want to know, it all began with the wireless.

Yes. The daily heavenly voices rattling the room.

Yes, those, and the silence. The palms taking over in the sudden vacuum.

And I, at that table above the sea, calling out through the house full of leaves.

A bit nervous, I said, a little excited, not that I expected anything but an evening or two of company, but we lead a quiet life here, and there is the business of food.

So that's how it started, I said. From here, I said. With me shouting towards that doorway, like this: "Naibusi–O!"

BROWNE

The house endures.

Under the palm-fronds, under the wind, signed by rain with marks of a daily kind, like time. It has stained the timber walls with trails of black and slimegreen. The stilts on which the house stands drop pale gobbets of themselves on the chicken-raked mud. In the high wooden steps to the veranda the termites feed.

The palms above the house submerge the rooms in their surf of sound. Creakings and susurrations drop from the air. The palms wander in the bare wooden passages, in the gaunt living room wide open to the sea. Sudden gusts send them streaming, grey-green plumes against a grey-blue sky.

Time has not smoothed or mellowed the fabric of the house. Grey splinters fur the walls of the central room, where maps and ships' pennants fade to a neutral dun. A smell of mildew circulates, from chests and cupboards where clothes, bedding, papers moulder in the hot damp.

The grass mats shine a little in the greenish light from the shutters. They show the path of someone who walks day after day

9

between the windows, who leans day after day on the splintery sills to watch the sea.

A house is a castle; it defends. A house is a conch.

Under the palms, the house lies turbulent and still.

SALIBA

When Misa Makadoneli called to Naibusi she had her hands in water, and I said: "I will go, Naibus'."

"No," said Naibusi, "he will abuse us both."

"I am not afraid because of Misa Makadoneli," I said. And then he called again, very loud: "Naibusi–O!"

"E, go then Salib'," Naibusi said. "If he calls you a fat pig, I will call him something."

So I went running from the cookhouse, across the veranda and down the passage, though he tells me not to run in the house because I will break it.

Misa Makadoneli was walking up and down in the room, by the shutter there, and muttering. He took off his glasses and wiped them on the handkerchief that he wears around his neck. Then he put them on again and looked at me.

"What, taubada?" I said.

"O," he said, "you. Do not shout, I hear you. I do not want you. Where is Naibus'?"

"She is coming," I said. "Already she has come."

He never hears Naibusi, she walks so softly. When she was in the room he moved his glasses again to see her better. Sometimes they stare at one another, Naibusi and Misa Makadoneli.

I think I do not understand the minds of people who are old. But everyone knows what there was between Misa Makadoneli and Naibusi, long ago. So I think when they stare like that they are looking for the people who were young.

"Taubada?" said Naibusi.

"Ki, Naibus'!" said Misa Makadoneli. "You have shaved your head."

"E, taubada," said Naibusi. "It is mourning."

"Truly?" said Misa Makadoneli. "Then who has died?"

"Bakalu'osi, taubada.'

"Ah, my grief for him," said Misa Makadoneli, shaking his head. "He was my friend, that old man."

All the time Misa Makadoneli looked at the eyes of Naibusi, while Naibusi tugged at the blue dress Misa Makadoneli gave her, that is too tight. Under that dress Naibusi's chest is flat like a boy.

"Taubada," Naibusi said, "you called."

"E," said Misa Makadoneli, like a man whose spirit had been away. "Naibusi, the wireless has spoken. Soon some taubadas will come. Make ready the beds in that room and this room."

I called out: "How many taubadas?" and Naibusi hissed at me and said: "Enough, Salib'."

"Two," said Misa Makadoneli. "One is that young Misa Kodo from Osiwa. The other I do not know."

"O," I said, "Misa Kodo. He has a benevolent face."

Misa Makadoneli said to me: "Much you care about his face." But he and the old woman were thinking about other things.

"These taubadas," Naibusi said, "when will they come?"

"Soon. Before night."

"They will bring food perhaps? Dimdim food?"

"Perhaps."

"They might eat chicken," Naibusi said, wondering. "I do not know. The Dimdim yams are finished."

"E," said Misa Makadoneli, "green bananas then. They are the same as potatoes. And *lokwai*."

"They will eat *lokwai*?" said Naibusi. "Perhaps it is not their custom."

"My grief for them," Misa Makadoneli said, showing his teeth that he keeps very often in a glass of water, and that smile at me when I am making the bed. "Go now," said Misa Makadoneli, "see what there is in the cookhouse."

Then Naibusi went away, very quiet, saying: "E, taubad'," very quiet, and I could not hear her feet because of the sound of the palms. But I stayed to ask a question of Misa Makadoneli, who had gone to his table and sat in his chair, though he still looked after Naibusi down the long grey passage.

MACDONNELL

Not really what I expected, in a life devoted to escaping everything, to be left at the end of it the guardian and ward of an old woman with the head of a monk, and a back like a spear hardened in the fire.

11

Ah, Naibus'. You will bury me.

Well, that is something to be thought about, and something I was thinking then, sitting there among the bills and unanswered letters that the *Igau* had given a point to suddenly, and that were speaking to me in a language that cut me off from her. Yes, I thought, something will have to be done. Because how will she live, afterwards?

But the big girl slouched in the doorway was impatient with the silence, and bursting with a question. She screamed across the room: "Taubada."

"Do not shout," I shouted, "madwoman."

"That other taubada, what is his name?"

"I do not know."

"What is he like?"

I put down the pen and settled my spectacles, so that she could see that I was giving her all my attention, noting in passing that her breasts had come a long way since I last observed. "He is young," I said. "Yes, he is young. And very big. And insatiable. His organ is like the long yam —"

"O, taubada!" she shrieked. "O, your shame!"

Modesty struck the house like an earthquake and the floorboards juddered under her feet. She ran away from me, with a boiling skirt, down the passage towards Naibusi, to tell her of the organ that was to come.

"Sea-cow," I called after her. Even a household like mine has its rituals.

When she was gone, the palms returned to the room. I heard a ripe nut plump to the ground, muffled by grass, outside the shutter. At the table I was washed in the surge of palm-sound. But the sea below was still: a pond of turquoise deepening to indigo beyond the islet.

I said aloud, just to hear myself speak English: "Well before dark." And thinking of that, went back to my bills and cheque book, signing *MacDonnell of Kailuana*, as is my privilege.

DALWOOD

When we were in the lagoon it was green, a sort of milky opal-green, but after we rounded the horn of Vaimuna we were on the open sea, and the *Igau* wallowed. So of course I thought of him, wondering if he was sick. The lagoon shores of Vaimuna were lush, all palms, but there on the south coast it is terrible country. Waves from clear across the Solomon Sea pound at the cliffs. The rock is grey, it has teeth like a nutmeg-grater. The pandanus that clings to it is twisted every which way by the wind, and you wonder how it grew there, how it keeps hold. The sea and the wind will not leave the atoll alone. We passed so close that I noticed the silence in the forest. Every few feet there are shafts into the caves below.

The *Igau* had just been painted, she looked fine then, especially out there, on the darker sea. She was white as salt. White is the best colour. The *Eagle — Igau — Sooner or Later*, she is called.

I was always standing there, up ahead. He used to say who did I think I was, the figurehead or George Washington crossing the creek? It was because I wanted to be the first to see everything, and get the wind and spray on me. I used to feel sorry for him, wondering was he sick yet.

OSANA

Mister Dalwood's houseboy works hard. Mister Dalwood's clothes are always white. He is clean like a hospital. He looks as if they painted him, like the boat. I would not like to have blue eyes. They are not natural. I would not like to have big white teeth. They are like shells.

I asked the ADO how old was Mister Dalwood. The ADO said nineteen years. I said: "He is very big," and the ADO said: "You can say that again." I would not like to be big and clumsy like Mister Dalwood. He has the mind of a child.

I said to my wife: "Mister Dalwood is like a young dog," and she laughed. It is true. He was like a young dog with Mister Cawdor. Like a young dog with an old dog, but Mister Cawdor was not old. Twenty-seven, that is younger than I.

Once, on patrol, my feet hurt on the coral, and I said to Mister Cawdor: "I cannot walk any further." He said: "My grief for you," smiling, and told me to go on. So afterwards I used to look at him and say that with my eyes. My eyes said: "My grief for you," smiling, and he looked away.

DALWOOD

I always know when Osana is watching me. Today, in this room, he is watching. And that day, on the *Igau*, I felt his eyes on my back. I knew if I turned he would be sitting there, and so I wouldn't turn, not to give him the pleasure.

A while before I had said, not looking round: "How much longer?"

And he said: "Two hours, taubada."

Just the three words. But I couldn't help myself, suddenly I was face to face with him, looking into those eyes that don't seem to have any depth to them, but are flat and always insolent, in a way I can't put my finger on.

I never knew how to deal with it. I said: "Watch it, Osana."

And he did his usual stuff. "Taubada," very tolerant, drawing the word out, as if I was three years old.

"I won't take cheek," I said. "Just watch it."

And he said: "Yes, taubada," not exactly smiling, but I felt small.

It was always the same, and always I went on thinking and thinking about it. Of him, on the deck behind me. I kept thinking: I won't turn round to see; but I had to, I did again. And he was looking, sure enough, sitting there in a clump of Papuans, but not really with them, lording it over them in his navy-blue shirt and rami that show he's Government. A face like a smacked bottom, my old woman would say.

And then it all went sour. The sea and the trip and going to a new island, it didn't seem to matter, and I felt useless.

It can't be that I hate him, he's not worth it, he's something-nothing. But he poisons the air. And that day, I found myself going away; stumbling over someone's legs, feeling eight feet tall and spastic, the way he wanted me to feel. Scrambling down into the belly of the *Igau*.

What was it I used to go to him for? It can't have been comfort.

OSANA

Mister Cawdor was lying on the bench inside the belly of the *Igau*. A book was in front of his face. Mister Dalwood could not see his face. I could not see his face, either, looking in over the head of Sayam.

"Batman," said Mister Dalwood, in his loud voice, "have you ever noticed, Osana's got eyes like a snake. You can't see into them."

But Mister Cawdor was reading.

"Hey," said Mister Dalwood. "Misa Kodo."

Mister Cawdor's face, that we could not see, said: "Hullo."

Still Mister Dalwood was standing over the bench, with the look of a worried man. The next time he spoke to Mister Cawdor, it was like a question.

"Alistair?" said Mister Dalwood.

It was as if he thought that someone else might be behind Mister Cawdor's book.

Then at last Mister Cawdor began to speak, and said, not bothering with Mister Dalwood's stupid words: "Tim, you know the old *Chinampa*?"

"Sure," said Mister Dalwood, sounding glad, because he is always wanting to talk about boats. "I came on her from Samarai."

"You know what the word means?" said Mister Cawdor.

"Not a clue," said Mister Dalwood. "What is it: Motu?"

"No," said Mister Cawdor, "Aztec," and he sounded glad too. He began to read from the book to Mister Dalwood, about floating islands covered with flowers that are called *chinampa*. I did not think that Dimdims would believe in such things, which are like the rock-men in the sea that ignorant people believe in, but Mister Cawdor sounded glad.

When Mister Cawdor had stopped reading, Mister Dalwood said: "Gee, eh?"

"Isn't that a pretty thought," said Mister Cawdor, "a wandering garden delivering our stores."

"It's a wandering bloody distillery," said Mister Dalwood, "when your order comes. What's the book?"

"*The Conquest of Mexico*," said Mister Cawdor, and I could hear from his voice that he was reading again and wanted Mister Dalwood to go away.

"Well," said Mister Dalwood, "it makes a lousy megaphone."

When Mister Dalwood said that, Mister Cawdor sighed and put down the book, and looked up at Mister Dalwood, who was leaning over him like a big tree. I saw how Mister Dalwood's eyes, when he

15

looked at Mister Cawdor, got round and worried. But I and Mister Cawdor did not think anything of that, because it was something we saw many times.

DALWOOD

He shouldn't have looked like that, at his age. Sometimes, catching sight of him, I'd think: If I could get my hands on them. But he wouldn't have liked it. He told me once I had the temperament of a Nazi animal-lover.

At first he was always taking the piss.

I said: "Christ, you look terrible."

He didn't even mind. He said: "I'm a terrible sailor."

"No, it's more than that. Have you been taking those vitamin pills?"

But he always did think I was a joke, and just laughed, lying like spaghetti on a plate, holding the book to his chest.

Sometimes he reminded me of a horse, a high-strung horse in a storm. His eyes were too big, big brown wild eyes. Underneath there were dark marks, like stains. When he laughed, his mouth was tight over his teeth, and his face creased up like something that had had a long time in the desert, such as Leichardt's boot.

"Do you know what you look like?" I said.

"You've told me. 'Like a middle-aged teenager'."

"I've got a brother of your age —"

"You've got," he said, "more brothers than a rabbit."

"Well, listen: my brother isn't a mess like you."

But that was going too far, or coming too close to him. "We're all dying," he said. "Even you. So stop hanging around me like an undertaker."

"Look," I said, "you've got to be healthy in this job."

He said: "Don't tell me about this job, let me tell you."

He would do that, suddenly, pull rank on me. And it got me down, it never failed. I didn't say anything. I parked myself on the bench at his feet and sat looking out over the sky-glossy water, listening to the wash down the sides. His eyes were on me, thinking about me, but I wouldn't look that way.

"I can't get through to you," I said after a while. "You're killing yourself."

Then for a long time I heard nothing except the sea, and I knew that he had surrendered. So I turned to him to make sure I'd won, to show him my face, that I was serious. "Listen to me," I said.

"Yes," he said. "All right." And he sat up, serious then like me. I saw his face from a new angle, and more than ever he looked sick, sick to the bone.

His eyes had gone to old Sayam, where he stood at the wheel, looming out of a clump of Papuans. Sayam is the sea-god; they are the mortals, buying safety. He stands like an idol, with a crown of wire. You would think the people came to worship him. Every now and then they will give him something, some tobacco or betelnut, and he will take it, but he never thanks them, never looks to see where it came from.

Into the jumble of bodies Alistair shouted a name. He shouted: "Kailusa," and his houseboy jumped up and padded towards us, hunchbacked, in that rami of terrible mauve. His face was what I always thought of as a hunchback's face, tight-skinned and making you think of pain. He glided, Kailusa; always with his eyes fixed on Alistair, timid and stubborn with concern.

"Kailusa," Alistair said, "I want the little medicine box. I'm about to gorge myself on Misa Dolu'udi's nourishing pills."

I watched Kailusa, who never spoke if he could help it, turn away to the stacked patrol-boxes. He stood stooped over them with his brown shining hump pointed towards us, trying to picture everything inside them.

"By the way," Alistair said to me, "here's news for you. I don't seem to have had an anti-malarial for a month."

But I supposed he tried it on to get a rise. I said: "You need a keeper."

"That's what they must have reckoned in Samarai when they sent me you."

We weren't listening to ourselves. We watched Kailusa wavering among the patrol-boxes. He used to depend on remembering everything he had packed, its exact place, but that time he was beaten. "What box, taubada?" he called out, sounding peeved with the world.

Then suddenly he was coming towards me, he was falling at my feet and dragging out a leather suitcase from under the bench.

17

"Oh," he said, smiling with a sort of stiff kink in his face, proud of his memory. "Oh, sinabada's box."

And I wanted to hammer him through the boat and into the sea.

OSANA

Mister Cawdor's face did not look angry because Kailusa had said such a thing. He did not look at Kailusa, or at Mister Dalwood. He said: "The box is mine," and stood up and walked away.

Mister Cawdor went to the arse of the *Igau* and was staring into the wake.

Because I could not hear what Mister Dalwood would say to Kailusa, I climbed to the roof of the *Igau* and went down quietly to sit over Mister Cawdor's head.

I knew why Mister Cawdor was watching the water. He did not want to see Mister Dalwood, who is so stupid and young.

I heard Kailusa give a little cry, and I heard him whispering, or trying to whisper. "No, taubada," Kailusa was saying. "I forget, taubada. True."

Mister Dalwood cannot whisper, he does not know how. He said: "You sure you weren't being clever?"

"I forget, taubada," Kailusa said.

"Don't forget," Mister Dalwood said. "One more time, Kailusa. One more time."

And then I think Mister Cawdor was angry, and he called out: "Tim."

For a long time Mister Dalwood did not come. Mister Dalwood had his hand in Kailusa's hair and was staring at him. And Kailusa was nearly weeping, so Sayam told me, thinking that he had grieved Mister Cawdor.

Then I saw Mister Dalwood's head, leaning over the water as he stood beside Mister Cawdor, and I moved back on the roof of the *Igau*. Mister Dalwood and Mister Cawdor looked into the bubbling colours of the wake and the blue and white road behind. I saw Mister Dalwood's hand come out and take hold of the fishing-line. The line bit into the sea like a bushknife and smoked with water in the sun.

18

"What?" asked Mister Dalwood, very quiet then, so that I could hardly hear him because of the wash.

"Just a favour I wanted to ask," Mister Cawdor said. "Will you mind your own fucking business?"

As soon as I heard Mister Cawdor speak like that to Mister Dalwood, I went running quickly along the roof of the *Igau*, and when I saw in, over the head of Sayam, Mister Dalwood and Mister Cawdor were staring at each other's faces. Mister Cawdor was leaning his elbow on the side, and his face was quiet. But Mister Dalwood's face was red, and his hands moved as if he would hit Mister Cawdor.

"Don't worry," Mister Dalwood said, like someone with something in his throat. Then he went away from Mister Cawdor, very clumsy and angry. I saw him bend to pick up the book that he writes all his letters in, and I knew that he would be coming up to where I was.

I went on watching the back of Mister Cawdor while he stared at the sea. Mister Cawdor's clothes were white and his head was black and the sea was shining. I think now that Mister Cawdor was always lonely like he looked then.

DALWOOD

Of course I called him every kind of bastard. Arrogant ungrateful sod, I said. As if I needed to get mixed up in it. Some day he'll go too far, I said, and I'll knuckle him.

Osana was where I left him, watching a hazy grey lump of island on the horizon. "Kailuana, taubada," he said. Then he seemed to catch sight of my face, and took an interest. "There something wrong?"

I didn't answer. I sat down and watched the island, but couldn't stop myself from breathing hard.

"Mister Cawdor not seasick?" Osana checked.

I knew he hoped Mister Cawdor had puked up his toenails by then, so I said: "No, he's feeling fine."

"Not like usual," Osana said. "I think more better he go to another district. Too many islands here."

"You suggest it to him," I said; wishing he would, wanting to be there when it happened.

I kept thinking: Bastard, that bastard. Bastards, both of them. Some day it's going to blow up between that pair.

Hating the two of them about equally. Hating the country, life, everything that seemed to be ganged up to put me down. Not even the spray and the slap of the waves below could do me any good just then.

But suddenly behind me, the boat-boys and policemen started to sing. Somebody signalled, and they were away, belting out that tune that they sing at every anchorage when we say goodbye to the people. The soloist soared, up in the clouds somewhere, like an oboe against muffled drums.

"*Kayoni, kagu toki, veyogu-u-u* . . ."

Goodbye, thank you very much, my relations, he sings. Goodbye and thank you, my relations. I'm off, I'm homeward bound for Osiwa. Goodbye, my relations, thanking you.

Then they all jumped into the chorus, sharp as cymbals. "*Dumeraka, dumeraka, dumeraka, dumeraka* . . ." they sang, to that wildly jazzy tune which may have been a hymn once, and I could have sung it with them, after those weeks of patrolling. But what would Osana have made of that, behind my back?

They are my age, a lot of them. But I am something special, a *taubada*, a great man.

I twisted my neck to look at them. I saw them all sitting there, still. Their bare knees were drawn up and their eyes were on the sky while they sang. They didn't think about each other, but they were together, doing something together. It seemed a long time since life had been like that for me.

Then suddenly I saw the other one, that I had never seen before. And I felt cold.

OSANA

Mister Dalwood saw the madman. He looked into his eyes, and he was afraid.

They were all afraid when they looked into that man's eyes. So he stared back at Mister Dalwood, as he would have stared at any white man, protected by his eyes.

He said God gave him something. He said they saw it.

His mouth was open a little way. But it was not truly a smile. I knew what he was thinking: This young Dimdim's face is very red. He is very big. He cannot look away from me because he is afraid.

20

When Mister Dalwood spoke to me, in a small voice, the man watched his lips. I know now what he was thinking then. He thought: He talks in English and believes I do not understand. I do not understand everything. In time I will understand.

"For God's sake," Mister Dalwood said to me, or perhaps to himself, "who's that?"

"Which, taubada?" I said, pretending.

"That one," Mister Dalwood said. His finger pointed at the big-eyed man.

Then I looked, as if I had not known before. "Oh, him," I said. "People call him Two-bob. Some taubada name him Two-bob. Because his eyes, you see, like two shillings."

Mister Dalwood moved on his backside, in white shorts, as if the deck was too hard.

"What a funny-looking fella," he said. "Like a zombie."

"What that, taubada?" I said. Because I must learn the words.

"Oh – " he said, the way they say: "Oh" in English, meaning that they do not know what to say. "It doesn't matter," he said. "But why have we got him?"

I was tired of Mister Dalwood's questions, and moved my shoulders, since he was not seeing me. "I don't know, taubada," I said. Then I called to the man, in a voice to make him know that I was Government: "*Um valu ambes'*?"

The man did not look at me. He stared into the face of Mister Dalwood, a long time. When his mouth opened to speak, it was as if he was seeing it open and thinking of it. He said, not to me but only to Mister Dalwood: "*Yaegu* Metusela." When he saw that Mister Dalwood understood, he said: "*Ba ka'ita* Wayouyo."

Then his mouth closed. We watched it close.

DALWOOD

I'd never seen anything like it. They were the weirdest eyes I ever came across. The white went clear about the brown. And he never stopped looking, as if he knew, as if he was trying to put the wind up me.

And yet, it was only the eyes. God knows, there wasn't much more to him. A middle-aged shrimp of a man, with a mop of black curls, in old Army shorts so far gone that you could see the areca-sheath jockstrap he wore as a second line. But so still, as if he hadn't moved for hours. When he opened his mouth, and I saw the betelnut on his teeth and knew that he was going to speak to me, I was scared for a moment, the way you might be scared by noises in the night, even though you know you don't believe in ghosts.

His voice was very deep, very loud. He didn't think much of our Osana.

I said to Osana: "What was that last bit?"

Osana was put out, it was good to hear. "Oh, he just say this," he muttered. "He say: 'My name is Metusela. I'm going home to Wayouyo.' That Dipapa's village, taubada, on Kailuana island. I think he is crazy."

I said: "Sure he doesn't understand?"

"Him?" Osana said, grinning. "No. He nothing. Bush-kanaka," Osana said, laughing, and I was supposed to hear quotes around the words, but they were vicious.

Suddenly he shouted at the man: "*Ku la!* Go away."

"Now listen," I said. But Two-bob, Metusela, just smiled, raising his eyebrows a little, and got up. For a second he looked at Osana and at me. Then he padded away aft on skinny dusty legs.

"Well done, Osana," I said. "That was real sophisticated." Because he made me sick, sitting in his crowd of hangers-on like a Chief Justice. I turned my back on him, and took up the letter in the pad.

A crash-hot patrol, the letter drooled, in so many ways. Because that genius actually spoke the language, and they loved him, especially the old ladies. Whole villages of old ladies all trying to feed him up with great scungey grey yams out of their cooking-pots, and he politely drinking a bottle of rum instead. A hell of a good bloke. Hard to understand the mentality of anyone who could do this to him, such a hell of a good bloke . . .

I took out my pen to revise that, and then put it back. The island was dim and grey across the swell. I thought about the island, feeling my face stiff with salt.

I had known, anyway, all the time, I was stuck with it. He could talk to me like that, and I would still have to work with him, eat with him, travel with him, sleep in the same room. All day and every day, till my first leave, another year. There was no one else who spoke my language.

So I made a resolution, and stood up. As I stepped over their legs, the eyes of Osana and friends fixed on me, hopeful of entertainment. But I didn't fall in, climbing down again into the belly of the *Igau*.

OSANA

People were walking around on the veranda of the *Igau*. The sun was on Mister Cawdor, and the shadows of the people's legs moved over him.

I stood by Sayam, watching Mister Dalwood, who was searching for something. I saw him drag out a green coconut from the pile under the bench. As soon as he had it in his hand, some colours like a lot of parrots flew past me towards him. It was his houseboy, Biyu, wearing that Hawaii shirt that Mister Dalwood's aunt, whose name is Doris, sent to Mister Dalwood. Biyu was smiling and looking like an important man, with a bushknife in his hand.

"Thanks," said Mister Dalwood, and took the knife.

"I do it, taubada," Biyu said.

"Push off," Mister Dalwood said. "I do things myself."

Mister Dalwood hacked at the husk with the bushknife, while Biyu called: "Your hand, taubada," and the chips fell on the boards. Then Mister Dalwood went towards Mister Cawdor, slicing a lid off the coconut as he walked. "Alistair," he said.

Underneath his book, Mister Cawdor said: "Uh?"

"*Bwaibwaya*," said Mister Dalwood, which is number two of the five words that he knows in the language.

Mister Cawdor put down the book and sat up. He did not look at Mister Dalwood. He reached out for the coconut and leaned back his head to drink. The wind blew in Mister Cawdor's hair, which seemed to be very soft like the hair of some Dimdims, and the light of the water flashed on his skin, so that you could see that it was not like the skin of a Dimdim truly and would never turn red in the sun.

"Alistair," said Mister Dalwood, watching Mister Cawdor. "Sorry."

"That's all right," said Mister Cawdor, into the coconut, which echoed.

Mister Dalwood waited. When he had waited a while he began to grow hot in the face, and he said: "Aren't you going to say you're sorry too?"

"No," said Mister Cawdor.

23

"Here, give me that," Mister Dalwood said, and he grabbed the coconut out of Mister Cawdor's hands. "I opened it," Mister Dalwood said. He drank from the coconut until it was empty, then he put it down so as to see Mister Cawdor again.

"I'm not sorry," Mister Cawdor said, smiling at Mister Dalwood. "If you were me, wouldn't you have had enough?"

"Okay," said Mister Dalwood, "so I bungle. You've told me before." He was frowning down at Mister Cawdor and looking uncertain, as if he did not understand Mister Cawdor's mind.

"I know what you thought you were doing," Mister Cawdor said. "To that extent, thanks."

"Fine," said Mister Dalwood, with a serious face. "I'm glad you see it."

Mister Dalwood and Mister Cawdor looked at each other in the way that people half-look.

"I mean well," Mister Dalwood said. "You tell me I think with my muscles, but I mean well. I've been used to having people around me all the time, but here . . . We've got to get on, or nothing will work."

I saw that Mister Cawdor did not think the words of Mister Dalwood were important, though his face was kind. "It works," he said. Then he made his face more kind by wanting to, and said: "Let's have a row, say, every Wednesday."

When I saw Mister Dalwood looking so glad I guessed that he was thinking of those boxing-gloves that he cannot find anyone to hit with.

"You're on," Mister Dalwood said.

Then it was very quiet, and nothing was happening between the Dimdims, and I went to the side and looked at the island. The sea-haze was still in front of it, but I saw the tops of the palms and the sharp roof of Mister MacDonnell's house. So I was glad, thinking of the people and the parties.

But suddenly everybody went running down the boat. The crew, the policemen, the houseboys, they all ran to the arse of the *Igau*. "What's up?" cried Mister Dalwood, using his loud voice again; and he went with them, asking questions that nobody listened to. Over all the people Mister Dalwood waved his head like a tree, asking questions from side to side.

The arms of the people were reaching out to the line, and their voices were crying: "O! O!" I heard Mister Dalwood's cry, one foot

24

above them: "God Almighty!" Then they were all dancing, clubbing the leaping thing that had come into the boat. When their bodies moved away I saw Mister Dalwood crouching over the great fish.

"Jesus wept," said Mister Dalwood. "Isn't that just beautiful?"

The fish was like the tin toys that the children have in the ADO's house. Its belly was silver, its back was black. The sunlight leaned on it and made it burn. The fins of the fish were yellow like bananas, the streak on its side was butterfly-blue.

"Oh God, that's beautiful," Mister Dalwood kept saying, as he stroked it. "Hey, life's beautiful, did you know?"

"Kai for the MacDonnell," said Mister Cawdor. "We ought to take him something."

"How can you talk like that?" said Mister Dalwood. "Here's this magnificent thing come up from the bottom of the sea, and you're thinking about feeding the MacDonnell."

Mister Cawdor had not moved from the bench. He looked down at Mister Dalwood, who squatted among the brown legs, and I saw that he was a sad man, which I had forgotten. Mister Cawdor looked down at Mister Dalwood looking up at him. The sun on Mister Dalwood's face made his eyes small and shiny, and I saw the salt on his red skin. Because he was out of breath he showed many teeth, and he was laughing also.

"I was never so young in my life," said Mister Cawdor, and shook his head.

Then Mister Cawdor turned and leaned over the side to look at the island, which had turned from grey to green. Over his shoulder he said: "I can just make out the house," in a voice that sounded as if he did not care.

MACDONNELL

I had dozed in my chair, and woke slowly, bringing to the surface with me the memory of some sound. A breeze had come up, through the shutter, moving my hair and carrying with it a complicated sweetness. Fifty years I've been smelling it, crushed and warm from their bodies, yet can't place in my mind all the scents from my childhood that return. Anise? Lemon verbena? Thyme? No, scents are themselves. *Sulumwoya.*

25

The sound from my sleep came again, a scuff of bare feet. "Oh, you," I said, over the back of the chair.

Saliba was at the shutter, staring down on the sea. "Already they have come," she cried out.

The fresh sprigs of sulumwoya were wilting in her arm-bands. On her breasts a garland of bwita flowers looked pale and smelled heavy. There was a hibiscus flower in her hair. The dye of the red-and-yellow skirt had hardly had time to dry, and the skirt stood out from her hips in layer on layer, the work of weeks by the glare of the Tilley lamp, in this room. I saw that she could after all look graceful, and like her dead mother, and realized that she herself must all the time have known.

"Who will look at you?" I said, polishing my glasses.

"*Ku sasop'*," the girl said, meaning that I was lying, or was joking, or was honestly mistaken.

"Misa Kodo will not see you."

"*Ku sasop'*," she said again, and pulled a face. "Besides, I do not like the Dimdims."

"Oh," I said, "a black man, is it? A mainland man, a *polisimanu*."

"Ssss," she said. "I do not like those policemen." Then she exclaimed: "*Wa*! He is very big."

"Who is big?" I said.

"That one," she said, pointing at the sea.

I got up from the creaking chair and came to stand beside her at the window-place. By the islet the *Igau* lay at anchor. Two outrigger canoes that had hoisted their basketwork sails to make use of the sudden breeze were moving away from her, and in one of them a white man stood squinting under his raised hand at the house. Against the dun-coloured sail his clothes were dazzling.

"That is Misa Kodo?" I said.

"No," she said, scornful, drawing out the word. "You are a blind man. Misa Kodo is not so big."

"I am not a blind man," I said. "I am not a deaf man. *Ku sasop'*, Salib'."

She smiled, tolerant, all her attention on the canoes. As soon as the beach palms hid them she flared about and ran for the veranda. She was there, intent, and in the post of honour, when I came out with my hat on.

"Move," I said to her. "This is my house. Here I am commander." I took my place at the head of the splintering wooden steps.

26

"But old," I said, to her who believed it more easily than I did. "*Mtaga sena tomwoya.*"

BENONI

When people heard that the *Igau* was coming they went down to the beach-path. I was at Misa Makadoneli's house, speaking to the old woman Naibusi, and I went with them to see Misa Kodo, because I thought he was my friend. I stood by the path among the others and watched the people from Osiwa coming up from the beach. In front of them all walked Misa Kodo, because he was the leader, and behind Misa Kodo came a very big young Dimdim who is not truly a grown man yet, and is called Misa Dolu'udi. Misa Dolu'udi walked like a good-tempered man who was eager to go to a place. But Misa Kodo walked as if his legs were heavy.

When they came out of the shadow of the palm-grove they passed close by me, and in the sunlight I saw two or three white hairs on Misa Kodo's head, which was black, and the light shining on the hair which he had on his arms, like all the Dimdims. I was standing among other people, but taller than any of them, and I smiled at Misa Kodo. But he did not see me, and walked on, and my mind was heavy. When he was here before I said: "Are you my friend?" and he said: "Yes, truly," and gave me tobacco. So then my mind was heavy, because I thought he was my friend.

As Misa Dolu'udi passed me he stopped and looked back. He stepped out of the line and stood by the path, watching the other Osiwa people. Behind him was Osana, the interpreter of the Government, and behind Osana two men from the boat-crew were carrying a big fish on a pole. After the fish came a man with eyes like a fish, and Misa Dolu'udi was looking at the man and frowning.

Misa Dolu'udi spoke to Osana. "Has *he* joined us?" he said.

"Who, taubada?" said Osana, like a man talking to a child.

Misa Dolu'udi looked angry for an instant, then he said: "Two-bob. He's back there."

"He is walking home to his village," said Osana, "if I may make a suggestion."

"Well said," Misa Dolu'udi told Osana. "That was a good drop of English you turned on there." Then he turned to go away, but higher up the path he stopped again and stood watching.

27

The fish-eyed man went past me. I did not know who he was, or which his village could be. I had never seen him before, but his eyes and face made me feel strange.

Misa Kodo's boy was a hunchback, his name was Kailusa. On the steep path he walked like a crab, with his arms spread wide. His face looked as if something hurt him. He stared uphill all the time, towards his taubada.

Behind him I saw Biyu, wearing a Dimdim shirt of all colours. "O, Biyu," I called. "How are you? What are you doing here?"

"O, Benoni," Biyu said. "Does Dipapa exist? If not, are you chief of Kailuana?"

"He exists," I said, feeling angry with Biyu, who smiled too much.

"Nowadays I am Misa Dolu'udi's boy," Biyu said. Then he looked up the path and saw Misa Dolu'udi standing aside, gazing down, and he stopped smiling and grew worried. "Why is my taubada looking at us?" he said. "Did he call?"

"No," said Kailusa the hunchback, not caring about Biyu's taubada. "He is looking, that is all."

"Like a lizard," said old man Sayam, the skipper of the *Igau*. "He stares like a lizard. Go on, go on, little police-master."

"Not little," Biyu said. "Big. Very big."

"Little," Sayam said. "Later on he will be a grown man."

"Truly?" said Biyu, laughing. "Then we shall be afraid, as in the days of Dokonikan."

"I shall not be afraid because of Misa Dolu'udi," said Kailusa. "He is like a child."

"You lie," cried Biyu. "My taubada is strong, very strong. Your taubada —"

"Enough!" shouted Kailusa, swinging round towards Biyu. He had eyes that were hot and wet. "You shall not speak like that!"

Biyu muttered also: "Enough," and looked uncertain, because the hunchback was so passionate.

"Enough, both of you," Sayam said. "Go on, Kailusa. *Tonagowa*," he added, loud enough for Kailusa to hear. "Defective one."

And I saw Kailusa's face, which Sayam could not see, go stiff, and as he walked on he whispered: "You shall not speak like that, Sayam."

The people from Osiwa passed, carrying the boxes and all the other somethings that travel with the Dimdims. I thought: I do not think that I can talk now to Misa Kodo about my affair. Because of Misa Kodo my mind was heavy. I believed he was my friend.

DALWOOD

So the people turned out to line the path, staring at us, talking about us. And Misa Kodo strode on. A tall young bloke tried to catch his eye, but he didn't notice, and the bloke felt put down, I saw that. I thought of saying something, but then I thought: There is time. Ahead of me Alistair walked loose and mechanical, like a tired man with a job waiting.

I stood by the side of the path, watching the line. When I turned to follow, Alistair was gone. A clump of hibiscus bushes had hidden him at a turn in the path, and over the leaves I caught sight of the roof of the house, half-buried in palms. So I hurried to catch up with him, as I always did, because he was the only one who spoke my language.

Once round the bend, the house sprang up in front of me, sudden and close at hand.

I remember, before I came to this district, asking someone one time: "What happens there?" And he said: "It rains." Seeing the MacDonnell's house, on that clear evening, I felt surprised, as if it should have had its own cloud a few feet above the palms. Rain was written on everything, fifty years of rain. The wooden walls were grey with it and the edges of the iron roof had turned to rusty lace. Under the floorboards pigs were rooting in the mud and rubbing flakes of wood from the rotting stilts. Beyond, between the stilts, I had a glimpse of the old man's village: sago-leaf houses, grey-brown and rain-stained, fuming with smoke like steam. Cottages around a castle, I thought. And it *is* a castle: a sad mouldering castle that some day soon will collapse, as suddenly as Jericho, with a slow dank crunch into mud and leaves in the rain.

But then it was in the yellow-green light of a clear late afternoon, that made the most of the green in the palms sweeping over the roof. And somewhere in the grove two birds were calling, two of the little butcher-birds of these parts, echoing

29

the way in a plantation things do echo and hold on. It was the kind of evening when you feel that you could let all your thoughts go and empty yourself, and sit listening to your own silence like a shell.

So I came out of the sunlight, to the sodden grey house in the gloom of the trees. Steep grey steps led up from the rank grass to a veranda as deep as the building, dividing the kitchen quarters from the rest. Shadowy up there, silhouetted against a glow from behind, Alistair leaned on a veranda-post and talked to someone his body hid.

I looked at the steps, which seemed to have been built, like the island, by coral-insects, and thought that the heaviest man on the island was certainly me. With an eye on my feet, I went up to the veranda pound by pound.

And that way the MacDonnell was laid out for me, when Alistair moved away, from bottom to top, by instalments. There was first of all the MacDonnell's Army surplus boots, then a pair of puttees with nothing worth mentioning inside. Eighteen inches of pale pipe-cleaner legs got lost in flapping khaki shorts like a kilt. I followed up a narrow column of grey flannel singlet, and came to a pink silk scarf tied loose round a chicken-neck. Then I was looking into the MacDonnell's face: thin, old, innocent, with perfectly round blue eyes behind perfectly round glasses. On top of it all was a greasy grey businessman's hat. As I watched there was a sudden commotion in the air, and a white cockatoo came out of nowhere and skidded to a halt on the crown of the hat. In a high feeble voice it said to me: "Popu."

CAWDOR

That p.m. on the veranda, sea in front, jungle of pink frangipani behind. Inevitability. 50 years he has been here. TD's eyes on stalks at the sight of him. Yet the island took him in & digested him almost at first sight.

Think about that. The receptiveness. So many visitants coming, none that anyone knows of ever driven away.

Think about the history. A riddle, but one can guess.

1st. The mountains in the sea. Perhaps sudden, perhaps a storm of lava and steam. But time quietened them. Sea and wind, rain and ice.

Then birds, seeds, floating fruit, uprooted trees. Green. Coral in the shallows, silt and sediment in the lagoon.

Then the mountains sinking back into the sea, the coral struggling upward. Earth and seeds from the mountains lodging in the coral reefs, and the reefs becoming islands. The mountains disappearing, the ringed atolls left behind.

Then the earth, it must have been, heaving again, and the seas pounding. The coral walls breached, the lagoons rejoining the ocean. Water boiling through today's dripping caves. And the islands one after another going down, till Kailuana stood alone.

Can't even guess when people first came to Kailuana, how they came, where from. Probably in canoes blown by storms, lost and frightened. Perhaps the first were men without women, hunting, gathering food for a while, dying, leaving nothing. Or perhaps they did leave something: the megaliths. Because wouldn't I, if it was me, even if it was me by myself, want to build, leave a sign? And the sign, here, would have to be something simple, something like flat coral slabs stood on end.

But more must have called and passed on, and spread the news of Kailuana. So settlers then, with wives, food-plants, livestock. Making their gardens and burying their dead. Simple people, the first ones, but the next wave more sophisticated. They took the fruit-trees and pigs of the earlier people, declared themselves an aristocracy, made the others stoop. Because, they said, the world is divided into four clans, and we are the top people. So everyone in the world knew his place, and things went tidily.

Try to imagine all that when the first ship, the French one, bore down under full sail. The terror. Yet they coped, they cope with everything. "The world is divided into four clans." The Frenchmen fitted, they parted friends.

And the same, next century, with the sailors, traders, missionaries, Government officers. They dropped in for a day or two, never came back, but they fitted. And the same, fifty years ago, with young MacDonnell and his partner. They arrived and announced that they owned the islet. Nobody sweated. It was all in the scheme of things.

It's a comforting institution, that scheme of things. When the Japs dropped a bomb on the MacDonnell's copra shed, Kailuana laughed. Not that they wanted to see the MacDonnell done out of anything, but a copra shed exploding, that was funny. No one said: "What about me?"

Keep thinking about time, vast stretches of time, so as not to think: "What about me?" Where was I when the mountains came out of

31

the sea. Seize hold of that moment, concentrate on it, meditate on it. Then I know where I stand with time and it doesn't matter. It doesn't matter. Alistair, Alistair, she said, it doesn't matter. Don't think about it, it doesn't matter.

MACDONNELL

The huge pink youth stared and stared at me, with the bird on my hat, and I took him for a fool, as so many of them are; but he was never a fool, only innocent, a little innocent, as he thinks I am too, and he told me so one night, on the veranda, in that very place. He stared and stared at the bird, and then the wind-burnt face opened up on the big teeth and he said: "Do you always wear that?"

"Not if I can help it, old man," I said, "but he comes to have a look at the visitors and I don't see him coming. Go away, Popu," I said, shaking my head, and the bird flew out screeching into the grove.

"I am Dalwood," the boy said. "I go around with Misa Kodo doing good."

"Yes, I know," I said. "Popu means excrement. The women named him that because of his habits in the house. I am MacDonnell. But call me Mak. Where has Cawdor gone?"

"He is there," Dalwood said, and I turned and saw Cawdor at the other end of the veranda, looking down on my village, against the thicket of frangipani glowing pink in the last sun.

"Cawdor," I said, "you haven't introduced us, old man."

"Sorry," Cawdor said, coming back to us, his skin very dark. I used to wonder if there might be a touch of the tar-brush there, but that is not possible, he was a son of the manse, a dark Scot. "Tim Dalwood," he said, "the MacDonnell of Kailuana."

"Do you want a rinse, old man?" I said to Dalwood.

"Do I want a what?" he said.

"If you need to pumpship," I said, "do it over the veranda rail, planter's privilege here."

"'Pumpship'," Dalwood repeated. "Hey, Batman, listen to the words."

Cawdor said, looking absent: "Mak's always a year ahead of *Time* magazine with the slang."

"I haven't been off the island for seven years, old man," I said, "or out of the Territory for fourteen, and I haven't spoken English,

32

except to the wireless, since the *Chinampa* came three weeks ago, if you want to know."

"That's fantastic," Dalwood said, and I saw his fingers playing with the strap of the camera that he had slung over his left shoulder (is it part of the uniform of the new breed?) and his eyes arranging me in some grotesque pose, and waited for him to say: "Do you think I could —?"

"Do you think I could take a photo of the house?" he said. "And, oh — maybe you wouldn't mind —?"

"Please yourself, old man," I said, "but not me, not now, it's my time for a shower. No, you sit yourselves down at the table there, Naibusi will bring some rum. Cawdor, look after him, give Naibusi a shout." Then I went off to get out of my clothes, because it was six o'clock.

I heard Dalwood behind me spluttering and then choking with stupid laughter that he couldn't swallow, and Cawdor saying, half-laughing himself: "Where are your manners, you ape?" And the funny thing was that I felt rather pleased with him, the boy, for laughing at me that way, because I used to be like him at his age, and even later, when I first came to the island. But of course he couldn't have conceived of that, no one can conceive it, except sometimes Naibusi when she stops and looks.

DALWOOD

We sat at a table with a scarred plastic cloth on it, looking down on the sea, which was changing colour, and the dimming *Igau* by the islet. The palms kept up a slow sweeping on the roof, and the white bird somewhere out of sight was swearing to itself in one of those instant rages that cockatoos can turn on. A pawpaw tree beside me leaned in and drooped its fruit on the veranda rail. I thought of tight green breasts.

Corny. But that was the sort of thing I thought then a lot of the time, and thought it must be the same for him, not understanding that it was not that, never simple like that.

But then he was laughing and looked at home, at ease, the way he sometimes was when we were among new faces and not at home, and I thought perhaps, perhaps when we get back to Osiwa, this time, it will be over and he'll be like he was before, however that may have been.

He saw me looking at him, and scowled. "You still doing a project on me?" he said. Then he caught sight of something behind me, and his face went sort of gentle, and he stretched out an arm.

"O!" he called. "Naibus'."

An old woman in a blue dress, with her hair cropped to the scalp, came towards us over the veranda carrying a tray. A rather beautiful old woman, I remember thinking: very straight and young in her walk, her face worn and fine. She put down the tray on the table, and then did what I never saw any other woman do in these islands, held out her hand, and he took it and kept it for a moment, smiling into her eyes.

"How are you, old woman?" he said in the language. And she murmured: "*A bwoina wa'*, taubad'. I'm just fine."

"That is Misa Dolu'udi," he said, nodding my way, and she turned and bowed, taking me in for a second with deep eyes. "This is Naibusi, Tim, the woman of the house."

I said: "Hullo, Naibusi," and she murmured: "Taubada," bending to the tray and beginning to put out the things on the table. I saw that there was a bottle of O.P. rum there, with glasses and sugar and water, and a withered lemon on a plate that said *South Australian Government Railways*.

"But where is Saliba?" Alistair asked her. And as soon as the name was out, something violent happened in the passage leading to the cookhouse, an explosion of shrieks and giggles, screams of: "*Ku la*, Salib'!" Then there were sounds of fisticuffs on yielding surfaces, and one girl kept yelling out at the others. "*Inam!*" she shouted, and "*Wim!*" Then the force behind her had its way, and she came shooting across the veranda, still swearing, like a giggle-powered rocket.

"Saliba!" Misa Kodo sang out.

She was wearing all the flowers for miles around and smelt like a rich funeral, and had on arm-bands and leg-bands and red coral beads and a new skirt that seemed to be giving her a lot of trouble to control. She must have got dressed up for somebody, but it wasn't for Misa Kodo apparently, because when she saw him opening his arms for her all she had to say was: "*Kwim!*"

"Slut," he said. "Tim, this is Saliba."

She turned to look me over for a moment, the big motherly teenaged bosom thrusting against the flowers, and I thought I made out in her something that was in Naibusi too, a sort of restfulness.

34

Noisy as she was, quivering with bottled-up noise, there was a seriousness there too, in the plump blunt face and the eyes that seemed to be happy with everything they saw. I thought that somehow she was different from the rest, maybe not so pretty as the rest, but fuller, and kinder, and the only young one, probably, whose name and face I'd be able to remember when I'd gone.

Then he began to tell her something in the language about me and about the tax, how I'd come to help collect the tax, and she turned away from me and squatted down at his feet to listen, the fibres of the banana-leaf skirt parting over her thighs. But she was still thinking about me, I saw that, and it was some remark of hers to do with me that made him suddenly burst out laughing, and explain: "Saliba's the clown of the house." The other girls were laughing too, and began to press around us, and the hot sticky air was suddenly full of crushed sulumwoya leaves.

When the MacDonnell pushed his way through them on his way to the shower, none of the women turned or noticed.

"Hey," I said. The MacDonnell was stark naked.

"Got a drink, old man?" he sang out. "Help yourself. I'll be there in five minutes."

"Do you always get about like that?" I said, taking him in. Among the brown garlanded girls he was white like a woodgrub, and something of the same texture.

"All born in the house, old man," he said, waving at the girls. And he went off, with everything explained, at a jiggling trot, and disappeared on the cookhouse side.

"Good skin, hasn't he?" Alistair said, looking up for a second. Then he went back to talking to Saliba, having some conversation that they must have found pretty funny, because the dark creases kept coming back to his face and she quaked all over with that gurgling laugh. Rough, boisterous, tender. I thought what a household, and what might not happen in such a household, watching the girls, feeling tight.

Now all that evening seems so far away and sharp and bright it is as if I am watching through the wrong end of the binoculars and am outside but it is still going on. I drank too much and laughed till I got laughed at over jokes in a language I don't know. The cockatoo came home and sat on my head and cursed and screamed at Saliba, every feather on end. Mak joined us, dressed for dinner in striped pyjamas, and we ate chicken and yams and the leaves of some tree by

35

the light of a Tilley lamp that dropped fried insects on every plate. The palms turned blue, and the sea turned mauve, lilac, violet; the islet like a lump of coal floating on it, at the side of the ghostly *Igau*.

When we came afterwards into this terrible, dead, no, dying room, I did not notice what it looked like, there was so much talk and light. All the women came with us, the girls and Naibusi, to smoke and sing and make garlands in the hard white glare, the fireside of this house. They sat propped against one wall with their legs stretched straight ahead, teasing the old man, giving Alistair the local news, ogling me.

"O, *sena toveaka*," they said, making the shape of me in the air with their hands. "A very big man."

"Yes," I managed to say, "yes, truly, a very big man, me." Then they screamed and exclaimed, and I felt brilliant, because I was drunk with everything and still drinking.

And Alistair kept drinking too, and I saw him easing, coming to life, as if he was in his own house again after a long time away. It was when he was like that they opened up for him, they adopted him, like a clever kid or an amusing pet, with a kind of crooning. Well, they are sentimental; and I am sentimental too. We are treacherous, we sentimentalists, but I haven't known that long.

MACDONNELL

I had stopped drinking when I noticed it was seven o'clock, but Cawdor couldn't keep his hands off the bottle, and I wondered if I ought to do something, drop a hint or go to bed. Of course I hadn't heard then, I hear no news, but I saw that when he seemed to relax he was actually tightening, and could tell that Naibusi felt it too, the few things she said were so soothing. I should think the prodigal son was like that at first, too eager to please. But whatever the old woman and I thought, the boy thought that everything in the world was perfect, and he sat beaming, drinking himself asleep.

"Sunday tomorrow," I said. "No tax-gathering on the Sabbath. The idiocy. How much is it going to cost us to have you squeeze five bob a head a year out of these people? I'll tell you something, old man, if it wasn't for me buying copra there wouldn't *be* five bob in the villages. So what would you send to Konedobu then, coconuts?"

"It's the principle," Cawdor said. "They're calling it evolution towards self-government."

I turned and spat, not that it's a habit of mine but to make a point, through the open shutter, towards the ghostly palm-trunks that the lamplight dragged inwards from the dark. "Anyway," I said, "what are you doing tomorrow?"

"Well," he said, "I thought we might go to Kaga. Tim, shall we go to Kaga?"

"You'll see some self-government there," I said.

"Yes," he said, "that's what I wanted to talk to them about."

"This is great," the boy said, slurred. "This is the life. We say to Sayam: 'Take us to Kaga', and away we go. It's as good as being a pirate."

He laughed, and all the girls looked up at him, over their garlands and cigarettes and half-made skirts. "His legs," one of them said. "*Wa!* Like the piles of a yam-house."

"You watch out for Sayam," I said. "A vindictive old bugger, that one. There was an ADO at Osiwa one time, a friend of mine, very decent fellow. Sayam found he was breathing down his neck a bit too hard, so he made up a story about some funny business with Government stores. The next thing I heard, that ADO was out. That's what Sayam's like, old man, so don't say I didn't warn you."

"He manages the boat," Cawdor said, "I manage the rest. We don't clash."

"You clash with Osana," Dalwood said. "The slimy bastard."

"Osana," Saliba said, with a bray of contempt, and the boy glanced up eagerly and laughed at the tone in which she said the name. They seemed very pleased with each other suddenly, and I thought how young these white boys are, how long they go on being young, while she, at sixteen, was already mature and would soon begin to thicken.

"Mak," Cawdor said, "may I say something to you, you have the most extraordinary library. I can see both Kinsey Reports, and something about six inches thick called *Sexual Deviations*. How could you even know these things are in print?"

"To tell you the truth," I said, "it's because of that foreign fellow, that ethnographer, as he used to call himself, the one who wrote all the stuff about Osiwa. I forget what his name was, but he got it all wrong. So I've decided to write a book myself, and I can tell you this, old man, it's going to hit the world like a bomb. I've read Casanova and I've read Frank Harris, and they hadn't heard half of it. Of course it's a bit late, I'm seventy-four, wish I'd thought of

37

it earlier, but people ought to know these things, and they're not going to unless I tell them. So that's the reason for the racy stuff — I'm studying."

But Cawdor was hardly listening. Saliba had begun to pelt him and the boy with frangipani flowers, and the other girls had joined in, and he was looking at them, very steadily, as if trying to work out some problem in his mind.

"There's a lot of study we could do here," he said, towards Saliba rather than to me. "On the megaliths, for instance. Why are they there, who put them there? Are they temples, or what are they? Do you make anything of them, Mak?"

"Not a thing, old man," I said. "People here say their ancestors put them up, but I don't know about that. I think it was probably a different people altogether, but I haven't had any particular ideas about them."

"I think people who were fey," he said.

"'Fey'," I said. "Haven't heard that word for years. Well, you're a Scot, too, I suppose, with a name like that."

"Doomed to die," he said, still to Saliba, one would have thought. "When people were fey, their character was supposed to change. Mean men became generous, changes like that. I've always imagined some very ordinary blokes being marooned here and realizing that they'd never get away, and changing. Starting to know things about themselves and their place in the set-up. Getting a bit desperate, probably, but also — I should think — reverent. I can see them putting up those stones as an act of worship: not of anything in particular, but just worship. And to show that they'd been here, to leave something behind. Maybe they even thought of the stones as a signal for help."

"Never struck me that way, I must say," I said. "Very ordinary lumps of coral rock, I've always thought."

"Oh, yes, but," he said, "they didn't get there by themselves. And that may be the only message."

"All very interesting, old man," I said. "Nine o'clock, my time for bed. Are you turning in?"

"If I have to," he said, turning round at me and shrugging. "I know the laws of the house by now."

"Well," I said, "not such a bad place to be, bed." And was going on, dropping my voice: "I say, old chap, are you planning —" when he brought me up short.

38

"No," he said. "I'm sleeping alone, thanks."

"Oh, well," I said, "in your case —"

"And so's the kid," he broke in, nodding towards Dalwood. "Or I'll have the bastard up in front of the ADO."

"Please yourself, old man," I said. "Times have changed. Many's the ADO who's had his outlook broadened in this house, but enough said."

And then I was getting up to go and pumpship off the edge of the veranda, wondering what would become of the country when even the patrol officers were turning into missionaries. But suddenly all the women flew at me screaming like birds, and knocked me back on the sofa beside Cawdor again.

"*Avaka?*" I shouted at them, just as Dalwood, lurching to his feet, bounded into the middle of them.

"Fire!" bellowed Dalwood.

I said to Cawdor: "Which one this time?"

He leaned forward to see, and said: "It's Saliba. Seems someone dropped a match on her skirt."

"O, her new skirt," Naibusi cried. "O Saliba. Never mind."

"Salib'," Cawdor called out, "we will buy you a skirt in Wayouyo."

But Saliba was too busy to hear him, wrapped up in a battle which had been going on all this time between her and Dalwood. The boy was beating at the burning skirt, and she was shrieking: "Go away with your hands, ravisher!"

"I think he knows, old man," I said to Cawdor. "I think he's been there before."

He turned his head, with that peculiar, guileless expression on his face and laughed at me. "Ah, Mak," he said. "You're so abominable, you're irreplaceable."

"We're all irreplaceable," I said. "The Bible tells us so. As for abominable, I don't know what it means."

In the middle of the room Saliba broke away from Dalwood and ran for the passage, holding the blackened stubble together with her hands. From the doorway she screamed one word at Dalwood, who stood, huge and bewildered and pleased with himself, like a lighthouse among the waves of grass-skirted women.

"*Tokakaita!*" she shouted. "Insatiable fornicator."

Then she thundered away. We heard her laughing as far as the veranda steps.

SALIBA

That night Naibusi woke and called for me. She called from inside the hut: "Saliba, are you there?"

"Yes," I said. "I am here, outside the door. I cannot sleep."

In the light of the moon the house was nearly white, with black lines. The trunks of the palms were white too, and the branches were like feathers, white and black.

"What are you doing?" Naibusi called.

"Nothing," I said. "I am looking at the house, that is all. Misa Dolu'udi has put out his lamp."

Naibusi rolled over on her mat and laughed, inside the dark hut. "*Ki!*" she said; "you cannot sleep because of the young Dimdim?"

"*Ku sasop*', Naibus'," I said. "I cannot sleep because I am crying for my skirt."

"I have a skirt and will give it to you," Naibusi said. "Now come and lie down. It is the middle of the night."

"Very well," I said. "Thank you truly, Naibus'." Then I said: "Naibus', Misa Kodo cannot sleep, like me. He has not put out his lamp."

As I told Naibusi that, Misa Kodo came to the window of his room. He was there all black against the light of the lamp, looking out. I thought that he was looking towards me, and stepped back quickly into the door. But truly he could not have seen me, and why would he have tried? No. He was only standing there, staring out, with his forehead on the glass of the window that does not open. And all the time a big black moth that came from the frangipani flowers was beating and beating against the glass to get in.

DALWOOD

When you wake the air is already clammy, the sheet sticks to your back, but if there is a breeze your skin when you get up clenches as if with cold, and you feel new because the morning is so new. In this room, with the shutters open on the sea, there is always that dawn breeze, always the sound of palms, so that you hear the coolness at the same time as you feel it crawling over your hide. And that is the reason,

I suppose, that the old man is up and about before anybody, and wanders in here to lean on the sills and watch the sea.

When I opened my eyes he was there. I woke because he was there, and I lay in the musty camp-bed taking him in by the grey-blue light. I had to remember him, he was still strange, still a bit weird to me then. Stooped in front of the shutter, in shorts, with dead-white delicate skin, he made me think of some fragile kid, the kind that might grow up to be a genius if the big kids allow him to survive. That is the look he must always have had, of being breakable. I can guess that because I have seen his son, the only child, after all, he has ever fathered, who is as pretty as an angel and nearly forty.

I got up to join him, the grass matting cool under my feet and the breeze that had swept the night heat from the room cold on my sweat. When I came to the shutter beside him, he started and jerked about.

"*Avaela?*" he said. His eyes seemed for a moment as big and round as his glasses, baby-blue. Then: "Oh," he said. "Yes, yes. Young Dalwood."

"Sorry. I thought you'd heard me."

"Getting a bit deaf, old man," he said. "Forgot you were here, as a matter of fact. Sleep all right?"

I told him yes, stretching and shivering a little in the air from the wide shutters. "You don't stay long in the sack."

"It's the only time of day," he said, "for old men."

The rank grass under the palms was warming up with the morning, and the smell of it came in puffs into the room. Butcher-birds called and echoed. In spite of the breeze, the sea, of that turquoise of calm lagoons, looked congealed, like ice, and the white *Igau* sat fast in the mirror of her own shadow. On the islet behind her the palms in grey-green waves dipped and rolled.

"Campbell and I planted that lot," said the old man, pointing. "Fifty-one years ago, it must have been. Before your father was born, I dare say."

"Campbell?" I said. "Who is Campbell?"

"My partner," he said, "once upon a time. He stuck it out for a year. Then he took a trip with a trader, haven't heard from him since. Funny way to treat a friend."

"Perhaps he died," I said.

"Yes, probably. It was easy," he seemed to remember suddenly, "to die in those days."

I looked round at him for a clue how to take that remark, and went on looking. Apart from his glasses and Bombay bloomers he was naked. I thought of the White Rabbit, skinned.

"So he came with you in the beginning," I said. "The two of you built the house."

"No, we had a camp then," the old man said, "on the islet. But he would have, of course. We meant to, if he'd come back. I waited a fair time, a year, I think. Then I crossed over the lagoon and built here."

"Just you by yourself? You and the Kailuana people?"

"There was one foreigner, my houseboy, Naibusi's husband. He was a mainland man. But no white man, no. There's never been another white man on Kailuana."

All that time he went on gazing at the islet, as if it was a place he could never get to again.

"You must have missed him," I said. "Your partner, Campbell."

"I suppose, at first," he said, not much interested. "Because, you know, he was a white man. But soon that didn't matter. When I built the house, I meant it — d'you know? — to show him that I wouldn't need white men any more."

He had not sounded for some time as if it was me he was talking to, but all of a sudden he turned his head and glittered at me, through the thick lenses. He bared his mail order teeth. "You're a white man," he said. "Cawdor's not."

"What am I supposed to make of that?"

"Almost not. Not for much longer."

He was looking very significant. I pored over the tight old face, trying to make out what he might be hinting. "I don't get you," I said; and the bottled eyes, still on me, seemed to become for a moment almost fatherly, almost concerned. "I wouldn't," he said, "invest too much in Cawdor. He's a hobby with you. But he's going away."

"Alistair?" I said. "You're joking. Going where?"

"Just — away," the old man said, with a shrug. "I don't know how else to explain it." And by saying that he must have thought that he had rounded off the conversation rather neatly; and, besides, he was finished with me and the sea. "None of my business, after all," he said, wandering through the splintery room towards the

42

passage to the veranda. "Can't be bothered. That's what age does, old man, if you want to know. No curiosity any more."

"Mak," I said, "what are you getting at? Has he told you he's going?"

But he only called back from the doorway: "Kaikai on the veranda in half an hour." Then I heard his bare feet scuffing off over the grass mats, and was left staring at the last thing he had passed by, his little library of advanced sex, which it had been a mistake, apparently, to see as a sign of curiosity.

SALIBA

Benoni and Naibusi and I were sitting on the veranda beside the table where the Dimdims eat their food. Naibusi and I sat on the floor, but Benoni was sitting on Misa Makadoneli's chair, because he is of the family of chieftains and must keep his head above ours. But he was not proud, and had brought us betelnut which we were chewing, and talked to us while he smoked a cigarette.

Naibusi was cutting up sticks of tobacco very fine with the bread-knife. She was putting the shredded stuff into a Dimdim tobacco tin.

"Old woman," said Benoni, "I want a stick of tobacco."

"Not one stick," said Naibusi. "That is forbidden."

"Misa Makadoneli does not count all his tobacco," said Benoni.

"Truly, he does," said Naibusi, laughing. "But it is not his tobacco. Misa Kodo will smoke this here."

"No!" cried Benoni, showing his teeth. "Misa Kodo will smoke trade tobacco?"

"Yes," said Naibusi, "always. And he chews."

"I think," said Benoni, "I think that Misa Kodo is one of us. Some people say that he is a black man truly."

"That is gammon," I said. "His face is dark because of the sun, but I have watched him under the shower, through the hole in the cookhouse wall, and his arse is white like shells."

"Your shame, Saliba," said Naibusi.

"Why should I not watch the Dimdims?" I said. "All the women watch the Dimdims. Wa! Misa Dolu'udi has a cock as big as this."

"I have a cock as big as this," said Benoni.

"You lie," I said. "Let me see."

43

"*Ku la!*" cried Benoni, putting up his hands and pretending to be frightened. "I am not a *polisimanu*." All the men in the villages pretend to be frightened of the women in Misa Makadoneli's house, because of that night last year when we tore off the rami of a mainland policeman and raped him.

"Saliba," said Naibusi, "you have a bad tongue."

"I have not a tongue as bad as Misa Kodo," I said. "He knows that we watch him from the cookhouse when he is under the shower, and he turns his back and shouts shameful things."

"What does he say?" asked Benoni.

"I will not tell," I said. "His shame, to talk like that to a woman."

"Truly," said Benoni, "you are a crazy person, Salib'."

He leaned his arms on the Dimdims' table and yawned, and then stretched his neck to look over the veranda rail at the *Igau* below. In his hair he had a hibiscus flower, and on his chest the boar-tusk necklace that is worth more yams than a man could count.

"I am bored," he said. "When will Misa Kodo get up?"

Benoni is a most beautiful man. If he would sleep with me, I would tell everyone from Muyuwa to Dimdim.

"By and by he will get up," said Naibusi, still chopping Misa Kodo's tobacco, and rubbing it between her palms and packing it away. "Let him sleep. I think he is ill."

"He is different," Benoni agreed.

"I will speak to him," Naibusi said. "I will tell him he should swallow quinine, then he will be well."

I was going to say something to Benoni, to make him laugh, about Naibusi and her Dimdim magic, when I heard the old man's feet in the passage, dragging a little on the mats the way that they do. So I hissed to Benoni instead: "*Ku la. Misa Makadoneli bi ma.*"

"Truly?" whispered Benoni, and he stood up quickly and was going to go away down the steps. But Misa Makadoneli came suddenly out of the passage and saw him.

"You stay," Misa Makadoneli called out, and he sounded angry, because he has made this law that nobody may come on his veranda unless he says yes. "You stay. What man are you?"

So Benoni did not go away any more, but turned at the top of the steps to face Misa Makadoneli, looking very beautiful and tall against the sea.

44

"I," he said in a loud voice. "Benoni, taubada."

I looked at Misa Makadoneli, who is so little and shrivelled and white and old, and wondered that he was not ashamed to stand before Benoni. But he was not. He was only angry, and you could see how he hated Benoni. Because Benoni had been away to the Navy at Manus and spoke Pidgin and was respected in every village and did not respect Misa Makadoneli.

"Benoni?" said Misa Makadoneli, looking very fierce, and for a moment his glasses flashed like windows in the sun so that you would have thought he had eyes of fire. "What do you want here, Benoni?"

"I want to talk to my friend," said Benoni, "Misa Kodo."

"Talk with him in the village," said Misa Makadoneli. "I do not wish to see you in my house." Then he stretched out his arm, which is like the shoot of a yam before it has escaped to the light, and said: "Go, adulterer."

Benoni just smiled at Misa Makadoneli. "Very good," he said, but still his back was turned to the steps.

Then Naibusi spoke to Misa Makadoneli. She did not look at him, and her voice was so quiet that I did not think he would hear, yet he heard. "Taubada," she said, "do not abuse him. He is a good young man, and later he will command all the villages."

"That man?" said Misa Makadoneli, pointing at Benoni like a turd on the path. "He will command nothing. His uncle has said it, Dipapa has said it. He is unclean. He has slept with his uncle's wife."

I shouted at Misa Makadoneli: "Taubada, you talk gammon. Dipapa is too old to sleep with a woman, and Senubeta is an age like me. That old man has never slept with her. He did not marry her for that. He has thirteen wives so as to have fifty brothers-in-law to fill his yamhouse. I do not understand your mind. Do you want Senubeta never to have a man? I think truly she did love Benoni."

"Saliba, enough," said Benoni, sounding ashamed because I spoke of such things, and I think also because he did not any longer love his uncle's wife.

"Yes, truly, enough," said Misa Makadoneli. "Go to the cook-house, Saliba, to your work. You are insulting. And you, Benoni, go to your house, if you have a house. I know that Dipapa forbids you to live at Wayouyo."

"You are wrong, taubada," Benoni said, and he smiled at Misa Makadoneli. "My house is again at Wayouyo. My uncle has forgotten — those doings."

"I think you are lying," said Misa Makadoneli. "Dipapa told me you will never command the villages. He told me that when he dies there will be no chief. Dipapa is the last chief of Kailuana. Like me. I am the last King."

"That is my uncle's word, taubada," Benoni said; "but it is not my uncle's affair."

"Ssss," said Misa Makadoneli. "So it is your affair, *ki*?"

"Taubada," Benoni said, "while my uncle is alive, he talks. While you are alive, you talk. When the time comes that you do not exist, that my uncle does not exist, you will not be talking, you two. If the people want a chief, there will be a chief. If they want a Dimdim King, there will be a King. The villages do not hear dead men."

"Do not quarrel with him, taubada," Naibusi said. "That is not gammon. Everything will be different when we are not here, you and I."

But the old man was passionate because a black man had spoken to him so proudly, and because he does love the people and wishes that the villages should always be like today and like yesterday. It is craziness, the craziness of old men. Better for him and Dipapa that they said in their mind: "We shall not command in the time when we are at Budibudi." But they hated Benoni's thoughts, that he brought from Manus with his Pidgin, and their desire was that when they were dead the villages should turn to stone.

"Benoni," the old man said, "go. You shall not speak with anyone in my house. You shall not walk on the ground of my village. You are not of a chief's family, not now. You are a commoner and a shamed man. Go to your house."

But Benoni still smiled, and talked to the old man in a gentle voice. "Taubada," he said, "do not be afraid because of me. I am a benevolent man and like your nephew. Now you understand my mind."

Then Benoni turned and went down the steps. I saw his thighs, and then his shoulders, and at last his beautiful head, shining against the sea.

DALWOOD

I went down the passage and knocked on Alistair's door. A grey door, like all the rest in the house, furry as a copper-stick, set a little askew in a grey wall.

I was still hot with the MacDonnell, for he seemed to be one more who thought that life was all way above my head, and by then I would have liked the chance to say some of the things I was muttering in my mind. Such as that it was tough on the young, this generation-gap, because by the time I was his age and fit to be talked to, he would be a hundred and twenty-nine, and all that much more experienced.

I heard Alistair behind the door shout something in the language, thinking probably that it was Naibusi or Saliba, and lifted the rust-eaten latch and went in. The window of the little room, the only one in the house with glass, was not built to be opened. The air held the heat of the day before, and it smelt of mildew.

He lay on yellowed sheets, in a grey bed, puffing the smoke of his nailrod tobacco at a ceiling that was a mirror-image of the floor. He lay inside a cube of grey boards whose lines went round and round him like a cage. I thought that if it had been me, I would have been out and away from a room like that as soon as I was conscious. But not him; he sprawled there in his underpants like a zoo animal that had given up.

"You sure you can breathe?" I said.

He turned his head on the yam-coloured pillow and just looked at me, impartially, in a way I was used to.

"You don't like it here?" he said at last.

"Yeah, I like it. Man, it's interesting."

"Good. You ready for Kaga?"

"Well, I've showered and so on. I don't see any feverish activity in here."

"It's the Sabbath," he said, leaning over to an up-ended kerosene case beside the bed and stubbing out his cigarette in the clam-shell that was there for the visitors. Then something caught his eye through the dusty window, the light on the pink frangipani flowers outside, and he lifted his head and looked at them, intently. He would do that. His eyes all of a sudden opened to something, his face changed. He concentrated like no one else I have ever seen, on things I never saw at all.

"Nice," he said. "Wish the window would get broken. The flowers might kill the mould."

47

"Alistair," I said, "why would Mak think that you're going away?"

He looked round at me over his shoulder, still with that intentness on his face. "Mak said that?"

"He said it. But it's not true, is it?"

"You know it isn't," he said. Then he turned his head again, but I heard in his voice that he was smiling to himself. "Mak thinks I'm going troppo."

"So do some people at Osiwa. If you'd just take some sort of ordinary care of yourself —"

"Ah, the people at Osiwa," he shrugged. "What would they do without me to talk about?" He rolled back on the pillow and examined the ceiling, his hands behind his head. "Troppo," he said to himself. "*Ma non troppo. Agitato ma non troppo.*"

"What are you raving about?"

"*Troppo,*" he explained. "Too much."

"I know what it means," I said. "Jesus, you talk to me as if I was some bush-kanaka just come in from the back of Wabag."

"All right," he said, "if you know so much, have you ever heard a piece of music marked *troppo agitato?*"

"I don't think it's possible," I said.

"I think it is. I want to hear it. At the end, all the instruments would be in bits."

"I'll bet it's been done," I said.

"Ah, but this would be tropical," he said. "I can see it," he said. "The glue would melt in the heat, and the wood would warp, and the strings would rot away with damp and snap, one after another. The brass would turn green, and mildew would be growing on the woodwinds. When it was finished, the instruments would be thrown in a heap, and they'd begin to sprout and turn into the trees they were made from. And reeds and vines, and the wind would blow through them and the birds would come. That part I'd mark *finito*, or *troppo troppo.*"

"You know something?" I said. "This is a University-refectory-type conversation you're having."

Then he made the noise that he made sometimes when I actually got through to him, that went something like: "Wo-o-oh," grinning at me from the pillow and looking pretty much like anyone else.

Watching him, I tried to remember what he had been like when I first set eyes on him. Was he better, had I done him any good? And it seemed to me that he was, that I had. Because that first evening he had been far gone, like one of his cracking instruments, ready to fly apart. I remembered standing by a shutter in the big room, our living-room at Osiwa, looking out on the lagoon in the last of the light, hearing the voices in his bedroom. I listened to Kailusa trying, in the language, to persuade him to come out and take delivery of me, and to him saying, I could guess pretty rude things about the snotty-nosed cadet he'd never wanted to have and had tried to keep away. At last Kailusa came back with the lamp into the dim room, and said to me: "Taubada come, taubada," and I looked and he was there. His stockings were round his ankles and his hair was on end, and his eyes were like that man Two-bob's, Metusela's, so wide that they showed white around the brown. Even at that hour, six in the evening, he had a bouquet of rum. For a long time, half a minute, we stared at each other, with Kailusa between us holding the lamp, and the first thing I thought was: he's dangerous.

But that morning, in the MacDonnell's mouldering spare room, before we left for Kaga, he looked simply tired, no longer wild inside. And I thought: He's got used to it, he's going back, to the way it must have been before.

"Tim," he said, "you *want* to go to Kaga, do you?"

"You know me, I want to go everywhere."

"It's not work," he said, "just a Sunday drive. I found something in an old patrol report I've been planning to ask them about."

"I won't understand a word," I said, "but I'll get to see Kaga."

"That's my boy adventurer," he said. "Listen, you go and have kai, then check that Sayam and the crew are ready to leave. And chase up Osana."

"Ah, shit, Alistair. Do we have to take Osana with us, even on a Sunday?"

"Yeah, we do. Otherwise his belly will be red-hot. It's called diplomacy."

"Okay," I said, "I'll sort it," letting him see my martyr's face through the closing door. "Oh, let me tell you something that's in store for you: the MacDonnell's small-house."

"I know it well," he said. "A man of your size ought to get danger money."

49

"There's a pit in the coral that goes clear to the centre of the earth, and it looks like nothing's keeping the seat up but the white ants holding hands."

"That's the way the MacDonnell's going to go when he goes. Poor old bugger, what a tomb."

That must have come over to him as a vivid picture, because when I left him he was lying back laughing, looking about twelve years old.

A gust of wind came down the passage as I turned from the door, all the scents of the morning on it, the sea and the grass, frangipani flowers and chickens, the leaves that have every smell between vanilla and hay. On the veranda I filled my lungs with it, the sweetness and saltness of the island after dawn. I sat at the table by the edge of the veranda and gazed down, through the rough flapping leaves of a pawpaw, on the bright lagoon, and the spotless *Igau* that was going to take us through all that freshness to something fresh again.

From where I was I could smell ripe pawpaws among the leaves. Then another scent cut across that, and I looked round and saw the girl behind me, the greyish sprigs of sulumwoya withering in her arm-bands.

"Hi, Saliba," I said. "Have a good night?"

The English words must have meant something to her. Her face, which might be plain if it ever had time to be, began to beam good will, and she laughed all over.

"Good," she said. Her voice is deep and high at the same time, coming from the back of her throat. "You good, taubada?"

"Good too much," I said. "Saliba, you me go long Kaga?"

"E-e-e-e," she cried, giving wild nods of her head, skirt and everything. "*Bi ta los'*," she said, which I knew by that time meant: "Let's go."

In her hands was a tray which she held pressed hard to her diaphragm, with two breasts on it and half a pawpaw on the plate that said *South Australian Government Railways*. She came beside me and put down the tray on the table. As she reached to set the plate in my place, I leaned down and rubbed my cheek against a brown susu.

"Taubada!" she yelled, and leaped away, nearly shapeless with giggles. "*Kam mwasila*!"

Then we looked each other over, quite a time, I innocent, she modest as a flower.

50

She must have been searching for the words, and at last found them, and murmured shyly, in English: "Taubada, you fuck off."

SALIBA

O, Kaga. O, the sea that day when we went to Kaga. The wind all the time blowing over the *Igau*, the frigate-birds following. The shouting and the bustle of the people going to Kaga that morning. And Timi telling me with his eyes that he wanted me, and I saying, by looking: I do not know, perhaps.

All the people were singing. Even Alistea, Misa Kodo, he was singing with the people, lying on the roof of the *Igau*. And the people lit a fire at the front of the *Igau* and cooked yams in a pot, and Timi and Alistea ate yams with the people. Osana said: "Soon Misa Kodo will puke like Mount Lamington," but Alistea did not, he sang.

And when we came to Kaga, under the cliff, it was like flowers and lories in the water. The sea was like the window in Misa Makadoneli's house when we have washed it, and the corals and the fish were different from in any other place, so bright, because the water is not so clear in any other place. And the people of Kaga were shouting on the cliffs and scrambling down their ladders, and jumping up and down on the rocks, full of joy and not truly able to believe what their eyes saw: a Dimdim boat, with Dimdims, and tobacco, that none of them had smoked for two years.

When the dinghy was in the water Alistea and Timi got into it. I was still standing on the veranda of the *Igau*, looking at the corals and the fish, and I was getting ready to jump and swim. But Timi stretched out his arm to me, and said: "Saliba, *ku ma*." So I put my hand in his hand and looked down into his face, which is not beautiful but was kind then, a Dimdim's face, red, with sky-coloured eyes, very strange. I held his hand and looked at his face turned up towards me and was frightened suddenly, and thought: He will not look after me, he will not care. But he smiled at me with his big teeth, and I thought: This is a benevolent man truly. So I jumped down into his arms and sat in the dinghy where he pointed, and I and Timi rowed to Kaga side by side.

OSANA

The people of Kaga are more ignorant than a pig. They know

nothing, they see nobody. No white man goes to Kaga, it is too far, and there is no beach and no anchorage, and besides no water and no food. They live like gulls or crabs, those people, drinking coconut-milk, eating fish. But a long time ago some white sailors came and taught them to smoke tobacco, and now always they sit on the top of their cliffs biting their fingernails and saying: When will we smoke again, this year, next year, ever? O, they say, our desire is very strong that a steamer should come, full to the deck with tobacco, before the year after next. And because once, all that long time ago, they gave chickens to the sailors and had tobacco for their reward, they care jealously for the chickens that they do not kill, and gather up and hoard the eggs that they do not eat, and it is a crazy place. There are more chickens on Kaga than there are people, and more hens' eggs in the grass than nits' eggs in the people's hair. They were idiots always, but I did not know how crazy until Mister Cawdor, reading from his book, began to ask questions. And then everybody knew, and those madmen of Kaga were ready to jump off their cliffs with shame.

When we came ashore from the dinghy the old headman of the village was still climbing down the ladder, and I thought he would fall and break his neck on the rocks, he was in so much hurry for the tobacco he expected Mister Cawdor to bring. He came down the palm-trunks and the ledges like a monitor lizard. They can only come to the sea by those notched palm-trunks, the Kaga people. Their village is up above, in the centre of the island, which is hollowed like a bird's nest. That is where they scratch around together, trying to grow tobacco and stealing it from one another as soon as a leaf shows above ground; and that is where they came cackling from when they saw the Dimdim boat. Or perhaps Mister Cawdor was right, that they began to run long before, when they smelled his cigarette.

They are very poor, those people, it is disgusting to see them, so poor and ignorant. The men did not have a rami or a pair of shorts among them, not even the headman. Every man was dressed in a yavi, without even a leather belt or a twist of cloth to hold it up, and their ignorant manners and the way they said their words made me laugh.

52

"Taubada," I said to Mister Cawdor, "how do you say yavi in English?"

Mister Dalwood said: "Bulletproof jockstrap," and grinned at his joke, whatever it was.

On the little piece of beach, under a mango tree whose shadow covered all of it, the Kaga people came panting to meet the Dimdims. They came bent to the ground, and crouched low at the Dimdims' feet, because to people like that any Dimdim is a greater chief than Dipapa, and no common man's head is allowed to be as high. The old headman crouched among the rest, and looked up at Mister Cawdor as if he hoped to become his wife.

"Taubada," that old man said at last, "the people are very glad." At least, that is what it was in his mind to say, but he spoke it this way: "The peopen an vanny ganad."

The headman talked only to Mister Cawdor, and looked only at him, because anybody could see that Mister Cawdor was the leader and would have the most tobacco. But the other men hardly looked at Mister Cawdor, even for politeness, they were so amazed by Mister Dalwood, and everywhere I heard them whispering and exclaiming that the young Dimdim was like a house.

"Yes, truly, my nephew is like a house," said Mister Cawdor, "but he is a child yet, and will grow. Later on he will be as tall as Darkness-of-Evening, the yam-house of Dipapa."

That was the kind of nonsense that Mister Cawdor talked in the villages, and he thought too that it was nonsense, but he did it to astonish the people. And always it made us laugh, the ones who came with him.

When he began to speak, I and Mister Dalwood and Kailusa and Biyu, we all turned to look at the faces of the men squatting around him.

At first their faces said: This Dimdim is talking, we must pretend to listen, and by and by somebody will interpret.

Then their faces said: What was that word that the Dimdim spoke?

Then their faces said: O! we understand every word that he speaks! "Listen," they called, "he is talking the language."

And in the end it was like in every village the first time. They were shouting and laughing, and going *Wa*! and *Sssss*! and smiling at him like a relation. Their bellies were moved towards him, it is the way with ignorant people. Many of them came sidling up to him

53

and touched his hand, or stroked the Dimdim hair on his arms and legs, which all such people find so strange. It was very comical and stupid to see, and even the miserable Kailusa was smiling, pleased with himself because other people were pleased with his taubada. It was for that that Sayam called him Misa Kodo's mother.

"They are so *soppy*," Mister Dalwood cried out, and I decided that I would ask Mister Cawdor the meaning of that word, because Mister Dalwood could never explain.

And meanwhile Mister Cawdor went on talking in the language with the headman. He said that he did not come as Government, because Kaga was not the business of Osiwa, but only to see the island and gossip a little with the people. And the headman said that he was as pleased to see Mister Cawdor as if Mister Cawdor was a *kula* partner bringing a famous arm-shell.

Then the headman said that he had a message for the King: that the VC, his own brother, was dead a year ago, and that the people wanted that man's son to wear the King's badge and be the next VC if the King would say yes, and that he wished the King to send a new rami and shirt for the VC because the old ones had rotted away. Mister Cawdor said that he would tell that message to the Government, and that the King had been dead for seven years, and that the commander of all villages was now a woman, the Kuwini. When they heard that the men became very excited, and asked questions about the Queen and about her husband, and told Mister Cawdor of their contempt for such a person who would let his wife command everything. But Mister Cawdor said what he always said: Our custom is different. And they all nodded their heads and looked wise and said: Yes, truly, it is different, your custom.

Then Mister Cawdor said: "Let us go, let us see your village." And over his shoulder he called: "Kailusa, go to the dinghy, bring the small tin box. In it there is tobacco."

O my lord Jesus, what a sigh went up under the mango tree. I thought we should all be buried alive in leaves.

DALWOOD

After Alistair and the headman had gone up the first ladder and were on the ledge, I said to Saliba: "You go now," pointing, and she looked at me half refusing, and then just moved her eyes towards Osana. I knew what she was saying, the danger from that bastard if he thought something was going to happen, but I wanted just that chance to see her before me in the line. Not my boss, trailing me in his wake, but her, thinking of me. And she saw that I meant it, and turned, and went up the notched pole as neat as a bush-rat up a tree. I watched her skirt with the stiff waistband flicking from side to side and her rounded brown calves marked with drying sea-water and sand. And I thought if I take the risk I will be someone to somebody, I will be more true. If I am real to her, if a woman like this can care.

From the ledge she looked back and down at me, so serious, her face was changed. And I thought yes, yes, she will care, I will be a man to her. Only for a little while, but she will care.

So I felt an excitement, climbing the pole, because even at that moment I was going to join her and she was waiting, and nobody knew of the going and the waiting but the two of us there on the cliff. And I thought of what might be ahead, too, but not much then of her, hardly of her at all, except that she seemed kind, and of course I would be kind.

When I came to the top of the cliff she had not waited for me, but had gone on after Alistair and the headman and was walking behind them on the path. And I let the distance between us stay, because Osana was following, and because, anyway, neither of us had anything yet to say, or a language to say it in. I kept my place in the line and watched them ahead, the black-headed man in white clothes and the brown girl in the flicking red skirt. I saw how soft the skirt was as it brushed the backs of her knees, and seemed to feel it myself when the waistband dipped and rose with the swing of her hips.

I couldn't have said, then, why I watched them so possessively, those two. But I think now that he had already told me. Because once he said to me that the most tender word in their language was *yamata*, which is to keep watch over, guard, and has in it the word for hand. So to watch over someone was to handle or stretch out a hand, he said, and also, he thought, to hold in one's hands, to have one's hands full. That, anyway, is what he made of it; and I think when I looked after them and thought about them in that way I was holding them too, so as not to be empty-handed.

The path we walked on was cropped and green, springy under my feet in shoes, springier to her bare soles. But the palms that bordered it were stunted and poor. Somehow the whole island, the

55

earth of it, seemed starved. For more than a week there had been no rain, and the mean scrub of the fallow gardens had shrivelled and the grass had dried. In the middle of the brilliant, empty sea the island was like a drab backyard that man had made and never looked at since with more than half an eye.

But the headman loved it, that was evident. At the entrance to his village, standing aside from the path, he threw out his arm like an immense gate that he had been keeping closed till then so as to stun us at the last minute. He flung open his arm for us, and we filed past it, and came out in the centre of a circle of houses much like any other houses, but poorer than most, where chickens scratched and women cooked and one pig foraged on the barren swept ground.

The long line behind me caught up and milled around us, guiding us towards the thatched platform outside the headman's house, where an old woman who must have been the headman's wife was spreading grass mats, and beaming. Small boys darted from the trees with green coconuts and screamed at their fathers to hack them open so that the Dimdims could drink. Half the village had a chicken under one arm, and the other half had a bamboo pipe in one hand, and the word on every lip was *pwa'iki*, to smoke tobacco. Even the animals came running to look at us, and the hens shrieked and fell about as the pigs charged through.

Through all the commotion Kailusa moved like a priest, carrying the sacrament in a padlocked tin box.

SALIBA

E, the crazy people. I laughed so much that Alistea turned round and told me enough. But who would not have laughed at them, all talking about the tobacco they were going to have. And the wife of Punutala, the old commander of the village, she kept shouting at him to ask the Dimdims if they would buy this thing or that thing, and if they would calaboose the person who was stealing her seedlings of tobacco in the night. That was when I laughed most, thinking of that robber in the night. I thought that in two years he would have enough seedlings for a cigarette, and then would have to sail to another island to smoke it.

And the things that they brought to sell, where had they got them? These are the things they wanted Alistea and Timi to buy: two forks and two spoons, a live crab, a pair of glasses

56

like Misa Makadoneli's with no glass, a battery for Misa Makadoneli's torch, a live grasshopper for eating, the skin of a python, a green parrot, a little new pig, and a piece of something that nobody could say what it was, but Timi thought it was a part of a Dimdim machine called a squeezebox. All these things the Kaga people thought that Alistea would wish to buy with his tobacco.

But Alistea told them, no, he wanted nothing, only to talk with them. But he said if they would talk, he would buy one chicken from each man, for one stick each. And so they said: "O taubada, our very great thanks," and Kailusa gave every man one stick, and soon it was as if the whole island was burning.

Then Alistea said that he wanted to talk only with the men, the women and children should go away. When they heard that the women muttered and were angry, and would only go after the men had given them half of their tobacco. And they said to Alistea: "And her, taubada," pointing at me. But he said: "She is not a Kaga woman," and so I stayed with the Dimdims and the men, after the women had hustled each other away to smoke in the grove.

As soon as they were gone Alistea opened a little book and spoke to the men from the platform where he and Timi sat. He said that they would not like to hear what he was going to say, but that it was nothing, it was all over, they were not to be afraid, he only wanted them to talk with him.

Then he said: "Seventeen years ago, in the war, at Misima, a man called Buriga began to talk to the people. Buriga told the people that if all the Dimdims were killed the world would turn over, and any Dimdim that remained would be changed into a native, and all the natives would be changed into Dimdims. And because of Buriga's talk, a soldier and a trader and some other Dimdims were murdered.

"Later on some canoes came to Misima from Muyuwa and heard Buriga's talk and took it back with them to Muyuwa. And with the talk they took a man called Taudoga. We do not know this man Taudoga, where he was born or where he is now. He was not a Misima man and not a Muyuwa man. Perhaps he was a Kaga man. We only know these things about him: he believed in Buriga's talk, and he was mad, and he wanted to kill.

"In the same year a Kaga canoe went to the village of Boagis on Muyuwa and heard the talk of Taudoga. And when the men returned to Kaga they brought Taudoga with them.

"The first thing that Taudoga did when he came to Kaga was to make himself King of it. These were the people in the Government of Taudoga's kingdom:

King: Taudoga
Number Two King: Mewabusi
Governor: Okamtaitu
Boss: Toselebu
Doctor: Peleidi
Sergeant: Kakapoi
Policemen: Naluga
            Monayai . . ."

By that time none of the Kaga men was looking at Alistea. They were looking at their hands, or the ground. And I and Osana were laughing and laughing and could not stop.

But Alistea went on.

"Resident Magistrates: Tamayuyu
                         Kalovakoya
                         Punutala . . ."

"O, Punutala," cried Osana to the headman, "were you nothing better than a Resident Magistrate?"

"Shut up, Osana," Alistea said in English. And once more he read from the book.

"Assistant Resident Magistrates: Polonai
                                 Kovaniko
                                 Tokalabu

Storemen: Toyobwaga
            To'uduya
Motor Drivers . . ."

"Motor Drivers!" I and Osana called out together. But Alistea frowned, and we covered our faces in our arms.

Alistea said again:

"Motor Drivers: Gumabudi and Gudisei."

Then the names were finished, and Alistea looked up from the book. "That was the Government," he said. "We do not know very much about the doings of that Government, but we do know what Taudoga said. He told you people of Kaga that once your ancestors had made the world turn over, everything would begin again. He said that your ancestors would come to life again and give you everything that you wanted: food, white men's somethings, every-

58

thing. And so you people of Kaga, you went to your gardens and destroyed them, you cut down your palms and fruit-trees, you emptied your yam-houses into the sea. You said to the ancestors: 'See, we have nothing.' And truly you had nothing. But still the world did not turn over."

We looked at the men of Kaga, I and Osana, and we could not see one face. Their heads were down towards the ground, and all their happiness about the tobacco was gone.

"I do not speak of this to shame you," Alistea said. "Three of you have been in the calaboose in Misima because of it. It has been forgotten for thirteen years. But the Patrol Officer who heard of it and punished those three men could not find Taudoga. He was gone. So I am asking you, when everyone else has forgotten: What did you do when he was King? And where is Taudoga today?"

At last one face was lifted up among the heads of the crouching people. It was the old one, Punutala. He said: "Taubada, Taudoga vanished. In the night, we do not know how. No one saw him again."

"*Ki?*" Alistea said. "And his customs? What did you do in the time when Taudoga was King?"

But the old man would not speak another word. He hid his face, and the silence went on and on.

"Very well," said Alistea, swinging down his legs from the platform and standing among the men, "we will not talk any more. I am sorry that I have made you feel shame. It was long ago. I thought that you would make me understand. Now I see that I will never understand. Well, we others, we must return now to Kailuana. So let it disappear from your minds, and come, all of you, and say goodbye to us under the mango tree."

I saw that he felt pity for those men, and I felt pity too, they were so quiet and so shamed before us and one another. Only Osana kept on laughing to himself, and muttering: "Idiots."

"Okay, Tim," Alistea said, and moved his head, and went away. And Timi, who had not understood one word of all that talk, jumped down from the platform and hurried after him, looking surprised and a little stupid, the way he often looked in those days, but today no more.

Side by side, in white clothes, Alistea and Timi were walking across the emptiness of the village place. Then Kailusa went, and I and Osana and Biyu followed. Behind us the village was still as if a great disease had suddenly killed it; but all those eyes, I knew, were looking at our backs.

And I thought: Shame is very strong, shame is terrible, most of all the shame of a man. I thought: That is a thing that can kill, the shame of a man.

DALWOOD

I hadn't understood anything that he said, but I saw the men freeze under his words, and when we left it was like saying goodbye to a ghost village that had nothing to offer us any more.

But that was only the men. From the grove the women and children caught sight of us, and came running. They massed in the path behind us, marching in step. Or else burst suddenly from the bushes ahead, to stand big-eyed beside the track and drink in the picture of us from front and side and rear.

"O, *sena toveaka*," they told each other, and I knew that that was me. A very big man, so they said everywhere.

And I thought for his sake, to lighten the atmosphere, I would do my act for them, Dolu'udi the Dimdim clown.

"E, *mokita*," I called to them. "*Sena toveaka yaegu.*" And it brought the house down, as always, it had them screaming and slapping themselves with laughter. They shouted the news down the length of the line that I had agreed I was truly a big man.

Only Misa Kodo, stumping the path ahead of me, was not bowled over by the joke, having heard it a few times before.

After a while the applause died away into mutters and whispers, and I knew that behind me there would be a clustering of people around Osana or Biyu, full of questions. Were we kind, were we clever, were we just? Because I had made us human to them, by sounding like an idiot, and they would want to know more.

And then it seemed that the air changed. Over and over I heard the same phrase being whispered, and it sounded like a phrase that I had heard before, had heard often, always on those walks between villages, always in a whisper. It sounded like something that we were not supposed to hear or understand. And to show them that I had my ears about me, to scandalize them, I shouted it out.

"*La kwava i paek'.*"

And the whole world seemed to die, with a little gasp.

I saw Alistair pause in mid-step. His head moved and he looked

60

at me. Unbelieving. As if I had put a spear in his back. Then he turned and walked on, faster than before.

I went after him, half-running, with that silence around me. I said to the back of his neck: "Alistair — what did I say?"

"Don't you know?" he said, speaking straight ahead.

"You know I don't know, I just said what they were saying. You've got to tell me."

He dropped his voice, though no one within earshot could have understood the English. "You said: 'His wife refused.'"

The quietness seemed to hit me in the head and in the gut, like a rush of blood brought on by fear or shame.

Yet we were still ridiculously striding on, in single file, an engine with one truck.

"I didn't know," I said.

"It's their idiom," he said, "didn't I tell you? As we might say: 'His wife took a powder.'"

"Alistair," I said. I came beside him and put one arm round his shoulder. But he broke away and went on.

"It's nothing new," he said. "Wherever we go, any village, I hear that in the background. It goes on as long as I'm there. And then all the discussions, all the arguments, about what went wrong."

"How do they know?"

"Osana tells them. Or Sayam, or Biyu. Everybody's interested. A great old Dimdim comedy."

"*Why* should it matter so much? It's happened to plenty of other people, plenty of *them*."

"Oh, yes, but," he said, "I'm a Dimdim, and you don't often see a Dimdim so — at such a disadvantage. And they have theories, you know, about me. Have they ever got theories. She'd be amazed. I'm amazed."

He never turned, but went striding on, the shadows of the palms sliding down his white clothes and falling on the green ground.

"I never would," I tried to tell him, "I never would —"

Still moving, he reached back an arm and grabbed me by the scruff of the neck. "Come on," he said dragging me after him, "walk beside me. Dimdims shall be seen to be the best of mates at all times. Forget it, it's something-nothing. My wife refused, but what the hell. I'll write South for another one. What else did they say?"

"I don't remember," I said, not wanting to remember. "Oh,

except — something, they said, they thought was very big. *Kala mwasila*, they said. *Kala mwasila sena kwaiveaka, a dok'*."

"'His shame,'" Alistair said, towards the gap in the palms ahead, where the *Igau* showed, asleep on the wheat-green water. "'His shame, I think, must be very great.'"

"It's mad," I said. "Their idea of shame —"

"Of course it is," he said. "But that's just them. Our custom is different."

OSANA

When I and Saliba came to the beach Mister Cawdor and Mister Dalwood were sitting in the sand under the mango tree, and Mister Cawdor was talking to a young Kaga man called Sagova. They were sitting with their backs to the rock and their legs stretched out in front of them. But when Saliba walked near them to go to the dinghy Sagova jumped to his feet, because the sand was so narrow that he saw she would have to step over their legs almost, and he was nervous. And he kept looking down at Mister Cawdor and Mister Dalwood and muttering: "Taubada, taubada," until Mister Dalwood stood up too, though he did not understand the reason. But Mister Cawdor stayed where he was, and just nodded to Saliba as she passed.

When Sagova and Mister Dalwood had sat down again, Mister Cawdor said: "Why did you do that, Sagova?"

Sagova laughed and looked shy. "I was afraid," he said, "of being made impotent."

"O!" said Mister Cawdor. "Then, am I impotent now?"

"I don't know, taubada," Sagova said, full of shame. "Your custom is different. For us, if a woman's box passed over our legs like that, that would be the end."

"Sssss. You talk gammon," I said to Sagova.

"Osana, shut up," said Mister Cawdor.

"Very good, taubada," I said. "He does not talk gammon, and you are impotent."

And Mister Cawdor just looked at me quietly, smiling the way he often smiled, not really with his mouth but with his eyebrows.

His face changed like no other man's. One time you could hardly see his face. That was when the Dimdims at Osiwa were saying that he would have to be sent away to Dimdim, because he was always

62

drunk, not very drunk, but always. For a while he would not shave or wash or change his clothes, and Kailusa was in despair, because Mister Cawdor was his *vaigua*, his jewel, that ignorant hunchback. So Kailusa thought of a plan, but could not explain it to Mister Dalwood, and he came with Mister Dalwood to me, and asked me to interpret.

When I had told Mister Dalwood Kailusa's idea we both laughed very much, and I said I would like to see what they were going to do, and Mister Dalwood said that I might come with them. So we went to the big room in their house, and when Mister Cawdor came in, all dirty and with his face covered with hair, Mister Dalwood jumped on him and twisted his arms and they fell into a chair. Mister Cawdor was very angry and said filthy things, but when he saw Kailusa coming in with the hot water and the razor he began to laugh. So Kailusa put the soap on his face and shaved him, and all the time he just laughed, and sat quiet on Mister Dalwood's knees like a baby.

Then Kailusa brought a glass and held it in front of Mister Cawdor and said: "Now, taubada, you are a young man again."

And truly, after all that beard was gone, he was a very young man, and when he looked at his face in the glass it was as if he had forgotten. A long, long time he looked at his face in the glass, and then he said: "Very good, Kailusa, now cut my hair." And next he went and put out the wooden figures for the game called chess that he played with Mister Dalwood. So afterwards the Dimdims thought that he was like before, in the days when the sinabada lived with him. But I knew that that was not true, and that some day I would have to say.

All the time, while I was thinking about Mister Cawdor's face, the men from the village were passing with chickens. Some chickens were tied and some had green palm-fronds woven around them, and all of them were crying out. The dinghy was filled with them, there was a great pile of them on the shore, and old Sayam was stamping up and down, furious because of his boat.

"Taubada," Sayam called to Mister Cawdor, "how many chickens are going in the *Igau*?"

"I do not know," Mister Cawdor said. "You count."

"I counted already," Sayam said. "Taubada, seventy-three chickens."

"Very good," said Mister Cawdor. "We will eat, and these people will smoke."

"But seventy-three chickens, taubada," Sayam cried out. "They will shit everywhere, everywhere."

"E," said Mister Cawdor, moving his shoulders, "it is their custom."

Sayam looked for a little while at Mister Cawdor. Then he spat a lot of betelnut on the sand, and went out through the water to the dinghy, muttering: "Madness."

Mister Dalwood had found a little hermit crab without a house, and was searching for a shell to give it. When he did find a shell, the crab would not go into it, because there was another crab inside. So Mister Dalwood searched again, and at last found an empty shell. It was too big, but the crab got into it, and scuttled away.

"My good deed for the day," said Mister Dalwood.

Sagova said to Mister Cawdor: "You like to eat chicken, taubada?"

"Yes," Mister Cawdor said. But he lied, because he never liked to eat anything.

"You like to eat this, taubada?" Sagova said, and he opened a banana-leaf parcel and offered Mister Cawdor a boiled mango.

Mister Cawdor looked round for Kailusa, sighing a little. "Kailusa," he said, "give my companion a stick of tobacco." And to Sagova he said: "My very great thanks, but today I do not eat. However, my nephew will eat it." Then he spoke in English to Mister Dalwood, and said: "Right, Tim ram it down." That was Mister Dalwood's biggest work in the villages, to eat, and a ship could not contain all the yams and maize and sago dumplings and pig-fat that he has put into his belly this year, in order to look polite.

Mister Dalwood sighed too when Mister Cawdor said that, but ate the mango, making noises of joy. All the time Sagova stared at his throat, and looked proud whenever he saw Mister Dalwood swallow.

"Sagova," said Mister Cawdor, "speak to me. Do you remember Taudoga?"

"Oh, yes, taubada," Sagova said. "But I was a child then. I was not in those doings."

"What were they like," Mister Cawdor said, "those doings? Were they like Christians, like Church?"

"Truly, I do not know," Sagova said. "I did not see. But I know the reason. The older men did not want the young men to have the girls. So they called themselves sergeants and names like that, and said that the girls were only for them. They had dancing, taubada, but the young men were not allowed to see it. The older men and the girls danced in two circles, and when they stopped the man seized the girl facing him and took her away into the bush."

"That is like a game," I said, "that they play at the Mission. It is called Musical Chairs."

"True, Osana," Mister Cawdor said. "Sagova, you say: did Taudoga truly vanish? You did not hide him?"

"No, taubada. He did truly vanish. And when he was gone, that madness was over."

"You did not kill him, you Kaga people?"

"No, taubada!" Sagova cried out. "He just vanished, and afterwards nobody saw him. Taubada, I am not lying."

"I believe," Mister Cawdor said. "I believe your word. Well, enough of Taudoga. My talk is finished."

By that time Mister Dalwood had finished his mango, and threw the mango-stone at a gull. Then he walked in the sand, pulling the strings of the fruit out of his big teeth. "Very good," Mister Dalwood exclaimed, nodding to Sagova. But in English he said: "It wasn't too bad, but let's push off quick. I was watched. Any minute now we'll have the ladies from Meals on Wheels."

"Right," Mister Cawdor said, beginning to get up from the sand. "Sagova, our gratitude, and goodbye."

"Taubada," Sagova said, putting his hand on Mister Cawdor's arm, "wait a little. I want to ask a question. The people are talking about the star. Taubada, what is the star?"

"Star?" Mister Cawdor said. "Which star?"

"It flies," Sagova said. "It flew last night from the south-east wind to the north-east wind."

"Perhaps it is a *mulukwausi*," Mister Cawdor said, "a flying witch." And he laughed, as all the Dimdims do at the *mulukwausi* that ignorant people believe in, because they think it is funny that fire should stream from their women's parts.

"No, taubada," Sagova said, sounding annoyed. "Not *mulukwausi*, taubada. A star, that flies."

"E," said Mister Cawdor, "I will tell you my mind. I think it is a machine, a Dimdim machine, and its name is Sputnik. It does nobody any harm. It flies in the sky and shines, that is all, like one of those glass floats of the Japanese fishermen."

"True?" said Sagova. "Well, I will tell the people."

"Yes, tell them," said Mister Cawdor; "and tell them also that I am sorry that I spoke of what they did not want to remember. Well, the dinghy has come back. Goodbye, my friend. I will see you perhaps at Wayouyo when you come on the *kula*."

"Yes, perhaps," Sagova said, and he shook hands with Mister Cawdor and Mister Dalwood and me. Then we waded to the dinghy and rowed away, with chickens packed all around us like Dimdim cushions.

DALWOOD

In those first days the weather was like early mornings when I was a kid, the south-easterly blew quiet and cool, hardly marking the sea, and the clouds were fairweather wisps along the horizons. That evening, between Kaga and Kailuana, the sea died to a smooth curve of bottomless blue, and the blue of the sky faded and changed to green: an apple-green peacock-green sky pouring down a pink and golden light. The *Igau* turned rosy in the glow, which coloured the sea, too, so that it passed through lavender to deep violet, while the faces and shapes of the people became ghostly and strange.

Sayam stood at the wheel wearing the face of a Mexican god, and listened to the plop of eggs behind him. Seventy-three eggs must have been dropped that evening in the belly of the fresh-painted *Igau*. So Sayam scowled and snapped at his admirers, steering that enormous omelette through the purple sea.

I thought Alistair would be asleep, I was so nearly asleep myself, and everything was so quiet, and I felt so alone. When the singing began I didn't even wonder about it, it just seemed right, and meant for me. I lay by Alistair on the decking over Sayam's head and let the song come to me.

"I attempt from Love's sickness
To fly in vain,
Since I am myself my own fever,
Since I am myself my own fever and pain."

66

Hard to believe that he understood perhaps four words of that, he sang with such passionate sadness. When it struck me, I scrambled to my knees and stared at him: coal-black in that light, his mauve rami burning. Cross-legged near Alistair's head, singing to Alistair.

I thought of the music books in the cupboard where he had thrown all her things, and knew that the song would be there, inside one of the books with her maiden-name on the cover.

"Kailusa," I said.

Alistair's hand came away from his eyes. "Very good, Kailusa," he said. "Another time." And the boy (that boy of round about forty) lifted his head and began again, out of that broad deep chest that had something to do with his deformity. Over the ghostly *Igau* on the empty sea the words hung like frigate-birds.

"Since I am myself my own fever,
Since I am myself my own fever and pain."

SALIBA

The sea was pale when we came to Kailuana again, but the island was black. We could tell where the house was among the palms because one shutter was full of light, and we knew that Misa Makadoneli would be standing there, looking for us, seeing us black like the island on the pale sea.

When the people came back he and Naibusi were waiting on the veranda, and he said to Alistea: "You're late, old man, you've been holding us up." He was dressed in his pyjamas that he puts on at six o'clock, and he had his rum and his pipe that Naibusi brings at half past six, and he sat at the table by the lamp wearing his hat, because the cockatoo likes to sit on his head at that time, and looked cross.

Because he was in a bad humour Alistea was gentle with him, and said we had been delayed by a *vineilida*, one of those rocks that are alive and live at the bottom of the sea. Then Popu flew down on to the table and began to drink Timi's rum, and Timi let him drink it, and soon Popu was drunk.

Popu staggered around the table flapping his wings and screaming, with all his feathers standing up, until he could not walk any more. Then he lay on his back and cried his name very pitifully, like a baby. Timi was laughing and laughing, and soon he was drunk too, and kept looking at me. So I said to Misa Makadoneli that I felt sick, and I went down the back steps to the village and stayed in Naibusi's house, to stop Timi from looking at me, because nothing can happen in the big house that Misa Makadoneli does not see.

Afterwards, when it was nine o'clock and Misa Makadoneli was in his bed, I went to help Naibusi in the cookhouse. Naibusi was making bread and her hands were covered with flour. "O," she said, "Misa Kodo wants his tobacco that I cut tonight. You take it to him, I have too much work. He is in his room."

I went to Alistea's door and knocked and he called to me to come in. He was lying on his bed and reading a book, and he looked very hot.

"O, Saliba," he said. "Shall we sleep?"

"Ssss," I said. "Anyway, I do not think you want to sleep with me."

"You are very pleasing," he said, "O face-like-the-moon." But he was smiling, and I did not think he truly thought I was pleasing, though he liked to be my friend.

"It is hot," he said. "The window will not open?"

"No," I said. "Here is your tobacco that Naibusi sent."

"Put it there," he said, pointing at the box beside his bed, "and say to Naibusi my thanks. E, I do not like this room. It smells. It smells of rot."

"The name of the house is Rotten Wood," I said.

"That is the truth," he said. "But your garland smells very good."

I was stooping to set down his tin of tobacco on the box, and he put his arms around my body and his face against my garland of bwita flowers.

I was not angry, I did not move away, but I said: "Taubada, I do not want that." Still I thought: He is my friend. But I did not like his body, which had black hair on it like so many Dimdims, though not like Timi, and his face was rough with hair and hurt my skin. "Taubada," I said, "I will go."

"No," he said, "stay a little." He turned his face upwards to look at my face, and his face was very young, he seemed like a boy. "Nowadays," he said, "I have no woman."

"I know," I said. "I heard the people talking. My grief for you."

"Sometimes," he said, "my mind is heavy. Yet truly, I was not happy before, when the sinabada was with me."

"Why?" I said.

"I do not know," he said. "We were not happy. Perhaps I am not a good lover."

"Truly?" I said. "In what way are you not a good lover?" Then I saw in his face that he had wanted me to think that he was joking, and because I thought he was not joking his eyes went dark and small.

"It is bad," he said. "I talk too much." And he stopped holding me and lay back on the bed, in his white Dimdim yavi, with hairs on his chest and belly.

"You are my friend?" he said, with his eyes on my eyes.

"Yes, truly," I said, and with one finger I stroked his arm, till he closed his hand around my finger and held it. "Alistea," I said.

"Salib'," he said, smiling because I had called him by his other name that I had never said before. And we stayed like that, very quiet and friendly, for a little while, until the door that was half open creaked all the way into the room, and Misa Makadoneli cried out: "O! Pardon me, old man."

MACDONNELL

Saliba sprang into the air like a wallaby, tearing away her hand from Cawdor. "Peeping man!" she screamed in my ear as she thudded past me at the door.

"Well, I'm sorry about that," I said to Cawdor. "I had no idea, old man, no idea at all."

"Nothing was happening, Mak," Cawdor said. "Relax. You haven't missed a thing."

"You might be civil," I said. "She is my servant."

"Yeah, and she's in the house after sundown," he said. "I could Court you for that."

"She's in the house because she was born and bred in the house," I said. "God knows who makes these ordinances. Some withered old nancy at Konedobu. The whole country's going to pot. If I could still do it I'd be doing it, and not think of your Court, old man."

"It would make a lovely trial," he said.

In the hot room the scent of the girl's flowers still hung on the air. I let him see me sniffing at it. "Like a whorehouse in here," I said.

"Mak," he said, picking up a book from the bed, "isn't it after lights out for you? I'm not really tuned in for this kind of chat."

"Well, of course, old man," I said, "I know nothing was going on, really, it was just my joke. The girl's a good-natured girl, but she's plain, they're all plain nowadays, and you've got other things to think about. I don't know why you don't bring her with you, she'd certainly be most welcome in the house."

He put down the book and faced me from the pillow, very hard and level. "Bring who?" he said, sounding sharp and tired at the same time.

"Why, your sinabada, old man. Quite a doll, that's what young Johnston from Muyuwa said."

He went on looking at me for so long that I began to know that something was up. Then he said: "Have you really not heard?"

"Heard what, old man?"

"No," he said to himself, studying my face. "No, you haven't. Well, Mak, my doll of a sinabada shot through two months ago with the Osiwa doctor."

"Oh," I said. "Sorry to hear that."

"They went out on the same plane. He was going on leave, she was going to the dentist in Moresby. So she told me. They wrote from Tokyo. They were having a honeymoon."

"Oh," I said. "Well, all I can say is it's a pretty poor show."

"Sometimes I think so," he said. "Sometimes I feel a bit restless. A bit taken for granted – you know the feeling? When I write to my wife, for instance, Mrs Alistair Cawdor, and have to address it to Mrs John Philipson. She gets worried about her reputation. Well, you wouldn't know, but neighbours can be beastly."

I went and sat on the bed, so as to see him better. His face, filmed with sweat, looked stiff, and very dark.

"You'll divorce her?" I said.

"Yes," he said. "I'll get round to that, in time."

"You wouldn't take her back? Just supposing."

"She wouldn't come. It's not her kind of place, the Territory. Especially not Osiwa. She never went much on tennis or Scrabble."

70

"Cawdor," I said, "I'm very sorry, old man. Never been married myself, but it must make a man feel —"

"Don't worry your head about it," he said. "It's all right. I shall have mistresses. Like you, you historic old ram."

"That's what you should have done in the first place," I said. And out of politeness he smiled, still with the stiffness in his face. "You're young, you've plenty of time. How old are you, by the way?"

"Twenty-seven," he said.

"And she?"

"Thirty-two. Which was the point, maybe."

"I don't quite read you, old man."

"Of marrying me," he said. "At least, I sometimes wondered."

He rolled over, so that his cheek was on the pillow, and began to talk past me, into the corner of the room. "In my second stint up here," he said, "I was twelve months alone on a patrol post. I never saw anyone to talk to, it was just me and the locals. Everyone said how can you stand it? I thought I stood it pretty well, I thought I was happy, I guess I was. But when I went South on leave, first of all I couldn't stop talking, it was like a disease, but there was no one to talk to. So I shut up, and then I couldn't talk at all. I couldn't talk and I couldn't know anybody. I went South to have a good time, spend my money, but I couldn't know anybody. So I went to ground in my father's house in Sydney, because of that — because I knew him, more or less. Then this girl, this woman, started coming. He asked her to come, I think. And I could talk to her, and she talked to me. So I asked her to marry me. You won't understand this, but it was *that* that I wanted, to be married. So we did marry and came to Osiwa and it didn't work and she went and it's finished. Now you know. It's going to be my leave again soon, but this time I won't take it. I'm not going to take any leave again. I'm going to stay here, in these islands, and if they transfer me I'll resign and be a trader or something, but I'm not leaving. I can't know anybody. I only ever knew her, and she never had any idea what she wanted, and she wouldn't try. Christ, Mak, I'm sorry, you don't want to hear this."

"It's all right," I said. "But don't let's have any more of it. You get too excited."

71

"Yes," he said, with a kind of laugh at the corner of the room. "I do. I get excited."

"And you've drunk a fair bit tonight."

"Yeah," he said. "I do that too."

"I'd change my mind about that leave, if I were you."

"Ah," he said, into the pillow. Then I saw that his eyes were closed, and he looked to have fallen, really fallen, asleep, still with his mouth open from making that sound. It seemed to bear out how young he was. And I thought he will get over this, perhaps, and Dalwood is a Samaritan happy in his work, and at this end of my life it is only humility to say it has nothing to do with me. So I turned to go, but when I was at the door he said quietly after me: "Tomorrow, Mak, you never heard me, understand?"

SALIBA

I called to Naibusi: "Very well, I will go, I will sleep now." And I went down the steps from the veranda and was on the path to our house, Naibusi's and mine, when a voice from the dark whispered my name.

I did not see him at first, I did not see him for a long time. He was underneath the house, where the boxes and the kerosene drums are, sitting on a drum. I would not have seen him at all, but two thin lines of light were on him, the light of Alistea's lamp, shining through cracks in the floorboards in Alistea's room above his head.

"You come, Salib'," he said.

He had waited very long, since he had been under the shower, and still had a white towel wrapped around him like a rami, stained with rust from the drum.

"Salib'," he said.

"No," I said. "No, taubada. I am afraid."

But he did not understand that word, and stood up, very tall, with the lines of light on him, expecting.

"I do not know," I said.

He said again: "You come," and one would not have thought that his voice could sound like that, so deep.

Then slowly I did go to him, not truly understanding my own mind, but because he said. And under the two lines of

72

light he seized me and held me against his skin, which was hot and cool.

"You are good, Salib'," he said, because those were all the words he knew. "Salib', you are very good." He kissed me on the mouth, and I held his back, and felt him trembling.

And then I knew that he too was afraid, this Dimdim, he was afraid that I might hurt him. And when I knew that, there was no difference and no strangeness any more, there was only like one person there in the dark, whispering: "Timi," and "Saliba."

II

VISITANTS

MACDONNELL

Of course, if you have the Government to stay with you, for a while you can't call your house your own. All those boxes, all those people: policemen, houseboys, boat-crew. And without fail that pain in the neck Osana, making sure that he doesn't pass unobserved. He had been busy somewhere all that weekend, daunting the maries with his high office and his keyhole-glimpses of Dimdim life. But before I was out of my bed on that Monday morning he was back, shouting orders in the village. And so I decided to stay where I was, till the organizing would be over, the patrol ready to set out.

And besides, they tire me nowadays, white men. I liked young Dalwood, and even Cawdor, but they tired me. To deal with white men — here, at my age — takes thought, a lot of thought.

When most of the shouting had died down I came out on to the veranda. Osana and the bearers, surrounded by their baggage, were milling around among the huts below, and Saliba, on the back steps, was watching them and playing a bit of a tune on a pawpaw-stalk, bending and slackening it to get the notes. An irritating noise, I've always thought. I said to her: "You have no work today?"

She looked at me, surprised, and then shouted: "Today I work for the Government."

"Oh?" I said. "Then the Government can feed you, I think."

She pulled a face at me, and went back to her aimless piping, through the green tube.

On the other side of the veranda Cawdor was still at the table, finishing a mug of tea. Dalwood leaned on the rail and was studying

77

the *Igau*, like something that he had made himself and in time would get perfect. In his clean white clothes, he could have been bound for an operating theatre. But on his back, I saw as I came nearer, were little red-brown stains; and you needn't have been fifty-one years on Kailuana to know what that means.

He turned as I came up, and said: "Ah, 'morning, Mak."

"Just a minute," I said. "Turn round." And as he did, not wanting to, but not quite sure that he hadn't a tarantula on him, I ripped his shirt out of his shorts and showed Cawdor the claw-marks running down his back.

"Dear me," I said.

Cawdor had his mug in front of his mouth, I could only see his eyes over it, fixed on mine. "That's what I've been saying to myself," he said.

"Jesus," Dalwood muttered, and backed off from me, tucking in his shirt again, too fast not to do some damage to his houseboy's ironing. I saw his eyes move towards the steps where Saliba had been, but they came back. She was gone, apparently. He turned on me, hot in the face, and demanded: "What did you get out of that? That was pretty sick, in my book."

"Now don't be so puritanical, old man," I said.

But already he had decided to transfer his indignation from me to Cawdor, and in a couple of strides was at the table, his fists on the plastic cover and his shadow, in the early sun, darkening the slighter man, who was already dark, and cool.

"All right," he said, "what have *you* got to say about it?"

"Not a thing," Cawdor said, looking up at him. "What were you expecting?"

"Nothing," Dalwood said. "Not a thing will do."

For a moment he had seemed to be spoiling for a row, a tremendous row, there was lightning in the air around him. But Cawdor, who had drained his mug and put it down, only looked at him with his usual detachment; which was taking, I thought, a certain amount of concentration.

"Right, then," he said, standing up. "You ready to go?"

"I've been ready for half a fucking hour," Dalwood said.

"More fool you," Cawdor said. "You only start getting paid at a quarter to eight."

"It's twenty-five to now, old man," I said. "Are you leaving already? What did Saliba mean about working for the Government today?"

"She wants to be a bearer," Cawdor said, "if that's all right. She'll be back at midday."

"Well, why not?" I said. "Let's be kind to them. I must tell Naibusi to cut her nails. Nasty habit, that. It's called *kimali*."

"There you are, Tim," Cawdor said. "You've learned a new word."

"I've had enough of this," the boy said, and he strode off. At the steps on the village side he called back: "Thanks, Mak, I'll see you in a few days." Then he sank out of sight, and I heard him shouting among the huts for his houseboy.

"It's all very sudden," I said to Cawdor. "Do you think it was the first time?"

"Mak," Cawdor said, "in your studies have you come across the word voyeur?"

"Well, of course," I said.

"I'm not one," Cawdor said. "So let's pull the chain on that subject."

"I say, Cawdor," I said, "that's a bit offensive. And besides, I'm responsible for that girl."

"No, you're not," he said. "She's been responsible for herself a good four years now."

"That's all very well," I said, "but what if there's a child? What if she's in love with him?"

"You know there's never a child," he said. "And never much love, either. All there is is curiosity, and that doesn't leave any complications."

"Well, let's hope you're right," I said. "She thinks you're her friend now. We'll see if she has reason to change her mind."

"I'll talk to him," he said, "if I have to. But I don't think there's anything I can do. The news will be all over the island by tomorrow, and at Osiwa by next week. The ADO's easy-going, but if Osana turns nasty he could force his hand. I think the kid will be in another district by Christmas. He won't mind, she won't mind. And it's no business of yours or mine."

"In the old days," I said, "ADOs knew what to do with characters like Osana. What he needs is a hiding, old man. Why don't you drop him a hint?"

79

"That's what he's waiting for," he said. "For me to hit him. It's been very inconvenient for Osana, having a PO who speaks the language. His prestige is falling. For six months now he's been trying to drive me out, and he's still waiting for the moment when I overhear something that goes just a bit too far, and turn round and paste him. Then I'll probably be finished here, and he'll be back where he was: Prime Minister of Osiwa, the man the Paramount Chief comes to for favours."

"We can't have that, old man," I said. "Got to think of the future."

"I do think of it," he said. "But lately – I'm beginning to wonder if Osana's winning."

"There's a very simple solution," I said. "Why shouldn't there be an accident? With a revolver, for instance."

He turned away with a sort of laugh that he had at times, very uninfectious. "Ah, you old fossil," he said. "The days of the desperadoes are over. I think, Mak, it's time we left. Thanks for having us. We'll be back."

His manner didn't fit with his words. His voice had gone suddenly nervy and high, and as he shook hands with me his face was as it had been on the night before, strained with the attempt to find some humour in himself.

"Cawdor," I said, "what's the matter?"

"Let me tell you something funny," he said. "I couldn't shoot Osana. Do you know why? Because they took my revolver away from me and locked it up in the office safe. You see, I've got friends."

"You need friends," I said, looking at his eyes.

"Not all that much," he said. But he seemed to press my hand before dropping it, and that was rather touching and not like the man. I remember him very clearly at that moment, against the glow of the frangipani thicket. I remember thinking, as he walked away, that when a man has been humiliated too often, which of course is a matter of his own tolerance, then the place where it shows itself is in the shoulders.

DALWOOD

First of all in the line there was Saliba.

On her head she had the typewriter, a huge old office model, a

80

jalopy of a machine. It moved through the air in a straight line, without a wobble. On the five miles to Wayouyo she never raised a hand.

Once upon a time the MacDonnell's vehicles used to travel that path: a horse and cart in the early days, then a string of horseless carriages, all dead after the first breakdown. It is a highway of grass. Once a month the villagers still turn out to mow it, and if anyone asked them why, they would say: "It is the custom of Kailuana."

After the palms had been left behind, we moved into the smell of the grass and the hot leaves of the scrub in the fallow gardens. The scrub was flowering then with vincas and painted-lady and little convolvulus, purple and pink. Everywhere, cropping out of the grass on the thin brown soil, boulders of coral glared in the white light. The sky was hazing over, and no wind blew that day. It was sultry. Alistair's shirt was glued to his back with sweat and his skin shone through it.

And my shirt and my skin too. In the long line behind they were talking about me, and I could have understood, if I'd concentrated, from the few words I knew. But I wouldn't, I shut my mind, I thought about anything, the weather, plants, birds, rather than hear them. But about her, most of all, because of her long brown back ahead of me, tapering to the pandanus-leaf waistband of her flaring red skirt.

But it's hard, hard to be deaf when you want to be, and he knew the language. I thought of all the weeks I had walked behind him, just like that, with that whisper all around us, that meant nothing to me: *La kwava i paek'.*

SALIBA

Wayouyo is a pretty place, and I would live there if I did not live with Naibusi. It is old and shady and cool, and when you are there you know that people have been in that village many many years, but in Misa Makadoneli's village you know that it is new, although it is falling down. When you come to Wayouyo the path is smoother with people's feet, and the old palms come together over the path, and between the palms are hibiscus bushes planted in a line. At the end of the path is the grove that surrounds Wayouyo, very thick and very dark, and always blue in its darkest places with smoke from the cooking fires. The areca-palms wave and look spiky against the sky, higher than any other trees in the grove, and from a long way away you can hear the women and the children calling, and sometimes a man going *Ululu!* from the gardens.

But before we came into the shade of the grove Alistea called out: "Salib'," and I turned and saw him pointing, and Timi behind him, looking at me, with his eyes bright blue in his red face.

"What?" I said.

"To the resthouse, Salib'," Alistea said. "We will leave these things."

So I took the little path that he pointed to, between hibiscus and palms.

"Saliba," Alistea said after me, "you call."

"No," I said, "you call. Because you are a man."

"E, truly, you are a too shrinking woman," said Alistea. And he put his hands around his mouth and called, just like a black man: "*Ululu! Gu'umenti bi ma!*"

All the men behind us were laughing at that, and other men that we could not see began to shout back, very excited. And suddenly I was at the end of the path and in the clearing, which was full of people, before the resthouse.

You would have thought, from the work of those men, that the people of Wayouyo loved the Government like a new wife, they had done such things to make the Government's house beautiful. No Dimdim ever stayed at the resthouse before Alistea's time, it was better for Dimdims in Misa Makadoneli's house, and besides, Misa Makadoneli liked them to be where he could see them. So when Alistea came the first time to Wayouyo the resthouse was falling down, and the Wayouyo people were ashamed. That is what Dipapa said, he said: "I am ashamed." And he was more ashamed because Alistea said: "O, Dipapa, it is nothing, next time I will sleep in a tree."

When the Wayouyo people heard that the *Igau* had come again they went to the clearing, every one of them, and began to work. They mowed that whole clearing with their bushknives till the grass was like a mat, and thatched the roof again, and in the sleeping-room built two beds, very beautifully, with vines and cane. All round the veranda they hung branches of bananas as a present for the Dimdims, and made a yam-house for them with yams in it, and a new small-house which was strewed with bwita flowers and sulum-woya so that it would smell sweet. They put mats on the floor, but

82

not too many, because every one wanted to watch the Dimdims through the cracks between the planks. On the wall they hung a picture of the Kuwini that was given to Dipapa when he went to Port Moresby to speak with the Kuwini's husband, and in front of the house they put a very tall pole buried deep in the ground.

As I came into the clearing people were running in all directions, and you could not tell what was happening or what would happen next. Three or four men were blowing conches, and a lot more men were shouting, and women and children were laughing and exclaiming everywhere. Then I saw that in their running about they were making themselves into two lines. Suddenly it was finished, and they stood with their faces turned towards us, waiting, like a road for the Dimdims to walk along.

At the end of the two lines, in front of the pole, two men were standing as straight as they could stand, and each of them had one hand up to his forehead and the other hand at his side. One man was Boitoku, the old VC, and the second man was Benoni. They stood stiff like stones, staring under their hands at the Dimdims.

Behind me I heard Osana laughing, and then Alistea said: "Osana, shut up."

"Taubada," I said, "I do not understand this. What do you want me to do?"

"Wait a little," Alistea said. "Follow Misa Dolu'udi." Then he and Timi walked past me, and into the road of the people.

When they saw them coming, two men on each side of Boitoku and Benoni lifted their conches to their mouths and blew long notes, and at the same time a little boy began to climb the pole behind them. He climbed very fast, and when he was near the top he took a piece of cloth out of his belt and fastened it to the pole. It was somebody's rami, bright red and new, and it flapped and floated in the sky, very fine.

Osana was laughing near my back. "You look," he said to the policemen, "the flag of Dipapa. O, Biyu, tomorrow we will be saluting your shirt."

I felt angry with Osana for speaking like that and mocking Benoni, and said: "Fuck your mother, Osana."

"Okay, sinabada," Osana said, and the three policemen laughed.

"You know nothing," I said. "You have not been to Manus. You do not understand the customs of the Navy, not like Benoni."

Osana said to the policemen: "Benoni," and I heard him spit.

Suddenly Biyu cried out, very loud. "O!" he cried. "Benoni-O! He will fall! The child will fall!" And all the people who had been standing so still and neat, like a hedge, watching Alistea and Timi walk between them, looked up and began to call, until after a second there were no more lines, there was only like an ants'-nest of people, rushing about and holding their arms to the sky, while the pole with the boy sliding down it leaned and fell over on top of them.

But Timi pushed through them and reached up. He reached over all the people and picked the boy off the pole like a beetle. When the pole fell among the other men, the boy was still high in the sky, at the end of Timi's arms.

"Salib'," said Osana, laughing, "you are right, I do not understand the customs of the Navy. Why do they lower the flag at midday? I think it must be a mad place, Manus."

"O, enough, Osana," I said, feeling sad for Benoni, who had worked hard to make a great welcome for the Dimdims, like they would have in their own home.

Timi was still holding the little boy up in the air. When the pole was falling the boy had been brave, but as soon as he looked down and saw the face of a Dimdim, with big teeth, he began to moan a little and call for his father. But his father was laughing, and so he laughed too, and was calling to people from out of the sky. "E, you talk gammon," he was saying. "I do not think he is a cannibal. I think he is my friend. Besides, he will not eat me raw."

BENONI

Misa Kodo turned round among the people and looked at me over their heads. He was hot, but he was smiling, and he said to me: "O, Benoni, how are you?"

"I am well, taubada," I said, and felt pleased because he had not forgotten me.

"They are very fine, all these doings," he said. "The house is very fine. O, Boitoku, how are you? Where is Kailusa? Kailus', tell the people what to do with our somethings. And give Osana some tobacco. Saliba, you help in the house. Now we will go with Benoni to speak with Dipapa. Boitoku, you lead the way."

Old Boitoku, the VC, was smiling right round his head, and began to march across the clearing like a soldier, very important, sometimes stopping to make sure that we were following. And Misa Kodo and I walked side by side, with the young Dimdim and Osana behind.

"Taubada," I said, "what is the name of your companion?"

"Misa Dolu'udi," said Misa Kodo. "His years are nineteen. Now you are going to say: '*Wa!* he is very big.'"

"It is true," I said. "That is what I thought when I saw him first, by the beach."

"You were at the beach?" he said.

"E," I said, "and you did not speak to me or see me."

"Idiot," he said, "you did not call. I cannot see everybody. There are so many, many people."

Then he looked at my face, and saw that I did not like the way he spoke, and he laughed. "I talk gammon," he said. "You are my friend, Benoni, from before. Shall we go fishing by and by, we three? On the sea there are not so many people."

"Yes, good," I said. "Because, taubada, I want to talk, I want to ask for something."

"E," he said quietly, sighing, and when I looked at him he was sad.

"What, taubada?" I said.

"Nothing," he said. "Only that — everywhere it is: 'I want, I ask'. Well, it is my work," he said. And so we walked on across the clearing and into the grove of my uncle's part of the village, not speaking any more.

DALWOOD

When we came through the grove of huge old shade-trees and areca-palms to the place where the whole circle suddenly spreads out ahead, what I saw first was the famous yam-house, like a tower at the heart of the hamlet. The great logs of it, grooved and locked at the corners, were thick as palm-trunks and silvery-grey with age. But the thatch was new, and the old designs of dolphins on the gable-boards had been retouched with black and white and red. And strings of cowries were hung from them, so many that some had to be dangled from frayed rods sticking out from the eaves, the marks of a man of tremendous rank. In that setting it looked enormous. But also very peaceful, and pretty, rising out of its own neat lawn, with the palms behind it and a clump of poinsettia nearby blazing against the old cool grey of the wood.

"Hey," I said to Osana, "look at that for a house."

"It is not a house, taubada," he said, condescending. "It is a *bwaima*, for Dipapa's yams. He is very rich."

While he spoke he was listening to Alistair and Benoni and the old VC, who were pointing at the bwaima and talking about it.

"What are they saying?" I said.

"When Mister Cawdor was here before," Osana said, "the bwaima was all bugger-up, and Dipapa said nobody was allowed to mend it. Now Mister Cawdor saying it look very good, and Boitoku telling him Benoni fix it. And Benoni, he says: 'Now my uncle and me, we are very friends.'"

Alistair called to me: "Tim, this here is Darkness-of-Evening. So full of yams the light can't get through the logs. That's how rich Dipapa is."

"Why is he so rich?" I said.

"He married well," Alistair said, "thirteen times."

He was pointing, and I looked beyond the yam-house to a neat semi-circle of thirteen grey-brown huts, and facing them a big house, built like the resthouse with pandanus leaf walls, but shut like a safe against light and air.

"The palace," Alistair explained. "But the old man never entertains there. He eats a meal with each of the wives in turn, and locks himself up in the big house to sleep. It's sorcery-proof, they say."

As we walked on, Osana muttered in his democratic way: "Ignorance."

Skirting the poinsettia, we came into the segment of the village that was Dipapa's special ground. On one hand, the huts of the wives, each faced by its own yam-house; on the other, Dipapa's mansion, painted with dolphins and hung with shells, like the great bwaima. But at the peak of the roof, instead of rods, it had the propeller of a plane, and the pilot's seat stood like a throne on the small veranda by the axe-cut door. The door was closed, and there were no windows, and no stilts, either, for a breeze to wander through. The walls rose straight from a flower-bed of sulumwoya plants, with a tidy edging that glinted.

"Wait a minute," I said to Osana, "is that live ammunition?"

"Not now, taubada," he said, and he started to laugh. "But lots of people died at first, in the war. They were hammering those bullets to make bracelets, and the big ones, they would stick three in the ground and put a cooking-pot on them and light a fire between. There were big bangs then, taubada. But not now."

"Where did it all come from?" I said.

"Out of the sky, taubada," he said. "From their ancestors, they said then. It was a Spitfire, taubada, that crashed over that way, in the swamp. The Air Force thought it was in the sea, they did not know until after the war. And these people, they did not know what it was, they said: 'O, it is our ancestors, it is cargo.' Then their cargo went bang in their faces. Life is sad, taubada."

I didn't say anything, in case of saying too much, but walked a bit faster after the others, nearly colliding with them when they stopped. They had fetched up at a covered platform towards the centre of the hamlet, and Alistair was stooping in under the thatch and staring at something.

I came behind him and peered over his shoulder, and was looking at an old dry mummy laid out on a mat.

"*I masisi*," the VC whispered. "He's asleep."

"Tim," Alistair said, also whispering, "we'll come back later."

But suddenly, as he was turning, someone else was there. He must have been sitting on the ground, at the far end of the platform, hidden from us, and only then stood up, half stooped, and looked at us across the body of the old chief. I could have sworn that his eyes had grown, in the few days since he had put the wind up me on board the *Igau*.

"Hey, look," I said, "it's Two-bob. Is this where he lives?"

Then I got shoved aside, as Alistair swung round to speak to Benoni. Though he kept his voice down, the questions sounded urgent, a bit angry. And Benoni and Boitoku, answering him, could have been nervous.

But Osana only looked amused. His face was saying: Look at me being amused.

When Alistair turned back, Two-bob was still watching us, and poised, as if he had been expecting an order.

"Who is he?" I muttered to Alistair. "Does anyone know?"

"Not exactly," he said, too low for the others to hear, but not quite to me, either. "He calls himself Metusela now, but he says his name used to be Mwanebu. He says his mother was a sister of Dipapa's who married a Muyuwa man, and Dipapa says it's true.

87

But that's not what he told us. He said he was born in the other village, Obomatu, and went to work on a plantation when he was a young man."

I said: "I didn't know you'd talked to him."

"We had a letter about him," he said, "before he arrived in Osiwa. He's been in the calaboose at Esa'ala. Nothing serious — he joined in a metho party while he was working round a hospital, and some of the guests finished up blind or dead. Well, he can't do that again, not here. But why should he lie about where he came from?"

"Does it matter?" I said, wishing the man would do something, instead of just standing there with his arms dangling and his eyes eating us up.

"To someone it does," Alistair said. "I can't tell you here. But if he's who he says he is, well, he's in line to be the next chief."

"*Him?*" I said.

"Yeah," he said. "Funny thought, isn't it? But no gossiping, understand?"

"Who can *I* gossip with?" I started to say. But he had raised his head, and for the first time was acknowledging the man at the other end of the platform. "Metusela," he said, "okay."

Like a robot, still with his eyes on us, Metusela stretched out his arm. He began to tap with a fingernail on the platform beside the chief's ear. Everything was so quiet, I never heard a village so quiet: the five of us at one end, he at the other, in the midday silence, and the slow tap-tap-tap going on by that old mummy's skull.

And at last Dipapa's spirit came back again. It heard the tapping, from wherever it is that spirits go, and it turned for home, hurrying, towards Metusela's nail. While we watched, the old man's spirit flew into the old man's head, and pushed up his eyelids, and he lay staring at the thatch.

OSANA

We watched Dipapa wake, and nobody said a word. He did not stretch or yawn. It was like a snake waking. For a little while he lay with his eyes open, then he reared up, like a snake with loose skin.

Dipapa was perhaps the oldest man in the world. The Dimdims say they think he was more than eighty years.

When I was in other villages, I laughed at Dipapa. But when I was near him I was shy, and never spoke.

Once a man at Vaimuna said to Mister Cawdor: "Taubada, I wish that Dipapa was dead." And Mister Cawdor said: "No. Why do you speak like that? He is my friend, a good old man." "Oh yes, taubada," the Vaimuna man said, "by day he is a good old man. By night it is otherwise."

In Osiwa, when they talked of his sorcery, I said: "Ignorance." But when I was near him, I was never sure.

Who knows what is inside his house, all sealed like that so that nobody else's sorcery could get in? Some day, I thought, perhaps Benoni will know: the things, but never the words. No one will fear Benoni, he is not like a chief.

But everyone who saw Dipapa knew that he was a chief, and felt it, like a sound or the temperature of the air.

When Dipapa was awake he sat up on the platform and turned his face towards Mister Cawdor. He had no teeth, and his head was like a skull. He was always sucking in his cheeks, and moving his lips, which were thin, like a white man's lips. He looked a long time at Mister Cawdor with his big eyes, which were brighter than any other man's eyes, and yet cloudy.

"O Dipapa," Mister Cawdor said, "already I have returned."

"O Misa Kodo," Dipapa said, not moving his head or any part of him, but staring into Mister Cawdor's eyes. "Again I see you at Wayouyo."

"You are well?" said Mister Cawdor.

"I am well," said Dipapa, "except for the malaria. Perhaps —"

"Yes, certainly," Mister Cawdor said. "You shall have some bully-beef and rice soon, for the malaria."

"My great thanks," said Dipapa. Then he began to look, though his head did not move, at the face of Mister Dalwood.

"The name of my companion," Mister Cawdor said, "is Misa Dolu'udi. He is a benevolent man, as well as strong."

"I see," Dipapa said, nodding. But he muttered, as if he was not pleased: "He is very young."

"O Dipapa," Mister Cawdor said, "you know it, he will be old before long."

Dipapa smiled then, showing his red gums and his red tongue. "Misa Kodo," he said, patting the mat beside him, "come, sit. Will you drink, will you chew?" And as Mister Cawdor climbed up beside him, he said out of one corner of his mouth to Benoni and Boitoku: "They will drink," and out of the other corner of his

89

mouth to the madman Metusela: "They will chew." And Benoni and Boitoku ran away to get green coconuts, while Metusela dived under the platform and brought out Dipapa's lime-gourd and the bag with his betelnut and all the other things.

When Mister Dalwood saw the lime-gourd, he whispered to me: "What's that?"

"The lime-gourd of Dipapa's ancestors," I said. "When he walks, there is a man to carry it."

"Like a king," Mister Dalwood said, staring at the old man, who had in one hand the great yellow gourd, and in the other a great ebony spatula as long as a man's forearm, all carved with animals and birds and branches with leaves.

Mister Cawdor had been tearing the husk away from the betelnut that Dipapa had given him, using his teeth. He took the spatula from Dipapa and dug lime from the gourd and wrapped it in a pepper-leaf which he put into his mouth. While he chewed he nodded to Dipapa and looked grateful.

All the time Metusela had been pounding betelnut for Dipapa, who had no teeth, and he handed it to the old man in an ebony mortar carved like a war-canoe, with a tall smooth ebony mast which was the pestle.

"Look at that," Mister Dalwood said. "Alistair, look at that. That's beautiful."

He was speaking in his loud voice, and Dipapa, scooping the betelnut into his mouth, peered at him over the little boat and did not seem pleased.

"He says," Mister Cawdor told Dipapa, "that your mortar is very beautiful. All the Dimdims say that. They think it is very fine, the carved ebony of your people."

"You say?" said Dipapa. "Then I will give the boy something in ebony, a *kuto* or a *sabu*."

"*Kuto?*" Mister Cawdor said. "*Sabu?* I do not know those words." And he turned to me, and said: "Osana?"

That made me pleased, because Mister Cawdor thought he knew everything about the language, though he did not, and I said in a kind voice: "*Kuto*, taubada, it is like a sharp knife, carved in ebony. And *sabu* is a big knife of ebony, a sword."

"*E, mokita?*" cried Mister Cawdor, looking astonished. "A knife and a sword? But those are white men's words, the language of France."

"It is possible, taubada," I said.

Dipapa mumbled his betelnut between his gums and seemed sleepy, not interested in the talk of Mister Cawdor and me. But he said: "If you wish, Misa Kodo, I will show you a *sabu* which is not made of ebony, but of iron." And to Metusela he said: "Go, get the old *sabu*," and Metusela ran off.

We watched Metusela open the door of Dipapa's house and step into the darkness. We could see him still, through the doorway, feeling about, and I thought it very strange that he knew what was inside Dipapa's house, which certainly Benoni would not have known, or any of Dipapa's wives. In a minute he came out again and closed the door, and ran back to us, holding a long sword which shone.

Dipapa took the sword from Metusela and gave it to Mister Cawdor, who stared and stared at it, up and down. He ran his finger down the edge of it, which was all broken away, like a saw.

"Some white men in a ship," Dipapa said, "gave it to my ancestors. Long ago they cut down trees with it, but today no more."

"Good God," Mister Cawdor said in English, and Mister Dalwood too was staring.

"There is writing on it," Dipapa said.

"I saw," said Mister Cawdor. "O Dipapa, it is the mark of Louis, the King of France. I think in the year that his sailing-master gave the *sabu* to your ancestor, the people of Louis cut off his head."

"Truly?" said Dipapa. "Bad doings. Our custom is not like that."

"*Sabu*," Mister Cawdor said to himself. "*Kuto.*"

"Let me in on it," said Mister Dalwood, who was wanting to see the sword, but Mister Cawdor would not take any notice of his hand reaching out. "Alistair, what's it all about? Who gave it to them?"

Mister Cawdor said in English: "D'Entrecasteaux, I should think. In 1793. And some knives as well. And ever since they've been making copies of them in ebony."

"Fantastic," Mister Dalwood said, like Mister Cawdor looking very pleased. "How much does he want for it?"

But Mister Cawdor did not seem to hear, and went on gazing at the sword, and rubbing at the mark of the King of France with his thumb.

"They come, they go," Dipapa said, sucking his gums and looking towards the sky, like a man half asleep. "Black men, white men, canoes, steamers. They bring their somethings. But we — we stay and watch, that is all. Every day the same."

DALWOOD

Nobody would tell me what they were talking about. For a while they let me handle the sword, but then the old man asked for it back, and Metusela took it away and shut it in the house. Benoni and Boitoku came back with green coconuts and gave me a drink, and that was all rather ceremonious while it lasted, but obviously I didn't count for much so long as Misa Kodo was in the area.

"Alistair," I said, when everyone was quiet for a moment, "do I need to stay?"

"You bored?" he said, looking round. "Okay, go for a walk."

As he spoke I noticed his lips and teeth, bright red with betelnut. "By the way, you look disgusting," I said, and he lobbed a mouthful of crimson spit on the ground near my shoe.

Boitoku wanted to come with me, but I told him no, because they wear me out, these friendly old men, always pointing to something and trying to explain it with their fingers and eyebrows. I said: "No, thanks, I'll just take a walk by myself," and Osana translated that, probably rudely, and the sad old VC looked put down.

Every part of the village was deserted when I wandered through. The people were at the resthouse, exclaiming over our somethings and getting the news from the houseboys and policemen. I walked by the fabulous yam-house, and then turned aside towards a gap I noticed in the grove, where there seemed to be a road leading to a circle of palms.

The path was mown and edged with a coral wall planted with crotons, as neat as a town garden. At the end of it I came out in a mown clearing, and thought at first that perhaps they danced there, or played cricket, because some of them do play a kind of cricket, with homemade bats like they used in the Middle Ages, and about sixty men to a side. But the clearing was not an empty space, after all, and when I came by the last palm, I saw the house away to the left.

Then I wished Alistair was with me, it seemed too good a joke not to share. The house was a church, it had a cross at the peak of the gable. But all along the top of the pandanus-leaf half-wall were

92

shapes in wood, beautifully carved, brightly painted. Hearts, clubs, diamonds and spades.

I wondered if they had a native catechist for this casino, and then remembered Mak saying that on Kailuana God died in the Great War. Yet there the church was, in the fresh-mown grass, the paint of it still spanking new; and some people who had once played cards somewhere had worked hard for weeks or months to make it beautiful like that.

I walked nearer, and looked up the cross. It wasn't a cross at all. It was a plane, a nasty-looking sharklike plane, carved in ebony.

Inside, from all the rafters, planes hung from cords and revolved in the faint breeze. Planes of all sizes, painted bright colours, or of polished wood with patterns picked out in lime. There were shiny planes, too, built of tin cans, and some crude little ones in brass. I thought of the old ammo around Dipapa's flower-bed, and Osana saying: Then their cargo went bang in their faces.

The earth floor was bare, but at the end where an altar might have been in the God-times, a huge black plane, another ebony one, hung upright from a rope. As I came near a puff of wind hit the wings and twisted it round, and I was looking into eyes.

Cowrie-shell eyes, the underside of the shell, like puckered white lids with no eyeballs behind them. They stared back at me, out of an ebony face. It was a pilot, there could be no doubt about his being a pilot: he was wearing all his gear, I made out the straps of his parachute and the goggles, pushed up on his helmet. He hung there by the neck, with his arms stretched out, crucified on his plane.

I touched one wing-tip, and turned him away from me. I thought, I'd better go back now, anyway; and is this what they mean by horror? Because that big wooden doll was doing things to me inside that I'd never felt in my life before. It was the nails in his hands, and the thought of the cargo, that came from a Spitfire, flown by a man.

Behind me, something moved. My heart jumped, and seemed to have all my blood in it.

Metusela was standing in the middle of the church, clutching a dagger.

93

Just standing there, nothing more. With his shell-eyes seeing me, nothing more.

"What?" I said. It came out with too much breath.

He walked nearer, holding out his hand with the dagger in it, the handle towards me. "*Kuto*," he said, watching my face. "Present," he said.

Then it was me who must have seemed the freak, gaping at the ebony knife. At last I reached out and took it, still warm and marked with sweat from his fingers.

"Present," he said again. Coming from that pint-sized frame the voice was so deep it was shocking, and I seemed to feel all the strings of the revolving planes vibrate a little over our heads. "My friend," he said, gazing up.

"Thank you," I said. "It is very good."

He smiled at me. He had a mouth of that shape they call a Cupid's bow, and it didn't go with anything else he had. "Good ebony," he said. "Taubada, Misa Kodo say: You come."

"Yes," I said. "Okay. I was coming." And I started to go past him. But just then he moved into my path, though not meaning to, probably, and suddenly my hands were on his shoulders. I shoved him aside, and he staggered.

"Sorry," I said, when I had had time to think about it. "Sorry, Metusela."

"All right, taubada," he said, still smiling. "My friend. Okay. See you later." And he waved, as if I was a passing ship, as I went by.

But when I was at the open front of the church, he shouted after me again. "My friend," he called, and I looked back and he was up where the altar should have been, beside the dangling crucifix. He had his arm around it, as though around somebody's shoulders, and white eyes were watching me out of two black faces.

"You see?" he called. "You see this fellow?"

"Yes." I said. "Very good."

"This Jesus," he said. "Black man Jesus. No white man Jesus. Jesus black."

"Yeah," I said. "I see." And I turned to go again. But he had one more thing to tell me, and he yelled after me, not my friend this time, no, more rough with his voice than I had been with my hands when I pushed him half across the church.

"You hear," he shouted. He looked cute as a golliwog in his

94

khaki shorts and curls, but he was furious and the finger he pointed at me would have been loaded. In the shadow of the church the two pairs of white eyes caught all the light, like foam on the sea at night.

"You hear," he said more quietly. "One time you kill black man Jesus. Another time, no. Another time, no more."

BENONI

All the afternoon they sat on chairs at a table under a big tree, and on the grass in front of them the people of the village talked and smoked and chewed. Between them they had the old census book. When Misa Dolu'udi called out the names from the old book, people got up and came and talked with Misa Kodo. Then Misa Kodo wrote their names in the new book.

Towards the end of the afternoon Misa Dolu'udi called the names of a family of eight people. But only one old woman came forward, in a rough grass skirt and with soot on her body and her head shaved. She squatted in front of the table, hiding her face.

"What's this?" Misa Dolu'udi said, not understanding. And he called out all the names again, more loudly, and with each name the old woman's head sank lower, till her face was on the ground and she was crying into the grass.

Then Misa Kodo, who had been writing in the new book, looked up and understood. He called me to him, and whispered: "What has happened, Benoni? Two years ago there were eight people in this family. Where are they now?"

"Her husband has died, taubada," I said, "one month ago. Her first son was killed falling from a palm. His wife went to a new husband in Obomatu and took the child. Her second and third sons were drowned in their canoe. The second son's wife went back to her mother. Now there is only the old woman."

Misa Kodo went on looking and looking at the old woman hiding her face. At last he said: "Old woman, go now. Our shame, we two."

The old woman tried to say something kind to him, because she was a good-natured old woman, but she could not speak for crying, and stumbled away.

"Just the mother, is it?" Misa Dolu'udi said, and he crossed out the other names.

95

"Just the mother," Misa Kodo said, and he wrote the old woman's name all alone in the new book as a family.

When the census was finished, Misa Kodo sat back in his chair and looked at me. "Who cares for that old woman?" he said. "Who gardens for her? Who mends her roof?"

"I do not know, taubada," I said.

"No?" he said. "And yet you will command all the villages, you say."

"Perhaps," I said.

"Is she hungry?" he said. "Does her roof leak? Do you know?"

"No," I said. "I do not know."

"I am tired," Misa Kodo said, rubbing his forehead. "Ah, Benoni, there are many people in the world whose minds are heavy. Many, many. What shall we do? Shall we cry? Shall we go mad? What will you do when you are commander?"

"I do not know, taubada," I said. "But I will not cry or go mad. I will be hard, like a Dimdim."

"E, be hard," he said. "Have a hard mind, like a bush pig. Be like me. Benoni, do you know the story of Jesus?"

"A little," I said. "Not much. Why do you ask?"

"When Jesus was born," he said, "there was a census and a new tax, just like this. I think patrol officers were called publicans then. I think they wrote JOSEPH–MARY–JESUS in their book and never thought of it again. Do you suppose they looked at their faces, Mary and Jesus? Well, perhaps. And made jokes. That Joseph was not the father. Because we all make jokes sometimes, we publicans, it is our custom."

"Taubada," I said, "there was a star. Taubada, is that true? There was a star."

"Ah, yes," he said, "but they would not see it. They would be in the resthouse, drinking rum and writing letters."

Then I wanted to tell Misa Kodo something, but he got up and took the books from the table. He said to me: "Come with me, let us walk," and in English to Misa Dolu'udi he said the same thing. He said: "But first we will go to the resthouse bwaima and take three baskets of Dipapa's yams for that old woman. Then I will believe that I am a benevolent man and be better-tempered."

When we had come to the old woman's house, the three of us with baskets, two Dimdims and the nephew of Dipapa,

96

she could not speak, she could only crouch at our feet and smile.

"Old woman," Misa Kodo said, "your yams."

"O taubad'," cried the old woman, and laughed like a hen.

"How is your house?" asked Misa Kodo. "Is it strong?"

"E, strong," she cried.

"And you are content?" he said.

"I am an old woman, taubad'," she said. "Only an old woman. E. Today I am content."

"Good, then," said Misa Kodo. "Well, we are going. Goodbye, my mother."

The old woman laughed again, out of shyness, and Misa Kodo and I began to walk away. But Misa Dolu'udi hung back, digging in the pocket of his shorts, and found a two-shillings and gave it to the old woman, who did not know what it was. "Here, buy yourself a drink," said Misa Dolu'udi, and ran after us down the path, smiling like a clam.

"We are three good men," said Misa Kodo to us all. "If we did not exist, Dipapa's yams would be at home with Dipapa."

"I want to talk to Benoni," Misa Dolu'udi said to Misa Kodo. "How about you be Osana for a while?"

"Benoni speaks English," Misa Kodo said.

"No, taubada," I said, "not English. I talk Pidgin, a little, that is all."

"But you understand us?" Misa Kodo said.

"Sometimes," I said, "a little bit."

"Tell him this," said Misa Dolu'udi. And then Misa Kodo began to play a game that was very strange. It was as if there was no longer anyone in Misa Kodo's body. He was not like a person any more, he was like a machine, that walked between Misa Dolu'udi and me and changed our words into another language.

Misa Dolu'udi said to me, through the machine: "I think that man Two-bob, Metusela, I think he is mad."

"Perhaps," I said.

"But clever," Misa Dolu'udi said. "He understands some English. He talked to me. Sometimes it sounds like English that they learn at the Osiwa mission, sometimes like Pidgin."

"He has travelled everywhere, taubada," I said.

"Then, what was his work?" asked Misa Dolu'udi.

"I don't know, taubada," I said. "I think plantation work, boat-boy, houseboy, everything. But truly I do not know. He does not talk to me."

"But he talks to your uncle?" Misa Dolu'udi said.

"E, truly," I said. And then I began to speak to Misa Kodo, not Misa Dolu'udi, about what had been in my mind since he first came. "Taubada," I said, "I think my uncle wants to shame me. He pretends that we are friends. He tells the people so. But in his mind it is different. That day when you came, I thought I knew what was in his mind. I thought, when he knows that he is going to die, he will burn all the things of the chief, all the valuables, perhaps the house, perhaps Darkness-of-Evening itself. I thought, he will tell the people that he is the last chief. And he will tell them that he has taught his sorcery to other people, so that if they disobey him after he is dead his sorcery will still reach them in the middle of the night. So I wanted to tell you. Taubada, I wanted to tell the Government, because sorcery is bad, it is forbidden by the Government. Taubada, I want you to put my uncle in the calaboose."

Misa Kodo was still walking on with a quiet face, not seeming to notice my words. So I looked at him in surprise, and suddenly he jerked his head and was awake again. "O," he said. "I was thinking like an interpreter. It is different from thinking like a kiap. Well, Benoni, I am sorry for you, but I am not going to calaboose your uncle, because he is eighty yam-seasons old. But I will speak with him, and some other people."

"There is more, taubada," I said. "Since the day you came, it is different."

"E?" he said.

"There is Metusela," I said. "My uncle says that Metusela is his nephew too. It is a lie, but my uncle says it. Why does he say it?"

"You say," said Misa Kodo. "Why?"

"Because Metusela is a sorcerer like himself, and would be a chief like himself."

"Good, then," Misa Kodo said. "So you wish me to calaboose Metusela?"

"E," I said.

"Our talk is finished," Misa Kodo said. "It is finished this time. But say to your uncle that I said this to you: A man does not need big eyes to see."

98

"No, taubada," I said. "Then he would know that I talked with you. I would be afraid."

"Of his sorcery?" Misa Kodo said. "Why? You slept with his wife, and live."

"Not of sorcery only," I said. "There are other things. There is poison, and clubs, and the sword. I was not afraid before, but now there is Metusela. It is different because of Metusela. And Metusela is not eighty years old."

"I cannot do anything today or tomorrow," Misa Kodo said. "Because — what has Metusela done? Nothing. No, Benoni. Come back to Osiwa with us. You could work, you could be a boat-boy on the *Igau* for a while, until we understand these doings better."

"I will not leave Wayouyo," I said, "If I go, I will never return. I know it, taubada."

He looked at me seriously, believing what I told him, and at last said: "Guard yourself, my friend."

"I am a strong man," I said.

And then Misa Kodo changed himself into a machine again, and said to Misa Dolu'udi in English: "I am a strong man."

"*You* are a strong man," said Misa Dolu'udi to me, through the machine. "You are strong like a bandicoot." Suddenly he started dancing at me, and slapped me on the face, and then over the belly-button with the back of his hand. So I hit him too, and we danced all up and down the path, but he never reached me again, though I hit him often, not hard.

At last Misa Dolu'udi was tired, and his face was red and shining. He said to me, through Misa Kodo: "I am only half a man now, because of New Guinea."

"Then," I said, "I would be two men in Dimdim."

Misa Dolu'udi waved his hand at me and spoke, and Misa Kodo said: "You talk gammon." But I had heard Misa Dolu'udi's English words, and waved my hand like him and said them back to him. "Up yours," I said, and we all laughed, even Misa Kodo.

All that time we had been walking along the path that leads to the coral ridge and the jungle and the sea, and I thought that we were going to swim, and that Misa Dolu'udi would teach me more Dimdim games on the beach. But on the slope that leads down to where the jungle begins Misa Kodo turned off the path. And then we were on the dead land, all rock and burnt grass, that belongs to nobody and that nobody has ever gardened, where the stones are, the biggest ones, called Ukula'osi.

We stood in the middle of the widest circle, which is about four strides across for a tall man, and the wind blew on us over the jungle, out of a sky full of rain. At any time of day that place is ugly and lonely and children are afraid of it, and then it was growing dark. I did not want to be there, in the ring of lumps of rock. Misa Dolu'udi was gazing around him at the circle, and at the four tall pointed rocks that stand like men.

"What is this?" said Misa Dolu'udi, through the mouth of Misa Kodo.

"It is the stones called Ukula'osi," I said. "And the four standing stones have their own names, which I forget."

"It is a forbidden place?" asked Misa Dolu'udi.

"Yes," I said. "No one may touch these stones. Our ancestors placed them here. If anyone moved them, a great wind would come up and destroy the villages, and there would be a famine, and all the people would go mad. One time a man's dog began to dig beside a stone, and the man killed his dog. Another time a woman called Olivilesi tried to move a stone. She went mad. It would be like that for all of us if the stones fell."

"I am afraid," said Misa Dolu'udi, but he laughed. "It is a place of spirits."

"Misa Kodo," I said, "Masta Interpreter, what do the Dimdims say about these stones?"

"O, many things," said Misa Kodo. "Some people say they were like a church, where people sang. Other people say chiefs were buried here."

"E?" I said. "And what else do they say?"

"Others say that the stones point to places in the sky where some stars first appear, that tell the people it is time to plant or harvest."

"If that is true," I said, "no old man remembers. What more do the Dimdims say?"

"Some think the stones are meant for reefs and islands, to teach young men how to sail between here and Muyuwa and Kinana."

"No, taubada," I said, "I do not believe that young men would learn like that. They learn by sailing with older men. Is that all that the Dimdims say?"

"Yes, that is all," Misa Kodo said. "Except — we have some crazy people in Dimdim."

"Then what do they say, the crazy ones?"

"They say," Misa Kodo said, smiling, "that there are people who come from the stars, flying in machines like the big tobacco-tins, and that these rings were like their air-strips, and that they will come again."

When he said that I felt a great fear, and cried out: "Taubad' —," staring at him.

"O, why do you look like that?" he said, surprised.

"Taubada, will they stop? Will they get out and walk in the villages?"

"E, you, mind-of-a-child," Misa Kodo said, and he was laughing at me. "It is a story, that is all. A Dimdim story, do you understand? There are no people in the stars."

I did not know how to tell it to him, to make him feel the fear, which had come back and in that place was worst of all. I said: "Taubada, I want to speak," but when he looked at me and waited I could not begin. "No," I said. "Not now. Now you would not believe. But tonight, I will come to the resthouse with some other men, to talk, to ask questions,"

"I know what you will say," he said. "I will show you a picture in a book, and you will not be afraid any more."

Then suddenly, over my shoulder, he saw what Misa Dolu'udi was doing, and began to shout, and I turned and saw and shouted even louder. "Forbidden, forbidden!" we screamed at Misa Dolu'udi. "Forbidden to piss on the stones!" And Misa Dolu'udi did not know at all what to do just then.

DALWOOD

When we were walking back to the resthouse, in the dusk, terrible screams broke out somewhere in the village, and I looked back at Alistair and Benoni, dawdling behind me, to know what was going on.

"Pig, taubada," Benoni said, in English. "You kaikai."

I saw that Alistair was trying to take no notice, but he was wearing his bad sailor's face.

"What are they doing to the thing?' I said to him. The screams were coming faster and louder. They didn't sound all that much like an animal.

"What?" he said. "The *bulukwa*? They're singeing the hair off it."

"*Alive?*" I said.

"It'll die as it cooks," he said. "They'll have speared it in the side."

Then I felt as queasy as he looked, and thought of going on strike. "I'm not eating any."

"You'll be given some," he said. "Better be polite. It's a big day for them, having meat."

Benoni was beaming at us, in the blue light, a blue tinge to his skin. I thought of the two of us fooling about on the path, pretending to box, and how he'd seemed such a nice ordinary young bloke, just like me, ordinary like me. And every scream of that animal was doing his heart good. Listen to what a good host I am, his face was saying; and he smiled at us, modestly, letting us know he had no doubt we'd have done the same for him.

OSANA

That evening they made a great feast in the village, and Mister Cawdor and Mister Dalwood sat beside Dipapa on his platform and had every kind of food brought to them. Mister Dalwood ate sago dumplings and yams and taro and mangoes and bananas and nearly everything that there was, except pig. Mister Cawdor only chewed a piece of sugar-cane, which would have hurt the feelings of the people if they had not had so much pleasure in feeding Mister Dalwood.

Some of the people were eating boiled bats. Benoni brought one to Mister Dalwood on a leaf, but Mister Dalwood said: "Thank you, no."

"You do not eat bats, taubada?" I said.

"No," said Mister Dalwood. "But once, with the black men in Dimdim, I ate a goanna."

After that I did not feel hungry for a long time, thinking of Mister Dalwood's disgusting customs.

When Mister Cawdor saw that there was no hope of putting more food into Mister Dalwood, he got down from the platform and said goodbye to Dipapa. This caused Dipapa to wake, and to say that he was enjoying Mister Cawdor's talk. Then Dipapa held out his hand to Mister Cawdor, and Mister Cawdor shook it and looked shy, more like a boy than a patrol officer. I thought that time: It is not only me, it is not only black men, it is everybody who is careful of Dipapa. Dipapa looked straight into Mister Cawdor's face; but Mister Cawdor never looked really at Dipapa, his eyes wandered away.

Afterwards we all went back to the resthouse, a great crowd of people, and especially a great crowd of girls, who crawled underneath the house and peered through the cracks in the floor, waiting for Mister Dalwood to take a shower. All the afternoon they had been talking about it, and they had hung the bucket-shower in a good place and filled it with water scented with flowers and sulumwoya. But Mister Dalwood sat down at the table on the veranda with Mister Cawdor and began to drink rum and would not take off his clothes. So the girls were bored, and started to sing, underneath the house, the song that they sing everywhere.

"Men's custom is this,
Men's custom is this,
When they see a hole
They have to fill it."

And the men, on the grass and on the veranda, sang back:

"Women's custom is this,
Women's custom is this,
When they see a banana
They have to swallow it."

Mister Dalwood, who seemed to be drunk, but he often seemed to be drunk without drinking anything, sang this song with the men, and Benoni, who was sitting at his feet, looked ashamed. I knew what Benoni was thinking. Because it happens to everybody, that one day they meet a Dimdim and think: At last, here is a Dimdim that is kind and clever and cheerful and will be like my brother to me. And always the Dimdim turns out to be the same as the rest, only an ignorant person after all.

The idiot Kailusa was one who never learned better. He was old enough to be Mister Cawdor's uncle, and that is what he was like: like a hunchbacked uncle with a handsome nephew. There was nothing in his mind but Mister Cawdor who never saw him. On the table where Mister Cawdor and Mister Dalwood sat that night was a wooden bowl, that went everywhere with Kailusa. In the bowl were the best flowers Kailusa could find. It was like a piece of Mister Cawdor's home, that travelled with him, whether he noticed or not. So Mister Cawdor dropped his cigarette butts among the flowers, because that was his custom, whether he noticed or not.

The flying ants swarmed in towards the Tilley lamp. Mister Cawdor and Mister Dalwood and Benoni were brushing ants away from their faces, and ants were burning and falling back from the lamp on to the table, with a bitter smell. Suddenly Biyu came running, all important, in his Hawaii shirt. Nobody wanted him or noticed him, but he came running, carrying an enamel basin full of water. Biyu unhooked the lamp and stood it in the basin, and ants began to fall into the water and to drown.

"What's happening to the light?" Mister Dalwood said, not bothering to look.

"Biyu's making an ant-trap," said Mister Cawdor.

"Biyu?" Mister Dalwood said. "Is he still about? I'm sick of being surrounded by Biyu."

Soon the water in the basin was like one crawling heap of ants, and Biyu set fire to a piece of newspaper and began to burn them.

"What's that stink?" Mister Dalwood cried, jumping up from his chair. "Biyu! Go and talk to some maries, we don't want you here."

So Biyu put out the fire, looking ashamed, and went away, and Benoni also looked ashamed because of his friend Mister Dalwood's bad temper.

"He was trying to be useful" Mister Cawdor said.

But Mister Dalwood muttered angrily: "I'll have to get rid of him. He can't do anything right."

"You're in a sweet mood," Mister Cawdor said. "Why don't you go to bed?"

"If I'm in a sweet mood," Mister Dalwood said, "you can bloody well lump it. I put up with plenty from you."

When Mister Dalwood was bad-tempered, it always made Mister Cawdor more cheerful, and he laughed and pushed the bottle towards Mister Dalwood. "Enjoy yourself," he said; "rot your stupid brain," and Mister Dalwood poured more rum.

Then Benoni got up from where he was sitting and stood behind Mister Cawdor's chair, leaning to whisper in his ear. Mister Cawdor seemed surprised, and his face turned, looking out from the lighted veranda to the darkness where all the people were. He spoke quietly to Benoni, and Benoni, also looking at the darkness, raised his arm and beckoned. Six or seven men came out of the clearing behind me, and mounted to the veranda and squatted at the Dimdims' feet.

BENONI

Misa Kodo, seeing the old VC among the men, said: "O, Boitoku, what is this trouble that makes the minds of the people heavy?" While he spoke, he and Misa Dolu'udi were both watching Metusela, who had come after the men into the light, and was standing in the grass by the corner of the veranda. The two Dimdims, and especially Misa Dolu'udi, did not seem to be able to move their eyes from the madman, though he was doing nothing, only standing there and listening. Misa Kodo, I saw in his face was thinking more about Metusela than about his words to the old man, and Misa Dolu'udi looked as if he would shout at Metusela to go away.

Boitoku was shy, and played with his badge. "It is difficult, taubada," he said. "Taubada, let Benoni speak."

"Well, Benoni?" Misa Kodo said.

"It is a question, taubada," I said. "Taubada, the war of the Dimdims with the people of Yapan is finished, isn't it?"

"E," Misa Kodo said. "Fourteen years ago."

"You see," I said to Boitoku, "I did not talk gammon."

"Good, then," Boitoku said with a shrug. "I was wrong. I have not been to Manus."

"Therefore," I said, "it is not a war-machine."

Misa Kodo was still watching Metusela. "What do you say, Beni?" he said. "What is not a war-machine?"

"The star," I said. "The star-machine."

Misa Kodo turned and stared at me, with great eyes. "The star-machine?" he said. "What is that, a star-machine?"

"It is like a star," I said, "at first, when it is far away in the sky. But when it comes close, it is a machine. With the brightest light, taubada, and people. Like a plane, taubada, but it is not a plane."

It was very extraordinary to see Misa Kodo's face. What was in his face was like joy.

His voice was strange too, with joy, or excitement. It was quiet, and as if his throat was tight.

"Tell me," he said. "Speak, Benoni."

"It comes in the night," I said. "It came eight nights ago. Then

105

it came six nights ago. It comes from the north-east, and it is like a star, but it moves like a feather. Sometimes it falls, sometimes it climbs. But always it is very fast."

"*Ki,*" Misa Kodo said, very quiet. "Go on."

"The first time," I said, "it came down out of the sky over Darkness-of-Evening, in the middle of the village. It had windows with lights, like a steamer. Suddenly a very bright light came out of it, like the sun. It was like daytime, taubada, in the village. All the people ran to their houses and peeped out at it. We saw men, taubada, looking at us from the windows. Then the big light went out, and the machine flew up into the sky and became a star again."

"And the look of it?" Misa Kodo said. "What is it like?"

I made the shape of it with my hands. "Like you said, taubada. Like a tobacco-tin, that flies."

"And the second time?" Misa Kodo said.

"That time," I said, "these five men here were coming home from fishing, in the dark. They were on the path near the stones, taubada, and carrying torches. I think the machine saw the flames. It came down over their heads and turned on its light and followed them when they ran. It chased them along the path, taubada, till they were near the village. Then it went dark, except for the windows, and flew away like a star."

"And you saw people?" Misa Kodo said, gazing at the five men. His face was moved, he was suddenly like a child. "In the star-machine, you saw people?"

The men began to stir, and murmur, and laugh uneasily. "We were very frightened," one of them said, and then they all laughed, ashamed of their fear. "We saw nothing," another of them said, "only the light. Taubada, the fear was very great."

"E," Misa Kodo said, nodding. "The fear, it would be great."

"But the first time, taubada," I said, "we saw people. Their heads and their shoulders and their arms. They were watching us, two or three of them, in the belly of the machine."

Then Misa Kodo said: "Tim!" and Misa Dolu'udi looked round from watching the madman. "Tim!" cried Misa Kodo, and he began to talk in English very fast, sometimes laughing in his excitement, and Misa Dolu'udi's strange blue eyes got big, and he began to laugh and chatter too. They kept saying to each other: "Boianai," which is a place in Kinana or Numa where some Osiwa men used to

106

go. They kept saying it over and over again, "Boianai!" and Misa Kodo sounded full of joy. But Misa Dolu'udi, though he was excited, shook his head sometimes, and said: "It can't be." When Misa Dolu'udi said that, Misa Kodo cried out: "It is, it is," sounding passionate, and then spoke some more, very fast.

At last Misa Dolu'udi said: "Then aren't you scared?"

"No, no," Misa Kodo cried. "Oh Christ, no. Don't you see?"

"It can't be," Misa Dolu'udi said again, and shook his head.

While the Dimdims were talking to each other, the rain began. One minute there was no rain, the next minute it broke like a wave. Metusela and Osana and all the people outside on the grass groaned and muttered and ran away. Soon there were only we few men on the veranda, and the chattering Dimdims.

"Taubada," I said to Misa Kodo, "what is the machine?"

"What?" he said, and it was as if he had forgotten that we were there. "Oh. Well, truly, Beni, I do not know. I think it is a machine of the Americans, or perhaps of a people whose country is called Russia. I think it will not hurt us. I think they are benevolent, those people." And then he went on, talking quicker and louder and more excited: "If it comes again, run to me, tell me. I want to speak with those people. It is my very strong desire. If I talk with those people, my joy will be great, very great."

"Then," I said, "even you, even the Dimdims, do not understand this machine."

"No," he said. "Not even I."

"They are not Americans," I said. "You talk gammon, taubada. They are people from the stars."

"I do not know," he said. "I will not say. I am an ignorant man too, Beni. Like all the men in the world. We live on the world like an island. Who can say he has seen every ship that sails on the sea?"

"You have lied to me, taubada," I said.

"No," he said. "I have said I am an ignorant man, and that is the truth."

Then he got up from his chair, full of restlessness, and said: "My friends, let us talk again tomorrow. Now I want to be alone. My very great thanks." He stood by the table looking down at us, with his eyes wide and his face moved and dark, and he said those words as if he believed what he said. "My very great thanks."

Now they are going to read from the book, where he slashed in the margin with a thick blue Department of Territories pencil.

He had the pencil stuck behind his ear. He lay reading, quiet in the bedroom, while I, at the table on the veranda, sat on alone, wondering what was in the business to stir him up like that. Him that I'd called anaemic because nothing thrilled him. I sat listening to his silence and the rain, measuring the time by the rum in my china mug.

The rain was a bead-curtain in front of the veranda. It drummed on the thatch. Suddenly two girls, hung with flowers and gasping, burst from the darkness and threw themselves on the boards near my feet. They crouched there, dripping and shining, and nodded to me casually, as if we were all where we belonged.

"What do you want?" I said.

But they didn't understand, and only smiled in a businesslike way.

"Alistair," I called out, "there's a pair of females here. What do I tell them?"

"Tell them you're engaged," he called back.

"You talk to them. Say it's time they went to bed."

"Okay," he said. "Are you ready?" And while I jerked my thumb towards the wall, his voice came over it: "*O, vivila! A doki tuta bu ku masis'.*"

The women looked at each other, and then at me. And one of them said, shyly: "*Ambesa magim bi ta masis'*?"

The translation came over the wall, deadpan. "They say: 'Where would you like us to sleep?'"

"With your mother," I shouted, standing up and pointing at the rain. "*Ku los'.* Fuck off." Before they had moved I unhooked the lamp and went to the bedroom, leaving them alone with each other's amazed faces.

Alistair was laid out on one of the neat bunks that Benoni had had built for us, wrapped in a tatty red trade-store blanket with a black tiger on it, nearly lifesize. "What are you doing in that?" I said.

"Feeling cold," he said.

"You'll be happy in hell," I said. But as I undressed I felt that it was, after all, a little cooler, and the air was so heavy with damp that it seemed surprising that the lamps could still burn. I put out the one on my bunk, and the insects that had come in with me went over to him and battered at his book.

"They've gone?" he said.

"I think so," I said. "They're probably under the floor now, looking up my leg."

"Osana sent them," he said.

"Osana did?" I said. "You're kidding."

"It's not the first time," he said. "Haven't you noticed? It's part of the Oust Cawdor campaign. He tells them we sent him to make a booking. He even pays them a bit on account. Poor stupid maries, it's rough on them. They arrive here all primed for an orgy, and you start screaming and abusing them."

"Well, I'm sorry about that," I said. "I didn't understand the situation. Do you feel like an orgy?"

"Constantly," he said.

"I've never had one," I said. "Why don't we?"

"That would be the happiest night in Osana's life," he said. And he went on reading.

"Hell, I didn't mean it," I said. "It was just stupid talk. It's this place, these islands. Everything's sex."

"And yams," he said. "Sex and yams. I spent a long time learning the language before I realized that was all there was to talk about."

"I wish I was going somewhere tomorrow," I said. "I wish I was going to Paris, or Las Vegas, or Bangkok."

"You're going to Obomatu," he said, "with me. To do a new census book, you lucky bugger."

I lay down on my bunk and watched him across the room. He had been reading most of the time when I was talking to him, but I was used to that.

I suppose I was drunk, that must have been why I thought all of a sudden of a story I'd heard in Moresby, and it seemed funny enough to snigger at.

"What appears to be the trouble?" he said, not looking up.

"Just a wet joke," I said. "There were these two troppo patrol officers living in a resthouse, week after week. One day a trader came to see them. 'Tell me something,' he said, 'what do you two fellas do about sex?' 'About sex?' they said. 'Oh, we lower the flag and have a glass of rum about sex.'"

"Very good," said Misa Kodo, in the best Misa Kodo manner.

I started to giggle, not because of the story but because of him. "You know this one?" I said. "There were these two troppo patrol officers sitting in the middle of a village, and a pigeon flew over and dropped a turd on the head of one of them. The VC gets very upset about this, and he says: 'Oh, taubada, I'll go away and get a piece of paper.' When he's gone, one patrol officer turns to the other and says: 'That's the stupidest kanaka I ever struck. By the time he gets back here with the paper, that bird will be miles away.'"

"You're a ball of fun tonight," Misa Kodo said. "It must be a riot, being two troppo patrol officers."

"Did you take the vitamin pills?" I said. "No, you didn't. Or the anti-malarial. That's why you're cold, you're getting malaria, you stupid bastard. What have you eaten today?"

"You're pissed," he said. "Go to sleep. Let's not have all that."

"I want to see you fit," I said.

He looked up at me at last, calm. "I'm pretty fit," he said. "And I'm glad you've got Saliba. Because there's something a bit sad about two troppo patrol officers worrying over each other's vitamin pills."

"You're not human," I said. "Okay. I don't care if you live or die. Just leave a note that it wasn't my fault, that's all, on account of public opinion."

Then I rolled over and turned my back on him, and did mean to go to sleep. But he must have gone on looking at me, and at last his voice said, thoughtfully: "*Tomitukwaibwoina yoku*. You are a benevolent man."

"Goodnight," I said.

"Listen," he said. "I want to read you something. Tim? Listen."

I heard the rain on the thatch. The rain on the thatch, and the insects bumping and scrabbling against the pages of his book. And his voice, rising, growing sharper as he read.

BROWNE

In the following years, three comets were seen; and not long before the coming of the Spaniards a strange light broke forth in the east. It spread broad at its base on the horizon, and rising in a pyramidal form tapered off as it approached the zenith. It resembled a vast sheet or flood of fire, or, as an old writer expresses it, "seemed thickly powdered with stars". At the same time, low voices were heard in the air, and doleful wailings, as if to announce some strange, mysterious calamity! The Aztec monarch, terrified at the apparitions in the heavens, took council of Nezahualpilli, who was a great proficient in the subtle science of astrology. But the royal sage cast a deeper cloud over his spirit, by reading in these prodigies the speedy downfall of the empire.

Such are the strange stories reported by the chroniclers, in which it is not impossible to detect the glimmerings of truth. Nearly thirty years had elapsed since the discovery of the islands by Columbus, and more than twenty since his visit to the American continent. Rumours, more or less distinct, of this wonderful appearance of the white men, bearing in their hands the thunder and the lightning, so like in many respects to the traditions of Quetzalcoatl, would naturally spread far and wide among the Indian nations. Such rumours, doubtless, long before the landing of the Spaniards in Mexico, found their way up the grand plateau, filling the minds of men with anticipations of the near coming of the period when the great deity was to return and receive his own again.

In the excited state of their imaginations, prodigies became a familiar occurrence. Or rather, events not very uncommon in themselves, seen through the discoloured medium of fear, were easily magnified into prodigies; and the accidental swell of the lake, the appearance of a comet, and the conflagration of a building, were all interpreted as the special annunciations of Heaven. Thus it happens in those great political convulsions which shake the foundations of society, – the mighty events that cast their shadows before them in the coming. Then it is that the atmosphere is agitated with the low, prophetic murmurs, with which nature, in the moral as in the physical world, announces the march of the hurricane:

"When from the shores
And forest-rustling mountains comes a voice,
That, solemn sounding, bids the world prepare!"

When tidings were brought to the capital of the landing of Grijalva on the coast, in the preceding year, the heart of Montezuma was filled with dismay. He felt as if the destinies which had so long brooded over the royal line of Mexico were to be accomplished, and the sceptre was to pass away from his house for ever.

111

DALWOOD

"You're asleep, of course," Alistair said. I heard him move in his bunk, reaching towards the lamp. Then the pressure hissed out of it, the light drained away, and the rain seemed all the louder because of the darkness and because we would not talk any more.

"I heard you," I said, inside the mosquito net I had arranged around me. "I don't understand you, that's all. Whose side are you on — the Martians?"

Then he said something that was covered by the rain. I couldn't hear the words, but I heard the tone of his voice, excited, as if he was impatient with waiting for something. I pulled back the net and called across the room: "What was that?"

And he shouted, in the roaring dark, while the rain came faster and the palms thrashed. "We're not alone," he shouted. "Ah, you thick lump, can't you see it? We're not alone."

OSANA

When I woke in the morning the rain was still falling as it had been when I went to sleep, and I said to the policemen: "We shall not go today to Obomatu. Sleep some more," I told them. "I am going to sleep, and no work can be done without me."

One of the policemen, Esau, said in Pidgin: "What is your work, bighead? Masta Alistair does your work."

"You shall see," I said. "Wait a little, Esau. You shall see."

When we had eaten we ran to the resthouse through the rain. There were no people about it, only the two Dimdims and Kailusa and Biyu on the veranda. Even an ignorant village like Wayouyo could not be interested in Dimdims when the weather was like that. The people had stayed in their houses, and the smoke from under their yam-pots climbed from the eaves into the rain, making the air of the village blue and the grove cloudy.

"It's nine o'clock," said Mister Dalwood to the three policemen and me.

Mister Dalwood sat in a chair on the veranda with an impatient face. But Mister Cawdor, in his chair, was reading a book and took no notice of us when we came.

"It is the rain, taubada," I said to Mister Dalwood. "We had much trouble because of the rain."

112

"Bullshit," said Mister Dalwood, speaking carefully, and the policemen laughed.

Biyu was waiting behind Mister Dalwood's chair. Biyu looked out across the clearing and said: "It rain, taubada," and then was so pleased with himself that he could not stop smiling, because he had said it in English.

"Is it?" said Mister Dalwood. "Hey, everybody. Biyu says it's raining."

That made the policemen laugh again, and the stupid Biyu was filled with shame and went away, and even Kailusa, who did not like him, seemed sorry.

Suddenly Mister Cawdor closed his book with a noise and looked angry at Mister Dalwood. He said: "Listen, will you stop trying to score off the kid."

"Well, he's such an idiot," Mister Dalwood complained. "Anyway, hell, who pays him?"

"Some time I'll have to tell you about shame in this part of the world," Mister Cawdor said. "That's if you don't want to see him shinning up a palm and jumping off."

When Mister Cawdor said that, Mister Dalwood went red like a flower and seemed more shamed even than Biyu, though no one had laughed at him. He said: "Yeah. Sorry. You don't tell me enough." And Mister Cawdor looked at him for a moment quite kindly, and then opened his book again.

"You're all right," Mister Cawdor said, while he read. "For a Dimdim, anyway."

Mister Dalwood did not answer, but gazed at his shoes and moved his shoulders like a modest man.

The policemen had not understood what the Dimdims said, but they saw Mister Dalwood's shame and were interested and sorry for him. Policemen and boat-boys are always fond of Mister Dalwood, because he is so childish and so strong. So the policemen went and squatted down beside him, and whenever he looked towards them they smiled very kindly, till I thought that Mister Dalwood would jump up and knock their heads together in his bad-temper.

Suddenly Kailusa said: "Taubada, people are coming." So we turned to see, and through the rain we made out four or five men crossing the clearing, moving at the pace of a very old man. Benoni was the first of them, and then we knew who was following, because in his hand he had the big yellow lime-gourd of Dipapa. But

113

Dipapa's head was hidden under the rain-mat that Boitoku and another old man held over him, so that we saw only his bent body and the ebony stick with which he walked, and the body of Metusela in his khaki shorts holding Dipapa's arm.

"Something must be up," Mister Cawdor said. "He never moves from that platform in front of his house."

Mister Cawdor stepped down from the veranda and went out into the rain to meet Dipapa. He stooped in under the rain-mat and spoke. Then he took the old man's other arm, and they all began to walk again, very slowly, towards the resthouse.

Kailusa and I sat with our heads low, pretending not to see, while the Dimdims pulled and pushed at Dipapa to get him up to the veranda. The old man was shaking. He fell into Mister Cawdor's chair, holding tight to his stick, and the shaking of his hands moved the stick like wind.

"Dipapa," Mister Cawdor said, "sit, rest. I am glad to see you here."

"My thanks," said Dipapa, who was out of breath.

"I have some good betelnut," Mister Cawdor said. "Kailusa, go and get it."

"By and by," the old man said. "By and by I will chew. Taubada, I am here to speak with you."

"Yes, good," said Mister Cawdor. "Speak, then."

But the old man was too tired, and he glanced towards Benoni and waved with his hand.

"Well, Benoni," Mister Cawdor said, turning. "What does your uncle have to say to me?"

Then I noticed Benoni's face for the first time. He was moved, he looked wild.

"They have come, taubada!" Benoni cried out.

And when he said that, Mister Cawdor's face changed too, and was excited and still.

"Who has come?" asked Mister Cawdor, very quiet. "Benoni, I do not understand your talk."

"The star-people," Benoni cried. "They have come to Budibudi."

Boitoku went *Ssss*, and the other old man shook his head, not believing. But Metusela believed. His eyes were huge and his big mouth smiled and smiled while he looked from Mister Cawdor to Benoni to Dipapa.

"I think you are mistaken," Mister Cawdor said; but he sounded

114

as though he too believed, and was glad."I do not think there are people in the stars."

"Taubada," Benoni said, "at Budibudi my uncle has a plantation of betelnut, the plantation of the chief. Three men live at Budibudi and care for the chief's plantation. E, yesterday my uncle sent two men in a canoe to get betelnut. For you, taubada, a present for you. And the three men are gone. Nothing else is gone, taubada, not their pots, nor their mats. Yams were cooking in one pot, though the fire had burned out. The two canoes were pulled up on the beach, and there were no footprints, no marks anywhere. Because those men have gone, taubada, with the star-people. They have gone into the sky."

I did not know what to believe. It made one afraid. And so many people everywhere were talking about the star-machine.

All the time Mister Cawdor was looking at Dipapa, with the same quiet face. "Well, Dipapa," he said at last, "what is your mind?"

"I do not know," the old man said. "I do not understand."

"You believe in the star-people?" Mister Cawdor said.

"Perhaps," said Dipapa. "Many things change. Today the Dimdims are here. Tomorrow, maybe, the star-people."

All of a sudden Metusela cried out a word, and everybody turned and stared at him.

"What did you say?" Mister Cawdor said. "Metusela, what did you say?"

"Angel," cried Metusela, looking mad and happy. "Those star-people, their name is angel. Now they come. Again they come. Ai! My belly is moved, because of those angel-people."

"Des'," Mister Cawdor said. "Enough. There are no star-people. Those three men had another canoe, they went in their canoe — somewhere — Vaimuna — I do not know. But we will hear of them. Or else they are drowned. Then we will not hear of them. But they did not go into the sky. Akh, Benoni, you talk gammon."

"Taubada," Benoni said, "you go, you see."

"Yes, truly," Mister Cawdor said. "We will go in the *Igau*, I and Misa Dolu'udi. We will search Budibudi, and we will ask for those men in all the islands. And I think we will find them, and you will be ashamed of your crazy talk. Now give me their names."

"You do not believe?" said Benoni, looking into Mister Cawdor's eyes. "You do not believe in the star-people?"

"No, my friend," said Mister Cawdor.

And then Benoni sighed. "I think you want to tell a lie, taubada," he said.

"Osana," said Mister Cawdor, as if he did not hear Benoni, "get those men's names, write them down. That is all. Well, Dipapa, shall we chew?"

But the old man was gazing across the clearing, through the rain, not listening, and he muttered to himself: "Now who is coming? O, Boitoku, who is that?"

Suddenly Mister Dalwood jumped to his feet, shouting: "Hey!"

All the policemen laughed. They were laughing at him and at Saliba, who was running so violently across the clearing, swinging her breasts and skirt. Over her head a big taro-leaf was nodding, held by the stalk, and the rain-drops bounced off that shiny green roof. She came bounding up on to the veranda, gasping and dripping and hitting herself on the bosom, which shook.

"*Wim!*" she panted. Then she noticed Dipapa, and sat down with a bump on the floor.

"Salib', be careful," Mister Cawdor said. "The Government's house is not so strong as Rotten Wood."

"You talk gammon," Saliba screamed, laughing and panting.

"Alistair, what does she want?" said Mister Dalwood, whose face looked as though he wished that Saliba would not talk and laugh so loud.

"I don't know," Mister Cawdor said. "Salib', what is your business?"

"O!" cried Saliba, beating her bosom. "I think I am going to die. Taubada, Misa Makadoneli has sent you some writing."

"Good, then," said Mister Cawdor. "Let me see."

"It is here," Saliba said, feeling in the waistband of her skirt. "*Wa*! It has fallen." She began fumbling about between her legs, and everybody stretched his neck and looked, even Dipapa. But Mister Dalwood did not look for long. His face went red and furious, and he turned away.

"E!" cried Saliba. "It is here." She took her hand out of her skirt and gave a piece of paper to Mister Cawdor, who opened it and read.

I watched Mister Cawdor's face. He was very angry. Too angry even to swear.

"Well?" said Mister Dalwood, turning back. "What's the news?"

"Short and sweet," muttered Mister Cawdor. "The King of Kailuana writes: *Sorry, old man: wireless message. They want you back at Osiwa immediately with 'Igau', Osana and policemen. Some visiting bureaucrats. What a farce. Stay here tonight. Yours aye, MacDonnell of Kailuana.*"

"O-o-o-o-o," went Mister Dalwood. He was not too angry to swear. He swore for a long time, and banged his head on the veranda-post, and even Dipapa laughed.

BENONI

In the afternoon everything that had been put up was taken down, and everything that had been unpacked was packed another time, and the Government went away. "We will come again," said Misa Kodo to my uncle, "soon." And my uncle nodded, still squatting on the veranda of the resthouse, out of the rain, with Metusela beside him, and looked after Misa Kodo, while he mumbled Misa Kodo's betelnut between his gums.

At the head of the line walked Saliba once more, the writing-machine on her head, a rain-mat covering it. Misa Kodo and Misa Dolu'udi followed one by one, in their pink clinging clothes, the rain running down their faces. Their faces were bad-tempered, and they did not talk, as if they were bad-tempered with one another. But Osana and the policemen were making jokes and laughing, and once Misa Dolu'udi turned back, angrily, and told them to stop, and then the bad-temper and the quietness went all along the line.

When they were leaving the Wayouyo lands I ran up beside the Dimdims and said: "Goodbye, Misa Kodo. Goodbye, Misa Dolu'udi. When will you come back?"

"Soon," Misa Kodo said. "A week, two weeks. Our work was not begun."

"Will you go to Budibudi, taubada?" I said. "Will you see?"

"Yes," he said. "In the morning, we will go and see."

"Taubada," I said, "say to Misa Dolu'udi that I regret him."

"Yes," Misa Kodo said. And he called back some words in English to Misa Dolu'udi. And then Misa Dolu'udi said: "So long, mate," and hit me on the shoulder with his hand. But it was not

117

like a game any more, it was not like the evening before, and in a moment Misa Dolu'udi had dropped his hand and walked on and forgot about me, as bad-tempered as when I spoke.

I watched them go, and I thought that I was sad. I thought then that I was sad. A'i.

They went winding away into the rain. The rain was grey and green, and at last so thick that it was like smoke, and I could not see even the white clothes of the Government any more.

SALIBA

And when we came to the house again, suddenly I had a feeling. The land around the house had all turned to mud and the rain rattled on the iron and the house was like a drum. I put down the machine on the veranda and went to the cookhouse where Naibusi was. "O Naibus'," I said, "we are home, we have come."

"They are wet," Naibusi said, "the Dimdims?"

"E," I said, "and their good white stockings are covered with mud. They say they will drink hot water and rum."

"Good, then," Naibusi said. "Salib', what is the matter?"

"I do not know," I said. "I am nervous."

"*You* are nervous?" Naibusi said. "Madwoman, you talk gammon. You were never nervous."

"I think I will go away," I said. "I think I will go back to Wayouyo, tonight. There is something in this house."

"It is *your* house," Naibusi said, "where you were born. Salib', I think you have a fever."

"No," I said, "it is not that. But something else. Something that I know. O Naibusi, I know I am going to be very unhappy."

Then Naibusi was worried, because I was crying, and she had not seen me cry for so long. She kept saying: "Salib', Salib', des'," and patting me, and still I went on crying and could not say why. I could not tell Naibusi because I did not know. All I knew was that the house was unfriendly and might hurt me.

MACDONNELL

Well, I said, it's good to see two young chaps who know how to make use of a rainy afternoon. I hadn't known that they were there. I had been lying on my bed, after a nap, listening to the weather, and then reading, and so the daylight had leaked away, one long racket of rain. But when at last I came out on the veranda, at a quarter to six, there they were at the table, in pullovers and swimming trunks, tight as ticks and twice as miserable.

"You'll make that boy an alcoholic," I said to Cawdor.

"What?" he said, looking up, vaguely."Oh. No. It's good for him. Takes his mind off his bloody vitamins."

"Hi, Mak," Dalwood said. "Is it sundowner time for you? Pull up a mug. It's on him."

I noticed that the pullover Cawdor wore was really Dalwood's, and that it must have come from Dalwood's old school. It made Cawdor look like a waif.

"Mak," Cawdor said, "I've had an idea. Why don't we all get disgustingly tiddly?"

"Well, I don't know, old man," I said. "Not a thing I've done for quite a while. It used to be a problem, you know. Falling over before breakfast and all that. No, I only drink from six to nine p.m. these days. I find it a healthy rule."

"Let's have an orgy," Cawdor said. "You know what, Mak, this character invited me last night to join him in an orgy."

"I didn't put it like that," Dalwood said. "Jesus, Cawdor, you don't know how often your risk your front teeth."

"An orgy," I said, thinking about it. "Yes, indeed, there've been some orgies in this house. So I've been told. Funny, though, it never feels like it. An orgy is something that happens somewhere else. Like the jungle, or the Outback. The real jungle and the real Outback are always a bit further on."

While I was talking I saw what a strange evening it had become: how the rain had turned blue, lashing at the grey-blue sea, where the *Igau* must have been wallowing, somewhere out of sight. The smell of chickens and rotting wood and wood-smoke were stronger for the wet. I thought of my first year here, after Campbell had gone, when things were new, and there seemed so much to be done and to control, and yet how often I just sat, like Cawdor, a glass in front of me, looking and breathing the air. Years can go away with a change in the air. And then, they both looked so young, lounging against the table, with their hair the way it had come out of a towel. How easy it is to forget one's age, faced with a change in the weather and the fact that there are people still around one as young as one ever was.

"Yes," I said, "let's make a night of it." But they were singing by then, to the tune of "Land of Hope and Glory":

"Fuck you, Konedobu,

Fuck you, Samarai,

Give us back our *Igau* . . ."

So I poured myself another drink from Cawdor's bottle, and helped them out with a rhyme when they seemed stuck. "'You can always fly'," I suggested. "At the taxpayers' expense, of course."

SALIBA

I said to Naibusi; "I will not go into the big room; I will wash the dishes, then sleep." The other girls were singing and laughing with the Dimdims, and sometimes Timi shouted down the passage: "Salib'–O!" but I went on washing the dishes as if I did not hear, and rattled with them to drown the voices. I spoke with Naibusi about the Wayouyo people and their doings and the talk of the star. "It is very strange," I said, "this talk of the star."

"It is very strange," agreed Naibusi. "What colour are these people from the stars? Are they black or white?"

"Nobody has seen them," I said. "Not truly. They do not come down from their machine."

"Good, then," said Naibusi. "I am content. I think I would not understand star-people. I do not understand Dimdims yet."

By that time Naibusi and I were finished and were hanging up the cloths and were going to go to the hut to sleep. But suddenly a huge noise came down the passage, like screams and whistles and music, and the girls were shouting and beating their hands.

"*Ki*!" cried Naibusi. "It is the radio."

"Not that one?" I said. "Not the new one?" Because Misa Makadoneli had sent for a new radio from Samarai when the old one broke, but the Samarai people put the radio in the mail-bag, and the pilot of the plane dropped the mail-bag near the front steps, like always.

"No, I think the old one," Naibusi said. And suddenly all the girls came running into the cookhouse, laughing and crying out.

"O!" they called. "Misa Dolu'udi has mended the radio."

And they said: "Salib', you come. Misa Dolu'udi says."

"He is going to dance," they said. "Salib', you come and dance with Misa Dolu'udi."

"I will not dance with a man," I said, shaking my head.

"Yes, you will dance," they cried. "Like a Dimdim, Salib'. Come and dance, O sinabada."

And then they were dragging me away. They were laughing, but it was not kind. Naibusi was calling: *"Des', des',* she is tired," and I was fighting them, but they were dragging me away from the cookhouse and across the veranda, and into the passage that was full of whistles and music.

In the big room they had closed the shutters because of the rain. It was hot, with the lamps and the people, and all the people were shining. And they were laughing and shouting, and the old radio on the table was screaming, and the air was full of smoke and the smell of flowers and the Dimdims' drink. I could not breathe in the room, and tried to go away, but all the girls were in the doorway.

Misa Makadoneli was sitting on a chair. His eyes were like blue beads behind his glasses, and he was smiling with all his teeth into the air.

Alistea's head was against the back of the sofa. He did not move. His eyes were open just a little way, like a dead man, and his face was an ugly colour, like soap.

But Timi was dancing, by himself, in the middle of the room. He was dancing a Dimdim dance to the music of the radio, wearing only his yavi that he swims in, and looked pink and glistening, but hard, like stone. He danced in his bare feet on the mats, and sometimes his feet caught in the edges and he stumbled across the room.

"Salib'!" Timi shouted.

He was smiling, with his big teeth and his blue eyes.

"No," I said. "Taubada," I called to Misa Makadoneli. But Misa Makadoneli was smiling too, and nodding his head, and said nothing.

I shouted at the girls: "I want to go," but they would not move from the door. They were yelling: "Dance, Salib', dance, we want to see," and suddenly people pushed me in the back, and I went running towards Timi.

I did not think he was cruel. I did not think he wanted to hurt me. But he did. He put his arms around me, and moved with me, among the screams and the laughter.

"No, no," I cried to him. "No. Your shame."

He was talking to me in English, and smiling, while I fought him.

"Why?" I kept crying to him. "Why? I am not a shamed woman. Taubada, why this?"

But he was like a deaf man. He did not hear, even, that I called him *taubada*. He went on holding me, and trying to move with me, and smiling. And suddenly he bent his head, so that I smelt the Dimdim drink on his breath, and kissed my mouth.

Then I must have screamed, and tore at his face with my nails, and he cried out too and stumbled back, with blood running down from near his eyes. He cried out: "Salib'!" sounding astonished, and lifted his hands to his eyes. So I pushed at him, and then ran towards the girls and scratched and beat at them till they let me through, and ran down the passage towards the veranda and the cookhouse.

When I was in the cookhouse Naibusi came after me. She said: "Put away the knife, Salib'."

"I am going to cut him," I said. "I am going to cut his face."

"No," said Naibusi. "That would be bad, Salib'."

"I am going to hurt him," I said. "He is a filthy man."

"No, " said Naibusi. "His mind is not bad. Only, their customs are different."

"O Naibus'," I said, "I will go away. I will go to Wayouyo. I do not want to see a Dimdim again. My shame is very great."

"Yes," Naibusi said, "go tomorrow. For a while. But give me the knife."

And then I was on my knees, weeping into Naibusi's skirt. "O Naibus'," I was saying. "O my mother." And Naibusi was stroking my head and saying: *"Des', desila*, my child. All will be well. You will see, how all will be well."

MACDONNELL

I had sat Dalwood down on my chair at the table, and had turned up his face towards the lamp to examine the scratches, when suddenly, beyond the lamplight, she materialized. In that old blue dress, stiff as a stake, with that old dried noble head on top of it.

"O Naibus'," I said. "Look what has happened. Go and get the box of medicine."

But she did not move. And when our eyes met, I saw that she had other things on her mind.

"Your shame," she hissed. "O, your shame."

"No, Naibus'," I said. "The girl did not understand. See, here. She has made him bleed."

She looked, not at the blood, but into his eyes, and he flinched. "Idiot," she said.

"What does she say?" he asked me. He sounded very subdued, and turned his head towards me to avoid the old woman.

"Naibus'," I said, pleading for him, "he is young, he is a young Dimdim. He wanted to dance a Dimdim dance. His custom is different. Old woman, you and I are going to quarrel by and by."

"Good, then," she said. "I am content. Let us quarrel. You are an idiot, like him. A *paek*'," she said, with eyes like bullets. "I refuse."

"You would not," I said. And believed and knew that she would not, but still the words clutched like cold hands. To die alone, in this house, without her, and she alone in some village. "No, Naibusi. You shall not speak like that."

"E, we shall see," she said, and shrugged. Then she was staring at the sofa, at Cawdor, who had been quiet and forgotten a long time. "He is asleep?" she said.

We turned to look. His eyes were closed, and suddenly we noticed how bad his colour was. "Hey, Alistair," Dalwood said, "are you all right?"

"Yes," he said, and his eyes opened and he was looking at Naibusi. "What, old woman?" he said, slurring the words.

"Why did you not speak?" she demanded.

"I did not see," he mumbled. "I did not truly see. Naibus'," he said, "I am ill, I think." He got to his feet, shakily, and stepped towards her. Then he staggered, and fell full-length on the floor.

Dalwood was making a great noise. "Jesus, Cawdor, you're paralytic."

But Naibusi wailed. Naibusi was on her haunches, holding Cawdor's head to her breast, and stroking it. *"Kapisila!"* she cried. "My grief for him! I did not understand. I do not want Misa Kodo to die."

SALIBA

When I went to Wayouyo in the night the rain had stopped for a while and the fireflies were burning in the dripping bushes. I was afraid in the dark, and sometimes I missed the path. But it was in the taller bushes by the path that the fireflies hung, and so I would find the road again by the little green flames among the leaves.

I did not weep after I left the house, but once I cried out, when the night-bird swooped by me and I felt the wind of its wings in my hair. I cried out and jumped away, thinking of bad luck, searching for the bird in the branches and the sky, in case it might come again. Then I saw the light. Just for a moment I saw the light, and I thought: It is them. I thought: It is them, and I was not sad any more. Let them come, I thought, and chase away the Dimdims. Let them kill the Dimdims, who bring nothing but disappointment and shame. I stared and stared at the sky, forgetting the bird, and though the light did not come again my mind was quiet.

DALWOOD

I turned over in the camp-bed, and the pillow rubbed across the scratches on my face and made them sting. So I woke, remembering. The room was dark, still shuttered, and the roof rattled with little gusts of rain. It was hot again, I was sweating, and my sweat in the marks of her nails brought back all the triumphs of the evening. For a while I wondered if what was making my head ache might be an obscure tropical disease, fatal with any luck, and okay for my mother to mention to her friends. But it just wasn't a room that it was possible to die in, stinking like that of tobacco and rum and flowers and the built-in mildew, and my watch said it was eight o'clock already, and we were due to sail at that time for Osiwa. So I rolled out, making plans to die at sea, and shambled down the passage towards the shower. Then I remembered Alistair.

He wasn't in his room, and nothing else was in his room. All packed and gone, and the bedding folded and stacked, the way Kailusa did it, Army-style.

Then he's all right, I thought. Of course, he was all right all along.

That poor old lady, getting herself into a state, just because a Dimdim drank himself under the table.

But I thought of the old man, too, after we had put the body to bed, gripping my elbow, all confidential, and suddenly stone-cold sober. "Dalwood," he said, "don't tell him what Naibusi's been saying. He thinks like a kanaka, in some ways. It would worry him."

124

Meaning that he, Mak, was worried. Meaning that *he* thought like a native in some ways. Because he does believe that Naibusi has a talent, like dogs or bees, that are supposed to know when a man is going to die.

I went out on to the veranda and Alistair was there, in clean clothes, showered and combed, at the rail with Mak, his back to me. And he looked so straight and sturdy beside the stalky old man that I thought: You gammon, Naibus'. They were talking quietly, watching the dinghy and canoes taking our gear out on the choppy sea to the *Igau*.

"Conscientious, aren't you?" I said behind him.

He turned back from the rail, looking greyish, though carefully shaved. Without a flicker of a smile he asked: "What have you done to your face?" He seemed honestly curious, and concerned.

"Not before breakfast, mate," I said. "I don't feel funny."

But the old man had been fascinated by the question, and jumped in to explain. "I say, Dalwood," he said, "Cawdor's had a blackout. Doesn't remember a thing. Sounds bad, don't you think?"

"Yeah," I said. "Sounds like another step along the road to Alcoholics Anonymous."

The MacDonnell went rambling on. "Ought to see a doctor, old chap. You'll be at Osiwa tonight. Drop in on the MO and ask him what he thinks."

"Mak," Alistair said, "we haven't got an MO at Osiwa just now. The MO at Osiwa was run away with by my wife."

"Oh," said the MacDonnell in confusion. "Sorry, old man. Thought you'd have had another one by this time."

I said to Alistair: "You enjoyed saying that, didn't you? You creep," I said, and he laughed as if he couldn't help it, though I saw that it hurt his head worse than mine.

"Time you got cracking," he said. "You look as if you'd been bombed. I'm not waiting round for you. I'm going aboard now. Where's Naibusi, Mak?"

The old man threw back his head and yelled, out of his chicken-neck: "Naibusi-O!" And the old woman was suddenly there among us, smiling, with a faint smell of yams, but no sound.

"I am leaving, Naibus'," Alistair said. "*Kayoni, kagu toki, numwoya.*"

"Goodbye," she said. "Taubada — when will you come again?"

"A week," he said. "Two weeks. Soon."

125

"Good," she said to herself. "Very good."

"Naibus'," he said, "why are you looking at me like that?"

"E, why would I not look at you?" she said. "Because you a very beautiful man, that is why."

Even with a hangover, when he laughed he could look like a kid. "O, my sweetheart," he said. "Well, I am going. But where is Salib'?"

The old woman, who hadn't seemed to see me before, managed to give the impression of seeing me a lot less, and murmured: "Salib'? E, Salib' has gone to Wayouyo. To her mother's sister. Next time she will be here."

"*Ki?*" said Misa Kodo thoughtfully.

"I'd better go and shower," I said, and grabbed my towel and went away down the veranda. Because Misa Kodo was observing me suddenly, as keenly as Naibusi wasn't, and the silence was loud with dropping pennies.

"He is young," I heard the MacDonnell say. "Naibusi, enough. It is finished."

Turning into the bathroom I risked a look back at them, the little group isolated at the edge of the long bare splintery deck. The sea behind them was hazed with rain and the rising steam of the grass. It was a funny lonely feeling, the feeling I had then, that by removing myself I'd somehow made the gathering complete. And although it was all baloney, although he didn't even know what they were thinking, it was funny too how they suggested, just by their attitudes, two devoted old parents making the most, while they had him, of their brave doomed bomber-pilot son.

OSANA

The *Igau* came to Budibudi shining with the wet, but the rain was over for the daytime, and the sea was green and flat. Steam was rising from the island as we came ashore in the dinghy, and the beach was smooth and hard with rain. On the beach two canoes were pulled up, and past them were the two huts where the three men had lived. A cooking-pot filled to the top with rainwater sat outside the huts on stones, over the wet ashes of a fire. There were yams in the pot, and the yams were done.

"No footprints, of course," Mister Cawdor said to himself. "Not even the men from Wayouyo."

126

"No, taubada, nothing," I said. "See, taubada," I told him, pointing to the grove, "there is Dipapa's betelnut plantation that the men guarded."

"E," said Mister Cawdor, and nodded his head. "Osana, were those men not afraid to live at Budibudi?"

"No, " I said. "There is nothing to be afraid of."

"Truly?" Mister Cawdor said. "Well, I think I might be afraid. But perhaps it is only we Dimdims who fear ghosts."

Then he picked open the door and we went into one house, and then the other house, gazing at the men's somethings by the light of the Government torch. There were the men's sleeping-mats and their lime-gourds and their water-bottles. There were their knives and bags and spears, their fishing-nets and shuttles and twine. Their footprints were still on the sand of the floors. Nothing was gone but the men.

"We shall see," Mister Cawdor said, coming out of the second house and staring about him. "We shall see, Osana. Meanwhile, do not talk."

"What do you think happened?" asked Mister Dalwood, in English.

"I don't think I'm ready to start thinking yet," said Mister Cawdor. "Maybe they wandered off down to the underworld, before their time."

"What 'underworld'?" Mister Dalwood said.

"The home of the dead," said Mister Cawdor. "Didn't I tell you? It's right here, under our feet."

He pointed to the tall trees that hid the mouth of the cave, and said: "There, Tim, that's the way to the afterlife. When you die, your relations build a little canoe for your soul, and launch it from the beach nearest your village. So your soul comes sailing here to Budibudi, and gets out and goes into that cave, and goes on down and down, till it comes to the other world, where the chief's name is Topileta. And that's where you stay, with Topileta, living pretty much as you live here, only more easily. You feast and you chew betelnut, and you don't worry anyone walking about up here. But now and again something happens, Topileta leaves a door open or something. And then people up here hear a funny sound, that they say is like a Dimdim bell."

"You tell a fantastic story," Mister Dalwood said. "Well, don't let's call off the manhunt without having a look at the underworld."

127

But Mister Cawdor did not answer, and only looked at me, and Mister Dalwood went on in a loud voice: "Alistair?"

"Perhaps I am afraid," said Mister Cawdor to me, but smiling.

"Why, taubada?" I said. "You do not believe."

"But many people believe," he said. "And you?"

"I am a Christian," I said, "like you, taubada, and Mister Dalwood."

"E," he said, "true. It is different for us, we Christians."

Then he turned back to Mister Dalwood, and said: "Okay, let's go. But do not tell anyone, Osana," he said to me, "where we have gone." And he moved away, swinging the torch, with Mister Dalwood behind him, into the shade and the wetness of Dipapa's plantation. They walked very quiet, and white like ghosts, through the thin palm-trunks, climbing to the rocky rise where the earth opened in the middle of a circle of trees.

DALWOOD

When we were among the trees he pointed to the narrow opening between the rocks. "Abandon hope," he said.

Out of the hole came a constant, echoing twittering. "It's full of budgies," I said.

"No," he said. "Bats."

We climbed down the rocks and stepped through the opening, and suddenly we were in a cathedral, under a great dome. Bats whirled in the light that seeped through the crannies in the coral, high up, and a steady drizzle fell as the soil of the island drained itself into the caves. The light from the opening stopped at a massive stalagmite. At the foot of it a clump of bracken glowed burning green.

"What do you think?" he asked, hushed, under the chirruping in the dome.

"It's — well, sort of grand," I said.

He kept moving on down, into the darkness, flashing the torch on fantastic columns and stalactites, slithering on the slimy ramp. Then we were beside a pool, that I heard before I saw it, from the slow plinking of water from the roof way overhead.

The smell of the mud and rock scoured my nostrils. "It does stink in here," I said.

"Bats' piss," he remarked expertly, and flashed the torch on a rock near me, and I saw little red beads on it, like blood.

"The things you know," I admitted.

He was going on, into the wetter and darker darkness. The sort of path he had found was narrowing. High sloping walls of rock closed in and loomed over our heads.

"They're all hollow," he was saying, "these islands. They were reefs once. The sea used to boil through here. Think of that. And before then there were mountains, but they all went down under the sea. Think of that, too."

Then he came to a sudden stop. Because golden eyes were swooping at us out of the dark, black furry bodies were zooming over our heads. "Flying-foxes," he called out, swinging round, following them with the torch, excited, like a kid. "Look at them, Tim. Look. Did you ever see so many?"

The beam swept about and caught, just for a moment, two golden headlamps bearing down on us like a train. Then the light went mad, and fell.

I heard a splash, and much silence.

"Hey, Misa Kodo," I said, "it's dark down here."

"Sorry," he muttered.

"You wouldn't maybe have a slight case of the shakes?"

"It looks like it," he said, sounding humbled. "Well, we'd better go back."

It was a darkness like I'd never seen before. It was perfect darkness. He was standing beside me, and I couldn't make out even a glimmer of his clothes.

"Alistair," I said, "you've got to go, you know."

"What?" he said. "Go where?"

"Away. Take sick leave. Christ knows, you look sick enough."

"What are you talking about?" he said. "I've got to be shipped out because I dropped a torch?"

"Forget the bloody torch," I said. "It's because you worry people. You worry me, you worry Kailusa. You even worry Mak a bit. And poor old Naibusi, last night —"

"What was wrong with Naibusi?"

"She thought you were dying. I wasn't supposed to tell you that, but you ought to know. It's not just your business, it involves other people."

He was thinking. And because he was thinking, I could hear the water dripping and the bats in the cave we had left behind. And him breathing, invisible at my side.

129

"I do know about it," he said at last. "About involving other people. But it's not a thing I ever asked for."

"Still, it happens," I said. "And if you're sick —"

"I'm not sick," he said. "But I would be if I hadn't had a job to do."

"Wait a minute," I said, "let me finish. If you're sick and carry on with it, you're not the only one who's going to suffer. If you care about these people, you ought to take a rest. I think you've thought that out for yourself."

He moved beside me, his shoes slipping on the rocks. "Yeah, sure," he said, suddenly and loudly, "that's fine for you to say. I know what you're thinking. Then you'd be out there on your own, patrolling, your own boss. But they wouldn't let you, not yet a while. And where am I supposed to go? Back to Dimdim, you'll tell me, but what is there for me down there?" He broke off for a moment, and then he said, in a strained voice: "This is my home. This is all I've got."

I don't know how I knew, but I knew, that something had happened, something had broken. I'd never thought before that he was weak, and I think now that he wasn't, till then, when I couldn't see.

I reached out and found his shoulders with my hands. "Let's get moving," I said. "You lead the way, I'll hang on to you."

"You'll trust me not to fall down a hole?" he said.

"I'll trust you," I said, "to give a piercing shriek as you go. Hey, what made that noise?"

"A python," he said.

"You don't mean that?"

"Yeah, I do. I heard it before."

"Oh Christ," I said. "It probably ate those three fellas. Did you think of that?"

"No, I didn't," he said. "Now, why didn't I think of it? It seems so obvious."

As we came nearer the big cave he was beginning to take shape in front of me. We were in a narrow slimy alley. His shirt formed itself, and I dropped my hands from his shoulders. Then we were both in the light.

"How'd you get like that?" I said. His face was smeared with slime and mud from his hands.

"The same way you did," he said. "This underworld's a scungey place."

Yet he had stopped, in the middle of the cave, and was looking up at the bats in the lighted dome and the stalactites and the dangling roots of trees, as if it was something he wanted to remember.

"What *do* you think?" I said. "Seriously, I mean. About those three blokes."

"I don't know," he said, still with his face lifted up to the portholes of light.

"You won't admit what you think, will you? About that flying saucer."

"I never mentioned the flying saucer," he said. "That was Benoni's theory."

"But you believe in it."

"In the star-machine? That it exists? Maybe."

"More than maybe," I said. "You're in love with that star-machine. It's crazy."

He shrugged, his back to me. "My father," he said, "believes that Jesus Christ was the son of God. Boy, is he crazy, but no one says so."

"You were talking last night," I said; and at that he turned and looked at me, sharply, out of his blackened face. "When we put you to bed, you were babbling away."

"Well?" he said, waiting for something painful. "What did I say?"

"I don't know. Nobody knew the language."

"Oh," he said, suddenly grinning, and glancing down. "Was I back at that ? Well, I didn't speak much English before the age of about seven."

"You were talking Martian," I said.

"What?" he said, staring at me, and starting to smile, in a puzzled way. "Explain that."

"You were talking Martian because you are a Martian. That's what I always thought. That's why the excitement over the saucer. It's got your people on board. People like you," I said, laughing at the idea, and yet it wasn't a joke, but something I'd seriously imagined, just before, in the dark. "Your folks," I said, thinking of his wife and what it must have been like for her, trying to talk to that, to love that, that visitant.

131

"Hey, Tim," he said, gazing at me, "hey — Tim. Are you feeling all right? If you could hear yourself, you'd be worried." And he was frowning and looking hurt, and that was something I'd never seen before, but I didn't care.

OSANA

I saw ahead of us, over the low sea, the north point of Vaimuna trailing away on the left hand, and on the other hand the high ridge and the jungle of Osiwa island, grey with sea-steam. So I knew that we would not be going around Vaimuna, but through that fast deep strait between the islands, the gut of Vilakota.

Mister Cawdor was lying on his back again, not reading, not sleeping, nothing. There was black mud still on his skin, though he and Mister Dalwood had washed themselves in the sea, leaning from the dinghy as we came back to the boat.

"We will anchor at Vilakota, taubada?" I said to him.

"Yes," he said.

"You like Vilakota, taubada? We always anchor there."

"Yes," he said. "It is like my own village. I would like to live there, and be an old man."

"E, taubad'," Kailusa called out, "let us garden at Vilakota, you and I."

Mister Cawdor did not really smile, but looked quite gently at the hunchback, and shook his head. "We are too young now," he said. "But later, Kailus', perhaps."

Then the hunchback wandered away, looking sad. But I stayed to talk to Mister Cawdor where he lay.

"Taubada," I said, "what did you find in the cave?"

"Nothing," he said. "Much darkness. That is all."

"But the men, taubada? Where are the men?"

"Gone," he said. "Vanished. I do not know. Soon I will make a report. Do not ask questions now."

So I too left him, and climbed out of the belly of the *Igau*, to go and sit behind Mister Dalwod and watch the land.

The village of Vilakota sits on the beach, at the end of Osiwa island. There are ten houses, fifteen houses, I do not remember. Behind them is a grey cliff, the sharp edge of the coral ridge and of the miles and miles of jungle that divide those houses from every other village on Osiwa. In front of Vilakota is the fast sea, boiling between the islands, and beyond that the low point of Vaimuna

132

with the wetter, more rotting jungle through which the Vilakota people walk to visit their relations of Vaimuna.

Usually there is a man with a canoe at one point or the other, waiting for people who want to cross the strait. I suppose he fishes, or hunts for shellfish, or sits in front of his house carving or mending nets, while he listens for a shout from the other shore. On that day too he was there, on the Vaimuna side, and before we saw the houses we saw his brown sail, then his darker body in front of it, waving at the Dimdim boat coming so fast towards him, fast as the sea, from the east.

The *Igau* went by with the man on one side, the village on the other. The man was shouting, and from the other shore people had run from their houses to call and wave. The *Igau* swept round the point into the blue-green milky water of the great lagoon that makes all the west of Vaimuna and Osiwa calm. Then the *Igau* was suddenly quiet, and we heard lories in the Vaimuna jungle, and frigate-birds in the sky.

When the dinghy was lowered, Mister Dalwood was the first man into it. He stood rocking on the sea, turning up his face so that I saw the mud in the roots of his hair which is coloured like rope.

"Come on," he shouted. "Where are you? Kailus', is your taubada asleep?"

"He is sick a bit," Kailusa said. Then Mister Cawdor came out of the belly of the *Igau* and dropped into the dinghy and sat down.

His legs were shaking. It was the sea. It made him shake and be sick and be sleepy. I was sorry sometimes.

"There's no hurry," he said. "We're nearly home. We won't stay here long. Just half an hour, to see."

Mister Dalwood said nothing, but was frowning about him, watching men get into the dinghy and seeming impatient with everyone, not only Mister Cawdor.

The smell of the jungle of Vaimuna came towards us in puffs. One minute you would say it was sweet, it was flowers or sweet berries or sweet leaves. Another minute it was bitter and rotten like disease.

"Will you come with us, Osana?" Mister Cawdor said to me.

"I would like to stay, taubada," I said, "with the men. I have goggles. We could hunt for turtles, taubada, in this water."

"Good, then," Mister Cawdor said. He had not looked at me or at Mister Dalwood or at anything except the trees ahead.

When the dinghy was near the muddy shore nobody moved but the two Dimdims, who were taking off their sandals, and among the trees the headman, the one from the canoe, who had crossed the point to come and wave.

"Look, taubada," I said to Mister Cawdor. "Your friend."

"Who is my friend?" Mister Cawdor said; then saw, and stood in the dinghy and called: "Keroni—O!"

That man Keroni, because Mister Cawdor had remembered his name, was like a madman. He burst out of the leaves and vines, he ran through the water. "O, my taubada," he was panting. "You have come back. O, my friend."

"E, I have come back," Mister Cawdor said, laughing at him. "Just for a little. Soon I must go, my friend."

"Come," Keroni cried, holding out his arms to Mister Cawdor. "I will take you. I will take you."

"Thank you," Mister Cawdor said, "but truly, I can walk to the land."

"No," Keroni cried, "taubada, no. There are stone-fish, taubada. There are sharks, taubada. Taubada, you seize my hand."

So Mister Cawdor put his hand in Keroni's hand, I think just for help while he jumped into the water. But Keroni caught him, and stood in the water holding him, like a baby, but as proud as if Mister Cawdor had been a huge bush-pig.

Mister Dalwood was looking amazed. "You know that bloke?" he said.

Mister Cawdor laughed, out of breath, and I think too weak to stop Keroni from doing what he wanted to do with him. "Yeah, I know him," he said. "But he hasn't done this before. Has he, Osana?"

He looked at me, and suddenly we both understood. Our two faces said: Yes, that is why Keroni would carry a Dimdim through the water. Because those other times it was the sinabada, Missus Cawdor, and Keroni carried her and had a rich reward.

"I do not know, taubada," I said. "I forget."

Already Mister Dalwood was splashing in the sea. The water was as deep as his knees as he ploughed towards the shore. "Come, come, come," he was saying, in the language. "Quick, quick, quick." And in English: "You pair of goons."

"You forget?" Mister Cawdor said in English to me.

"I forget everything," I said. "Now you, taubada."

"Perhaps," he said, with a still face, and turned his head.

Then he tried to stand in the water, but the headman still clung to him, muttering, and so he said: "Good, then, let us go," and he and Keroni went away through the narrow gap of sea, and into the green shadow where Mister Dalwood was waiting.

DALWOOD

And I thought: In this house there is peace. It was a house that nobody lived in, except the Government now and then, stopping off from a work-boat bound elsewhere. But they kept it in good repair, for the children to play in, perhaps, and the women to sit on rainy days making skirts or mats, looking out over the sea. The men mended the thatch, and the women and children came together under it. The great planks of the floor, hewn up in the coral ridge jungle, were polished by their sandy feet and their thighs and the sweat of their palms.

When we came across the strait from Vaimuna the women were already running to the house with sleeping-mats in rolls on their heads. They had carpeted the veranda for us by the time we reached the steps, and were crouched in the sand below, keeping their heads lower than ours, but nodding and beaming.

So we climbed the steps and sat down on the mats, enthroned at dead centre of that sandy spit, with the houses in a semi-circle behind us, and the cliff and the forest further back, the sea on either side, and ahead the strait and the Vaimuna jungle.

"It's quiet," I said, after a while. We were sitting cross-legged, looking down from a height on the Vilakota people, who squatted in the sand with their faces turned up to us. They were smiling, but they said nothing. They were quieter than the palms in the air behind and above.

"Yes," he said. "I'd like to spend a week or two here." He was watching the headman's wife come slowly up the stairs, and smiled at her as if they'd known each other a long time, but didn't speak. He just watched her hands, setting down a sort of carved oval tray in front of us, and pouring something hot and colourless out of a cheap enamel teapot into two tin cups.

"What is it?" I said. "How did she come by a teapot?"

135

But he wouldn't break the silence on my account. He lifted the cup and tasted it, while the woman studied his face. He said to her: "Our very great thanks," seriously, and she smiled, seriously, and edged away down the steps, with her back bowed and her head lower than ours.

I took the other cup and tasted. "It's hot water," I said.

"No," he said, "there's a flavour in it." And he went on sipping, gazing at the sea.

So I tried again, and did find in it, that time, something a bit sweet, a bit perfumed, maybe flowers or leaves, but faint, and hard to pin down.

"You know," I said, "you could have a week or two here by yourself, if you wanted."

"Not just yet," he said. "But I will take a break, at Christmas. I'll go to Jack Manson."

"Who's that?" I said. Because he had always seemed to have no friends, and nobody wrote to him: from embarassment, it could have been.

"A bloke who came up here when I did," he said. "He's at Vuna, not far away. He's got a wife who was a nurse, and she can cook."

"At last you're talking sense," I said.

"It's the nagging," he said. "It's worn me down."

All the time he had been watching the jungle on the other shore, and I turned my head to see what he saw. On the lagoon beach, hidden by the soggy undergrowth, someone had lit a fire and the smoke was rising, a little darker than the grey-white sky.

"What is it," I asked him, "a signal?"

"No," he said, still sipping at that petal-tea or whatever it was. "They've got their turtle."

"Oh God, no," I said. "No. I'm going to stop them."

"You're not," he said.

"Well, make them kill it, anyway. You know they'll be cooking the poor bloody thing alive."

And they cry, I was thinking, while I took my shirt off. Someone told me that. They cry like babies.

"Tim," he said, "you can't swim that. You'll be lost off the map, and then what will your hulking great brothers do to me?"

136

But I was already going down the steps, and muttered back at him: "I'll find out if I can swim it."

"It's too late," he said. "And what about the other turtles?"

"*What* other turtles?" I said.

"All of them," he said. "All the turtles in the Pacific."

"Ah," I said, "up your sweet reason." And I walked on, over the sand and up to my knees in the sea.

Then I knew, of course, that he was right. Between the two islands there was something like a canyon, and the tide-rip would have got hold of me and swept me far out, past the reefs of Vaimuna, where the bright white reef-herons were standing like the wreck of a fence. I knew he was right, because I remembered that bit of a rock-islet we'd seen from the *Igau*, with one little tree on it heavy with sea-birds' nests, and the sharks jumping out of the water and snapping.

So I stood where I'd stopped, staring at Keroni's canoe on the other side, which was empty because Keroni was enjoying the barbecue too, and I waited for a shout to let me down easy.

But there wasn't a shout, only a whisper. Keroni's wife, squatting at the edge of the water, was breathing: "Taubada, taubada," and pointing back towards the resthouse, towards him, meaning that I was ordered home.

Slowly I turned to face him, and suddenly it struck me how extraordinary it was, that geometrical arrangement that put him at the centre of the world.

Between me and the resthouse was a semi circle of people, their brown backs towards me. Behind the resthouse was an equal semi-circle of houses, rain-stained grey-brown. The houses followed the contour of the crescent of grey cliff, which was outlined against the sky with a crescent of forest.

The resthouse stood on stilts at an equal distance from two seas. On the right the water was dark and swelling, on the left flat and green. The open veranda of the resthouse was square, and was covered exactly with matting. At the centre of the matting Misa Kodo sat, cross-legged in white clothes, looking out.

I thought: Yes, that is what a king would look like. Not like Mak. Not like Dipapa, even. But remote like that. Alien like that. Now he looks like he must feel.

III
CARGO

SALIBA

When I came back to Wayouyo that first night I looked down from a high point on the path and saw a glow like a fire far away near the stones. I could not think what the fire might be, because all the bushes were still dripping with the rain, but I did not think it would be anything else but a fire.

My aunt was surprised when I scratched on her house-wall and hissed and called to her. I called: "It is I, Saliba," and heard her muttering inside: "Salib', Salib'," as if she did not believe. But soon she came to the doorway, and I said: "Aunt, I have come back to Wayouyo, I will stay here a while, I have quarrelled with Misa Makadoneli." So then she made kind noises, and led me into her house, and I lay down and slept where I used to sleep when I was small.

But the night was very unquiet, the rain was rough in the trees, and there were other sounds. Once I heard men's voices shouting, a long way off, and later men's feet running on the path. Then my aunt's husband came in, dripping with wet, and stumbled over my legs in the dark. "*Avae*'?" he cried out, and my aunt said, with sleep in her voice: "It is Salib', she will stay with us." "All right," he said, and groped his way towards his sleeping-mat and lay down. But he did not sleep for a long time, I heard that. Through all the sounds of the wind and rain I heard him lying there, awake.

CAWDOR

The first sign of activities near the stones was seen by SALIBA when she returned to Wayouyo from Mr MacDonnell's house in the early hours of

October 30th. She reports having seen a "fire", or "lights". This is not confirmed by any other witness, but she happens to have been alone, very late, at one of the few points of the island from which the area of the stones is visible from a distance. Her aunt's husband, TOBEBA'I, and the VC, BOITOKU, both deny having been there. So do all other Wayouyo males.

On the following day, SALIBA was bringing her aunt's water-bottles from the cave when she met BENONI on the path. They talked of her presence in the village, which she said was due to a misunderstanding with people in Mr MacDonnell's house. Then she asked him if he knew the reason for the noises in the night, mentioning that she had heard men running and shouting, and that her aunt had heard a conch being blown. She said that several women had heard these sounds and had been discussing them in the water-cave, and that they were "afraid of what the men will do".

Since his quarrel with DIPAPA, who disinherited him for alleged adultery and never formally re-instated him, BENONI has lived in the Mwamwada hamlet of Wayouyo. When METUSELA arrived in the village, DIPAPA gave him BENONI's former house in the chief's hamlet. This action caused something of a sensation in Wayouyo, and led to resentment and suspicion on the part of BENONI and his supporters, directed both at METUSELA (whom many described as "a deformity") and at DIPAPA himself.

From his house in the Mwamwada hamlet it would not have been possible for BENONI to hear the sounds described by SALIBA, since Mwamwada is removed from the chief's hamlet and from all the main paths. During that day, however, he had noticed a change in the attitude of some of the men towards himself. They were, he says, "whispering together" and "turning away from me". He also had the impression that "SALIBA was warning me".

SALIBA says that she had no such intention, that she assumed that BENONI would have been involved in any activity of the men, and was simply curious to see his reaction to her remarks. She was surprised that he seemed "very angry". When she reached her aunt's house, she noticed that he was walking towards the chief's hamlet. She called out: "Where are you going?" (a sort of politeness here) and he replied: "You will see, I will stop all the noises in the night."

BENONI

All his women were gone from their houses, to the gardens or to fetch water from the cave. The door of Metusela's house, that used to be mine, was fastened shut. There was nobody left but the old man, my uncle, like a roll of matting on the shaded platform in front of his house. He lay with his head in the curve of his ebony pillow, held up by the arms of little ebony men, his hands, on the mat, open like spiders, as if they were waiting for something alive to fall from the thatch.

I thought that he was deep asleep, as I might have been myself on a day like that, with the still heat and the white sky, and the smoke of the cooking-fires climbing straight up without a stir. But as I came close his eyelids quivered, and his eyes opened and were staring at me, cloudy and bright.

"Are you well?" I said.

For a long time he looked at me, he thought about me, before his face moved. Because he was old, so old that nobody could remember his childhood, his mouth had grown thin, and like rubber. When he spoke, all his skin stretched, and his whole face was different, more smooth.

"I am sick, a little," he said. "I am very old."

"Sleep, then," I said. "I will go."

But I did not mean to go, and he knew it. And at last he said: "What is your wish?"

"My uncle," I said, "the women are talking."

"Truly?" he said, and he almost laughed, meaning that I was a fool, that the women were always talking.

"Of sounds in the night," I said. "Men running and shouting. One heard a conch."

"I heard nothing," he said. "Only the rain."

"Myself," I said, "I heard nothing. But today men are talking about something. I see them muttering together."

"E?" the old man said. "Why do you tell me?"

"Because you know," I said. "These are some doings of yours."

My uncle lay still on his mat, his neck in the curve of his head-rest and his eyes never changing, though his mouth twisted a little, moving over his gums. "My nephew," he said, *"ku sasop'."*

"No," I said. "It is you who are lying, O Dipapa."

"Will you speak like that?" he said.

"Yes," I said. "I will speak like that."

Then it was so quiet that I noticed a pigeon in the bush beyond the village, and I could have forgotten about the old man, almost, wondering what was in the pots that his women had left untended in front of their houses.

"Good, then," he said at last. "Now tell me: what are these doings of mine?"

"I do not understand them. But I think Metusela understands."

"Then speak to Metusela," he said, "not to me. I am an old man. I sleep all day."

"And in the night?" I said.

"And in the night, too," he said, "I sleep."

I looked down into his old face, which was like a lizard's, and into his old sorcerer's eyes that would soon be blind.

"My uncle," I said, "I have waited a long time. Perhaps I will not wait till the end."

Then I saw a sort of smile in his eyes, but not in his face, because his lips were sliding around as he sucked his gums and his face was like water, no longer clear.

"Wait a little," he said. "A little more."

"For what?" I said.

"Perhaps for nothing," he said. "Who can say? In a little, my nephew, perhaps there will be nothing for you."

You would have thought from his words that he was angry, but his voice was soft, and while he was speaking his eyes closed again. He slipped back into sleep like a dying man, and as I was opening my mouth to answer him his mouth opened too, and a little snore came out of it, like you might hear from some small animal rooting in the bush at night.

CAWDOR

It is my opinion that the VC BOITOKU is the most obviously untrustworthy witness. Unlike anyone else involved in the case, he talks a great deal, I think on the principle of the octopus and the cloud of ink. To pay much attention to him would distort the picture that emerges from the evidence of more reliable witnesses, by whom I mean principally BENONI, SALIBA, and several women from Olumata and Obomatu, though I do not believe that even these have told me more than an inescapable minimum of the truth. BOITOKU's contribution seems to be aimed at excusing himself and taking the pressure off DIPAPA, who will not speak at all. If he were believed, he would deserve sympathy. He draws a moving picture of himself as a simple country policeman reading the Riot Act to Genghis Khan.

However, there seems no doubt that there was nothing premeditated about the events in the early evening of October 31st. The opportunity may have been seized, but it was not created by BOITOKU or any of his companions.

144

It arose out of a misunderstanding, which is excusable, on the part of the boys of Olumata regarding the intentions of a band of girls from Wayouyo who suddenly descended on them in the heat of a katuyausi *or courting expedition.*

SALIBA

The girls came into our part of the village twittering like bats and screaming like lories. All their skirts were new, and when they circled round me it was like a whirlwind smelling of bwita flowers and sulumwoya.

"Salib'," they called to me, "come with us to Olumata." They were dressed to look beautiful for the boys of Olumata, and they felt beautiful and wanted me to see.

"No," I said, "not this evening." I was standing over the cooking-pot and I knew that the smell of the smoke would be in my hair and on my skin. "I am cooking for my aunt," I said.

"O, come, Salib'," one girl said. "You are not an old woman yet."

But I said: "No, *des'*, another day." And because I was not happy, not like them, they all looked at each other and were tired of me, and ran away laughing over the green ground.

I went and sat on a stone by my aunt's yam-house, and watched the pot and thought my thoughts, while the light went out of the sky and the palms turned blue and grey.

It was nearly dark when the girls came back. My aunt and her husband and I were beginning to eat, at the door of the house, and my aunt said: "What is that crying?" and we stopped eating to listen, towards the path. We heard the girls calling out, and then their feet running, and then they burst into our part of the village, angry like gulls. "The Olumata boys insulted us," they shouted. "They seized us. They beat us." All kinds of things like that they were shouting, and after that they ran on, still screaming, to another part of Wayouyo.

All the boys and young men of our part had heard that, and were standing up or coming out of their houses.

"It is nothing," I said to my aunt's husband, who had growled. "I will tell you how it was. They met the boys on the path and were provoking to them and then ran away. So the boys chased after them and seized them, and the girls slapped the boys, and they all had a fight. It is often like that," I told him.

145

But our boys and young men were shouting that they would go and beat the Olumata boys. And my aunt's husband went into the house and brought out his shotgun, the iron part, that he uses to hit people over the head.

"Now there will be war," said my aunt with a sigh.

"E, truly," I said. Because already boys from the other part of Wayouyo were running through our part carrying sticks and clubs and torches, and more were gathering on the path to Olumata, with the girls behind them, yelling that the Olumata boys were bush-pigs and rapists and unnatural.

"You stay," my aunt said to her husband. But he looked away from her angrily, and went off to join the younger men, swinging his heavy gun.

"I will go too," I said. "It will make me laugh, this war."

And so I thought it would and was already laughing at my aunt's face and her sad noises. So when I saw Benoni hurrying towards the path I jumped up and ran after him, screaming like the other girls. "O Benoni!" I shouted. "O Benoni! I have been raped by forty Olumata boys. It was like a dream, Benoni—O!"

BENONI

"Crazy woman, Salib'," I said to her. But she could not make me laugh at her then, with the boys so angry and beginning to march, and the girls swearing and crying out all around them. I left her behind and pushed my way through the men, trying to talk to them, to make them peaceful. "It is bad," I told them, "war between villages." But they were excited, and would not listen to me. They began to call *ulululu*! and to whoop, swinging their sticks and torches. Then some began. to run, and soon everyone was running, boys and girls together, and I was caught up in them and had to run too. It was nearly dark then, and in the light of the torches the palm-trunks beside the path sprang out of the shadows of the bush like men or spirits, very pale.

The men of Olumata must have heard us or seen our lights from a long way, or perhaps they were waiting for us, because certainly the girls, whatever had happened there, would have run away threatening them that we would come. Halfway between the villages, where another track goes off towards Rotten Wood, we saw the torches of the Olumata people burning in the grass and against the low fronds of new palms, throwing a green light like fireflies, but growing red

146

as the holders of the torches stood up and moved together and waited in a line across the path.

I was trying to force my way to the head of the Wayouyo men, to hold them back and to speak to the Olumata people before the fighting began. But the bodies were so thick in the path, boys and girls too, that I could not get to the front, and they were shouting very loud and would not hear me. Then some of the men behind me left the path and ran through the bushes and came out ahead of the others, whooping and shouting insults. When they saw that, the men I was among broke into a fast run, and all the voices came together in one scream, and Wayouyo and Olumata met like two seas across a reef.

SALIBA

The Wayouyo girls scattered from the path to the bushes and the grass, as the Olumata women had done on the other side of the track to Rotten Wood. The Wayouyo girls and the Olumata women were screaming at each other, like white cockatoos in two close trees.

The noise of the fighting men was deeper. Some were calling out challenges, and others were grunting and groaning. The boys who had torches had given them to girls, and the girls were running up and down among the bushes, trying to see the fighting on the path but making everything dark by not being together.

Some Wayouyo men had hung back from the fighting as if they were afraid. Benoni was one of them. But with him it was not fear. Benoni was shouting and shouting through his hands but I could not hear what he said, and nobody else could have understood a word in his sounds because of the shrieking of the women.

A boy came staggering through the bushes where I was standing. Blood was running down his face, and shone in the light of my torch. He fell in the grass and lay there and was groaning. So I went to him, holding the torch above his head, and looked and saw that he was an Olumata boy, the same age as I.

"It hurts?" I said. "It is a bad hurt?"

"E," he said, "it hurts."

"You lie there," I said. "Lie quiet. It is madness, this."

"You say," he said, spitting and swallowing. "Ssss. Women."

Then he heard something, on the path, towards Wayouyo. "*Avak'*?" he said, sitting up, and looking at me, not trusting me.

"I do not know what it is," I said. "What did you hear?"

147

"A conch," he said. "Tell me — more men will come?"

"I do not know," I said. And then we heard the conches very clearly, more than one, and coming quickly from Wayouyo.

"I will go back," the boy muttered to himself. "What do they want? They will harm the village?"

"No," I said, "no," pushing him back in the grass. Blood was over all of his face and over most of his chest by then, and his voice sounded feeble. "Lie there," I said, "it is not war like that."

"Then," he said, "you go and look. There, by the path. You look out and tell me."

"All right," I said. "Now you see. I was not one of those girls."

When I told him that he smiled at me, weakly. "My thanks," he said. "O, Salib', did you think I did not know you? That night in the cookhouse at Rotten Wood, when the lamp went out, that was me."

"E, truly?" I cried out. "Then, what is your name?"

"Later I will say," he said. "Go now, Salib'. Keep watch."

But when I stood up, taking the light away from him, his eyes followed the light and me, and looked lonely and even a little afraid. So I hesitated, but he said: "Quickly," and lifted his arm to point where I should go. So I did what he said, though looking back at first, watching the light slide down him, and his body and the grass turning into darkness.

BENONI

It was the Olumata women who heard and saw first. Before I could hear anything, the women were running out of the bushes with their torches and clustering on the path towards Olumata, until their men were between them and what they were pointing at and calling out about, which was behind me somewhere, a long way.

As I was turning to see, the conches whooped. Not one but six or more of them together, and after them the high ululating of a crowd of men. Then the conches broke out again, booming and droning. On the palm-trunks leaning over the path I began to see the glow of moving torches, and later the flash of torches through gaps in the bushes. I saw the torches coming towards the last bend. The light spilled out ahead of them on the straight path. When the flames burst into the open, we saw who had come.

I thought: I do not know these men, what men are these? Their faces were painted white with black eyes and mouths. They had made their bushknives shine, like tin. They ran side by side, in line, four men after four men. As they ran, they howled.

Behind me everybody was quiet, the fighting had paused, there was only a little whimpering from the Olumata women.

I did not know one of them. They were coming towards me with their black eyes staring and the light on their white faces; coming from Wayouyo, yet there was not one I had seen before. They were all the same. Every man in a white yavi, every man with a silver bushknife, every man with a torch or a white conch in his other hand. They were all black and white, wearing tusks and arm-shells and garlands of white flowers, with white dancing-feathers shaking in their hair. As they ran they lifted their knees and stamped, and the conches blew. While they stamped, they howled.

I ran too, going towards them, shouting: "Who? who?" and spreading my arms in front of them, to stop them, to keep them from the fight. But the first men threw me out of the way, and others pushed me while I was stumbling, so that I fell and was lying in the deep grass at the side of the path. When I sat up, the last of them were going by me. I saw that the last ones were not young, and for the first time I understood what they were chanting. They were calling: "They will come." And then: "They will come here." And then: "They will come, the star-people."

SALIBA

The painted men smashed through the young men on the path. Wayouyo boys and Olumata boys, they all went sprawling. Not that the painted men hit them, they just came at a run, with a howl, and drove through. All the time the torches of the women dodged among the bushes and the voices of the women came out of the leaves in little wails of excitement and fear.

I could hear then what the painted men were calling. *"Bi meise! Bi meise besa! Bi meise Mina-utuyam!"*

149

Benoni had stood up and was staring down the path at the moving bodies and torches. I came beside him with my light, and he started.

"It is I," I said.

"Who are they?" he said. "Did you see?"

"They were moving," I said, "and they were painted. But I think I knew some. I think the old man Boitoku is there."

"Boitoku?" he said. *Ku sasop'*. He is the VC, he talks for the Government."

"Yes, but," I said, "he talks first of all for Dipapa."

By then the painted men were all together once more in their lines. Their torches were like a path in the middle of the path. Their conches sounded again, and their howls. They began to run.

"To Olumata," I said. "Why will they go to Olumata?"

But Benoni did not answer, and when I looked at him he was gazing after the lights going away from us, and the Wayouyo people and Olumata people falling in behind. He was gazing at the crowd that was trotting and running after the painted men, and biting his lip until I felt the pain.

"Benoni," I said to him, "what is it?"

"He will destroy it, " Benoni said.

"What?" I said. "Tell me, what will happen?"

"So that I may not have it," he said, shaking his head, as if he had grown very tired. "He will destroy everything."

BENONI

When we came into Olumata, Saliba and I, long after all the others had arrived there, the fires were just beginning.

But before the flames showed, we heard the noise. Pigs were screaming. They were being hacked to death with bushknives. Chickens were screaming. Boys were wringing their necks. Women and children were screaming, standing outside their houses, watching the fires spread slowly along the damp thatch.

Men with knives were running everywhere. Not only the painted men, but the Wayouyo boys, and many of the Olumata men too. Olumata men were setting fires, cutting down their own fruit-trees, laughing and shouting. Like the painted men, they were shouting: "They will come!" Only the mothers with their children, and the old women who had been dragged from their houses, were crying out and weeping and twisting their hands in front of their eyes.

150

And Boitoku, the old VC, painted like a skull, the white of his face growing redder as the fires spread, moved among them, telling a story.

CAWDOR

There is every reason to believe that the myth-basis of the movement has existed on the island for a very long time. Since my first visit, a year ago, I have been aware of the circulation of stories and traditions apparently influenced by or connected with some millennial cult which may have flourished here during the war years, when Mr MacDonnell was evacuated to Australia, or which may have been introduced (as myths pure and simple) from some area such as Kaga, where there has been an actual outbreak of "Vailala madness" or cargo-cult. I now think that the connection with Kaga has been proved, though I no longer feel certain of the physical reality of the vanished Kaga "King", TAUDOGA.

According to KALETA, an Olumata woman, BOITOKU went among the people who had refused to join in the destruction of their village, telling a "story" intended in part as an explanation of the events they were witnessing. As she told it to me, the story went like this:

"I will narrate. I will speak of TAUDOGA.

"A long time ago, TAUDOGA said this. He said: 'I am a native, you are natives, the Dimdims are the same as natives. In the olden days our ancestors and their ancestors came here together in two flying-machines. They crashed at Odakuna. So the survivors went into a cave. Oh, their hunger, having nothing to eat. Some died, others ate them. Then they saw that they could never leave the island. So they came up out of the ground and made their villages. They came up, they looked for village-land, they settled, one man after another. They settled the land all the way, as far as the coasts of Dimdim.'

"TAUDOGA also said this: 'So you see, the Dimdims went to Dimdim. But later they became envious. They said: 'It is our wish to return to Kailuana, to take away the land from the natives.'

"And TAUDOGA said this: 'This year war will break out. After three years, war will be ended, and I will go away.' And that year war with the people of Yapan broke out, and after three years TAUDOGA went away. Nobody can say if he died truly, he went away, that is all.

151

"But I am here to tell you this. He will come again. And today, in Wayouyo, we can hear his voice."

BENONI

I shouted over the women's heads: "This is gammon, Boitoku. Who is this Taudoga? Where did you hear his voice? Through Misa Makadoneli's wireless, *ki?*"

But Boitoku just looked at me with his painted face. That old man who used to be like my father to me when I was small, he just looked at me, and I knew from his eyes in their charcoal hollows what my uncle had it in his mind to do.

"You will come to Wayouyo," he called to all the people. "You will hear the voice of Taudoga. Dipapa has said."

And then he went away, towards the entrance to the village, where all the other men were gathering; and one by one the women wandered after, many still crying, talking of something precious that was gone, a pot that the men had broken, or a young pig that they had chopped up and thrown away, or the yam-harvest sizzling under the burning thatch.

So in the end Saliba and I were left alone, at the centre of the circle of fire, with blood and fallen fruit-trees on the ground around us.

"Salib'," I said.

"I am afraid," she said. "Beni, I am afraid for you."

All the village was deep in smoke. The smoke drifted between us, red, and the fires showed in the tears on her skin.

"Do not be afraid," I said. I reached out my arm to touch her shoulders, and then was holding her against my chest. She was crying, and I felt her mouth moving on my skin. My desire was very great, because my fear was great. "I will be strong, Salib'," I said. "O, all will be well."

SALIBA

I did not want to go back to Wayouyo, I was so happy. I said: "Let us go to Rotten Wood, we will tell Misa Makadoneli, he will talk through the wireless to the Dimdims." But Benoni said: "The Dimdims cannot settle this. This is work for me. Because soon, very soon, Salib', I shall command the villages."

Again we were on the path to Wayouyo, and on the high point of the path I saw for the second time the lights by the stones, and a long way off a glow in the sky.

"It is madness," I said. "The people have gone mad. There will be famine."

"Now Obomatu is burning," Benoni said. "They have destroyed two villages. There is only Wayouyo left, and Rotten Wood."

Then I felt afraid for Misa Makadoneli, and for Naibusi, who had kept his house safe with magic when Dipapa wanted to destroy it, in the Dimdim war. But Benoni was not in a mood to speak, and so I said nothing.

As we came into the boundaries of Wayouyo the mad people were returning from Obomatu. They were running wild through all the parts of the village, whooping and leaping, shouting of the star-machine. Some of them were Obomatu men, still bleeding from the fighting when they had tried to defend their village. But now they too were calling out about the star-people, like the Olumata men, who had helped destroy their own groves and houses, and then had gone to Obomatu and burned that too.

The women who followed them were weeping, and could not understand. They trailed behind the excited men with their children and their old people, crying out and sobbing because of all the things that were gone.

Boitoku ran among them, urging them on. He wanted them to go to where the church was, to hear some talk, some news. Dipapa was there, he said, and would speak to them. And they would hear something else, he said, yes, a thing never heard before. They would hear the talk of Taudoga, a man from the stars, who would come soon, when the world turned over, with cargo.

CAWDOR

The church at Wayouyo plays a rather mysterious role in the life of the community. The Methodist Mission on Osiwa Island was established in 1870, and at some time during that decade missionaries visited Kailuana and supervised the building of a church on the site of the present structure. It has been enlarged and rebuilt several times. For about twenty years a Polynesian or Osiwan catechist was in residence. Mr MacDonnell, when he arrived in 1908, immediately established hostile relations with the white missionaries on Osiwa, and his views seem to have spread to the Kailuana villages. The life of the native catechists became increasingly difficult, and after the 1914–18 War no more were sent to the island.

In the years since, however, singing and some form of worship has taken place in the building, often under the direction of someone who could be

153

called, in a general way, a religious leader. BOITOKU, who is the garden magician of a section of Wayouyo, has recently played this part. So, at some time or other, has DIPAPA. What they do during these ceremonies, apart from singing an eerie local version of "Daisy, Daisy", I have not been able to discover. It probably contains an element of Christianity, but certainly they acknowledge no debt to the Bible. There may be a clue in the fact that they claim "Daisy, Daisy" as an invention of their ancestors.

But the church was not the focus of this outbreak. As was known to the main actors in the cult, the "painted men", the centre of activities was the group of stones called Ukula'osi. It is only through the stones that one can explain the suddenness of the hysteria which took hold of the "painted men".

On October 29th a rumour went through the villages that a space-ship had taken away three men living on the island of Budibudi, where they guarded DIPAPA's betelnut plantation. This seems to have been interpreted (by DIPAPA first, I should say, and later by METUSELA and BOITOKU) as a hopeful sign, a sign that the visitants needed more information about Wayouyo and had taken the men aboard as guides.

When asked why they should connect the stones with the space-ship, all the men implicated said that they had heard of the connection from BENONI, who had heard it from me. I shall have to return to this, obviously.

On October 30th BOITOKU (acting for DIPAPA, I suspect) spread the "talk" through the group which became the hard core of the "painted men". There were perhaps twenty, perhaps forty of these, all men over 35, and all unfriendly to BENONI. Every one of them would have been familiar with the tradition attached to the stones: that if they were moved, a great wind would destroy the villages, that there would be famine, and that all the people would go mad.

Under the direction of METUSELA (I believe), these men went to the stones at Ukula'osi and moved them.

I consider this sufficient to explain the hysteria. They had expected to be destroyed instantly by a wind, and were not. They had expected to go mad, and in a sense did. They had accepted the possibility of a famine and were easily persuaded to set about creating one.

The stones, which formed a roughly oval pattern, were rearranged in a circle. The ground inside the circle was picked clean of weeds and pebbles, and swept ritually by a magician (presumably BOITOKU), in preparation for the space-craft which was to use it as a landmark.

Later they set about constructing a shed or warehouse for the cargo from the craft. Work continued on this throughout the next three days and nights.

154

When the violence began on the night of October 31st, it was the "painted men", in their almost intoxicated state, who spearheaded it. But they were very quickly joined by the majority of males in all three villages of Kailuana. I do not believe that this reaction had, at that stage, anything in particular to do with the "star-machine". I believe that myths and traditions of the "cargo" type are part of their experience, of their memory. But I may be wrong. I admit that I have good reason to doubt my own judgement on a number of matters.

After the burning of Obomatu, all returned to Wayouyo, where preparations had been made in and around the church for the next revelation. From this moment it becomes clear that the mind behind the destruction was that of the old chief, DIPAPA.

BENONI

In the clearing they had lighted a fire. It was the children who were feeding it at first, the small boys, running in out of the dark with bundles of wood and throwing them at the flames so that the sparks puffed upwards. Then they cheered and pushed each other about, full of excitement, but not knowing why or what to do.

All the time men and women were passing them by, going to join the crowd that pressed about the church. They were packed in front of it so thick that you could not see in, and at the sides the walls were bending under the weight of the taller men, who jostled each other to get a sight, over the top of the walls, of the things and the people inside. Their shoulders shone with the firelight and their faces shone with the torches they were staring towards. They would turn back and call and beckon to one another, their faces hot and moved like boys watching a fight.

Through the bodies came a quick, loud, confusing music, that was made, you knew, by people not listening to one another, but hearing only themselves; their own finger-drums, their own pan-pipes, or moaning to themselves the very old songs whose words nobody understands. It was a sound like I had never heard before, of very hungry, very lonely people. Now and again there was the sound of a conch, hollow and low.

I left Saliba to push my way through the men by the walls, to look in over their shoulders. In front of me, in the middle of the church, my uncle was sitting on a carved stool. The side of his head was towards me, the side with the tattered ear-lobe. He stared over the heads of the crowd at the glow of the fire, making munching movements sometimes with his lips, and twisting his fingers together round the top of an ebony walking-stick carved with the leaves and tendrils of yam-vines.

At each side of him, in two lines, the painted men sat cross-legged on the floor. They had driven their torches into the soft ground and the flames swayed in front of their faces. They were my uncle's men, all of them, none of them young and none of them friends of mine. Like him, they stared ahead of them, drumming or piping or droning their songs, each one quiet, but together loud and vague like the sea.

Near the back of the church the pilot was hanging from his rope, nailed to his aeroplane, which trembled. Because of the flickering of the light and the twisting of the rope his white eyes seemed to move and shine. Past him, against the back wall, someone had built a little hut of matting, round and pointed like a shell. Out of the hut, in the small silence between the other noises, came cries and moans, growing louder and faster: *Ai! A'i! A'a'i!* Then fading away: *A! A'o! A-a-a!*

SALIBA

Dipapa clenched his hands about his stick. He lifted himself to his feet, and stood looking at the people.

All the sounds stopped. Everything but the cries in the little house, which grew and grew.

"You hear," Dipapa called, in his tired, wandering old man's voice. "A man will appear. A man will speak."

Then a great shout pierced through the hut of matting, deep like a conch, and as Dipapa turned back to it a man burst out, pushing away the flaps that were its doors, and stumbled, reeling, between the torches, to the front of the church. His head was lifted very high, towards the stars, and his eyes were nearly closed. Only a little white showed between the lids. In his two hands, lifted to the sky, he held the old sword of the King of France. All his body was trembling, and he clung to the sword as if he was afraid of what was happening to him and only had trust in that.

Nobody said: It is Metusela. It was Metusela, and yet it was not.

Our bones were tight with fear. We did not seem to breathe.

"What man are you?" called Dipapa across the church. "Speak, tell us. What is your name?"

And then we heard the voice. Not Metusela's voice. Metusela's little body was shaking, the sweat made stripes on his face. But the voice that came out of his mouth was huge and deep and calm.

156

"I am Taudoga," it said. "A man of the stars."

Behind Metusela, over his head, the pilot looked down on us. The voice seemed to come from him, not from the frightened little man in the torn Dimdim shorts.

"Today I will speak to you," it said. "I will tell you of your ancestors and the ancestors of Dimdim.

"Two brothers came from the stars and crashed at Odakuna. The older brother was Kulua'ibu. The younger brother was Dovana.

"The older brother said: 'I will make a net and go fishing. You open the box, and build us a house here at Odakuna.'

"The older brother went away to fish. The younger brother opened their box of tools. In the box were nails, a hammer, a saw. He built a house and began to roof it, nailing down the corrugated iron.

"Later the older brother came back from fishing. He looked for his younger brother and could not find him. But he just thought: 'He is hiding from me,' and went away into the bush to gather vines.

"But soon he began to grow suspicious, he began to grow angry, his belly was hot. He shouted: 'While I was away, fishing for all of us, my brother was sleeping with my wife.'

"When the younger brother heard that, he was mad with rage. He said: 'Tomorrow I will pack up our belongings and go. If you take back what you said, I will give you the toolbox.' But the older brother was too angry, he would not take back what he said.

"So one day the younger brother, Dovana, and his mother and his sister, packed up the belongings and went away to Dimdim.

"And the older brother stayed. With vines alone he lashed together his house and his canoe. He went foraging in the forest and found nothing but vines.

"Because the younger brother had taken away the iron, the saw, the nails, the hammer, everything. He had taken them all away to Dimdim.

"That is why you have nothing. Your ancestor was foolish and angry, he let his younger brother take the things that belonged to him. The ancestor of the Dimdims was clever and a thief.

"And when other star-machines came, with bully-beef and knives and axes and trousers and all those somethings for your ancestor, Dovana's people tricked them into landing in Dimdim. They promised they would send those things to your people, but they stole them instead. So the Dimdims have everything, you have nothing.

"They will steal even what you have. Misa Makadoneli lives on your land. He gives you orders. Misa Kodo gives you orders. If you have money, Misa Kodo is going to take it for the Government. He will take your shillings and give you instead a piece of paper, with writing on it, saying to himself: You fools.

"But the people in the stars have found out what happened to the cargo they meant for Kailuana. We know that the Dimdims stole it. We are very angry.

"That is why we have told you to burn Olumata and Obomatu. You do not need those houses. You will have houses with roofs of iron. You do not need yams or banana-palms or betelnut. You will have bully-beef and tinned peaches and rum. Burn your houses. Burn your food. Burn your skirts and yavis and ramis. Go hungry till we come. Go naked till we come. Dance, sing, make love. We are very near. We may come tomorrow. We are coming with trucks and shotguns and bombs. We are bringing the children of Kulua'ibu their cargo."

CAWDOR

It has been very difficult to establish the substance of METUSELA's message. His own extraordinary excitement (witnesses who have seen cases of epilepsy say that he appeared to be in a fit) induced a rather similar state in most of his audience, and it is doubtful whether many followed the details of his talk. The story itself is an old one, possibly very old indeed. It tells how an older brother (black), through his impetuous behaviour, lost his inheritance to a younger brother (white), who took away the family's European tools and settled in Dimdim, the homeland of the Australians and various other white nations. As he also took away the mother and sister, these manufactured goods and skills have remained, quite properly, in Dimdim, descending in the female line. On to this story METUSELA then grafted another one, slightly adapted to the new phenomenon of the space-craft, telling how the cargo intended for the elder brother's descendants had been diverted and withheld by the Dimdims. His audience, if they followed him so far, would have found this quite credible. They do believe that a plane (and, presumably, a space-craft) has to be lured, like a bird, and that it is only the Dimdims who know the secret of the magic.

It has been even more difficult to find out what happened after METUSELA reached the climax of his story. The situation is rather like

158

the one which Dalwood and I struck at Kaga, very recently, when I put some questions about their comparatively long-lived "Government" during the war. No Kaga man would talk of it in front of anyone else; their "shame" was too great. In the same way, the Kailuana people cannot be made to speak. All I can do is put together a few hints and slips of the tongue that I noted in private conversations.

METUSELA came to the end of his speech in a frenzy. He was shaking and dripping with sweat. But the voice which he had assumed, the voice that was supposed to be TAUDOGA's, was not at all agitated. It was this peculiar contrast, between the hysteria of the little man and the calm (and very loud) authority of the voice, which seems to have had most effect on the crowd. They were convinced that they were hearing something uncanny. Even DIPAPA seems to have been unprepared for the power of METUSELA's performance, and BENONI describes him as looking "at first stunned, and later mad, like the others".

Towards the end of the message from TAUDOGA, METUSELA moved out into the crowd, still clinging to the sword, and walked through it until he had reached the bonfire. When he had finished speaking, he drove the point of the sword into the ground. Then he tore off his shorts and threw them on the fire.

I do not think that anyone was much surprised by this. If I am right, and all this has happened before, then it was probably one of the things they came to see. But it did certainly introduce a new element. As SALIBA puts it, in the rudest vernacular, ME-TUSELA was in a state of sexual arousal.

Up till this point, the crowd had been silent. But once METUSELA had made his gesture, a tremendous racket broke out; the "painted men" rushed from the church, beating finger-drums and blowing conches, the women began to scream, and the younger men ran about making the ululating noise common here. Then a second person stripped. I think it hardly coincidence that this should have been BOULATA, a wife of DIPAPA's, aged about 40.

After BOULATA had burned her skirt, most of the crowd swarmed to the fire and followed her example. BENONI gives a dry description of the effect of all this on DIPAPA. The old man, he says, was watching from the front of the church with an expression of such intense excitement that BENONI expected, and rather hoped, to see him sprint across the clearing and sacrifice the Government's rami, in which he received the Duke of Edinburgh at Port Moresby. But

159

the mood could not be sustained, apparently, and soon afterwards he hobbled back to his stool inside the church, where he seemed, Benoni says, to doze off, with his chin on his walking-stick.

I am not going to try to reconstruct what followed. BENONI is shy about describing it, even though he did not take part. Mr MacDonnell's opinion is that it could not be called an orgy, as Kailuana people lack the necessary imagination. Whatever it was, it was initiated by METUSELA and BOULATA, almost certainly with DIPAPA's blessing, and there are few people on the island who did not join in.

One who did not was SALIBA, and considering the normal tone of her conversation she expresses herself rather primly about it. She speaks of people behaving "like dogs" and "like pigs". She says she felt "very great shame" because BENONI was there and watching.

The shame was shared, for various complicated reasons to do with kinship and other existing relationships, by a number of individuals scattered through the crowd. Most of them were young, falling within the age-group of BENONI and SALIBA. I have the impression that something similar happened in the wild days at Kaga. Perhaps the young are more inhibited than the middle-aged; or perhaps they were frightened or embarrassed by the sudden change, amounting almost to a change of personality, in their elders. It was precisely the people who had taught them the taboos who were seen that night to be publicly breaking them, and there was a violence about the celebrations which scared the children, in particular. As BENONI was alone by the church, and obviously not intending to join in, these people, who included SALIBA, began to gravitate towards him. Whether or not one sees this as the beginning of an organized resistance depends on whose half-truths and whose denials one accepts.

SALIBA

When he said to me what he said we were in garden-land near the path, out of breath with running, because the girls and older children had begun to run, and I answered at first: "No. No, I could not."

Clouds were rushing across the sky, but every little while the moon broke through and shone on the white coral-lumps in the soil, and shone upwards from the coral into his face, which was stern and bright-eyed, while he held my shoulders.

"Why me?" I said. "Beni, there are others."

"No," he said. "There is only you. You are with me."

"But there are men," I said. "Over there, there is Tobeba'i, my aunt's husband. He is a strong man, and fond of you. He will do anything you say."

"No one is with me like you," he said. "Tobeba'i will help me later. But you must help us first."

He is very beautiful. That night in the moonlight he was beautiful like ebony.

"Ah, you speak like that," I said, "but how long will I be with you, after?"

"While we live," he said. "If you say no, perhaps I will not live long."

Around us, in the bushes, girls were hushing the children, and the men were muttering together, low and fierce.

"Now we have refused," Benoni said. "We have said no to Dipapa and gone away. Before the Dimdims hear of this and come, there is time for people to be killed. There is time for Wayouyo to be destroyed, and Rotten Wood. Do you want that — more hunger, more people sleeping in the rain, because you are afraid? Do you want me dead, Salib'?"

"It is not fear," I said. "It is — like sickness. My belly was sick when you spoke of it. I cannot."

"You will," he said, stroking my shoulder. "O, I have seen; you will." Suddenly his eyes were full of the moon and his teeth shone. "I am going with the men to Rotten Wood. I can trust only you. It is bad, but this is a bad time. You must have a hard mind, tonight, and later we can forget."

"If not —," I said. "If not, I—"

"We will forget," he said, "we two. When the sun rises tomorrow, all this will be finished. Do you hear that? — finished. Now you understand my mind."

Then he dropped his hand, brushing my arm, and turned away towards the shadow of a tree where Tobeba'i, my aunt's husband, was waiting. He went to lean on Tobeba'i's shoulder, and they were whispering together, like two small brothers with a secret behind a house. And I thought: No, no, I do not understand your mind. For a moment I had seemed to understand, but not then, hearing them laugh.

MACDONNELL

I must have rolled over in my sleep, and as I did the light hit my eyelids and startled me awake. Naibusi was beside my bed, a hissing lamp in her hand, dressed as if for the morning in her blue scarecrow's cassock, and looking down at me out of a face like a thoughtful prune.

"Naibus'!" I said. "What is it? Is the house on fire?"

"Not now," she said. "By and by."

"What are you saying? The house will be on fire by and by?"

"Yes," she said. "Soon Dipapa's people will burn it."

I couldn't doubt her or question that, hearing the calm rage in her voice. How she hated Dipapa. He was the enemy. Once before, she claims, while I was evacuated during the war, he planned to sack the place. Then she foiled him with magic. But bullets and strychnine, her face was saying that night, would make a cleaner solution the second time round.

As for me, I felt more surprise than funk. If the house didn't go up in flames, it was bound to go down, sooner or later, with white-ants. And Naibusi and I were on our way out, anyway. But old Dipapa, who couldn't hobble a yard without his walking-stalk — why should a ruin like that take it into his head to burn my bed under me?

"So there is trouble," I said.

"O, very great trouble," said Naibusi. "Madness. They have burned Olumata. They have burned Obomatu. Now they are all copulating together, like dogs."

"*Ki!* I would like to see that."

"There is no reason to laugh," she said. "It is truly disgusting. And they are going to burn Wayouyo too, I think tomorrow night."

"I am not laughing," I said. "Olumata and Obomatu both burned, you say? There is going to be hunger. And sickness too. The Government will be angry. The idiots. What is it — do they say Jesus is coming?"

"Perhaps," she said. "I have not asked. Taubada, it is better that we do not understand, we two."

"True," I said. "Well — what have you come to tell me to do, old woman?"

"Tomorrow," she said, "you will talk to the wireless, to Samarai."

"Yes," I said. "And now?"

"Give me the keys," she said, "for the store."

162

She knew where they were, under my pillow, with the revolver. I fished them out and dangled them between us, watching her face.

"Why?" I said.

"There are some men outside," she said. "They are going to surprise Dipapa."

"What men?" I said. "Benoni, eh? And which others?"

She shrugged her sharp shoulders. "I do not know all their names. There is Tobeba'i," she said, and I thought of course, there would be, smiling to think of him, still boisterous and eager, running with the younger ones until they had him panting. And if Tobeba'i, I thought, isn't copulating like a dog at Wayouyo, then there's something even more interesting in the wind, which Naibusi and I had better not know of, just in case.

"And the store?" I said to her. "What do you want there?"

"Some tools," she said, "Some tools. They will come back."

"Which tools?"

"Taubada," she said, "it is better that you do not know. They will come back, I promise."

"Good, then," I said, and I held out the bunch of keys to her. Her fingers, touching mine, were cool as if they had been in water. I looked a long time at her face, which had no kind of expression in it, and made me wonder what it was I was being shielded from.

"I will go," she said. "Thank you."

"Old woman," I said, "you are still a stranger to me."

"And you are a stranger to me," she said. The lamp swung at the end of her skinny arm, and she looked down on my body. half-smiling. "The skin of a stranger," she said. "O, your skin. There was nothing so smooth, long ago. You were like a newborn pig."

"You say?" I said. "E, I am a tough old pig now. And tired. So do not make fun of me."

"Sleep," she said. "I have gone already."

After the lamplight had withdrawn and was moving down the grey wall of the passage, I called to her: "Naibus'," and saw the light pause and wait. "Give them some more things," I said. "Give them tobacco. Give them one bottle of rum. And the old rifle, the one that is no good, I am angry with Dipapa. And I did not wake all night, do you understand?"

163

They were gone for so long that I began to wonder if Dipapa knew and had sent some men after them, across the gardens and through the bush, so that I would not have seen them from where I waited at the fork of the path. But it was only that the time went more slowly while I was alone and so nervous, longing for him to come again and yet dreading what he would say and think, now that it was done. The clouds had grown thick and the night was very dark. I had no torch. But a little way down the path there was a glow, the last flames of Olumata burning. And I thought I would go there and wait, and keep watch from there on a high place that their lights would have to come over on their way back from Rotten Wood.

I had not got into the village, even. It was by the first house of the circle, among the chopped-down areca-palms and banana-trees, that I saw him lying, half-buried in smouldering thatch.

I had forgotten him. Everyone had forgotten him, so much had happened since the moment when he came stumbling away from the fighting boys, with a bad wound on his head, and fell in the grass, and said to me: "Ssss – women." Probably he had not seen the painted men, or any of the things that followed. Because when he had looked at me, half-frightened, as I took away the light, it must have been that he was fainting, even while he said: "Salib', keep watch."

He knew my name. He did not tell me his name. But once, at Rotten Wood, he crept into the cookhouse while I was washing the dishes and put out the lamp, and then for a while we were laughing and struggling together in the black room, until I broke away and ran, screaming for Naibusi.

So he woke alone, in the bush, in the middle of the night. Nobody was keeping watch. He came staggering along the path towards his village, holding the pain in his head. But his village was empty and burning. His village was finished. So he fell down, fainting, in the cool banana leaves. And the fire crept over the ridgepole of the house beside him, till his lungs were full of smoke, and the blazing thatch fell on him, and his hair burned, and a fine ash covered the lids of his eyes and stained the teeth in his open mouth. Even the blood on his face had turned black and dull. The fire smothered and charred him, and no one was mourning or searching, and he died not knowing.

164

And then I knew that what I had done was right. Because the root of his dying, that young man, it was Dipapa and Metusela.

BENONI

We went through the village hamlet by hamlet, hunting him. Hiding behind trees, in shadows. Peering over the walls into the church, where naked people lay tangled asleep, as if a wind had knocked them down. Scratching on the wall of his house, whispering: "Metusela!", in fear of Dipapa, sealed inside his big house nearby. At the Government's house, where whole families from Olumata and Obomatu slept huddled together on the grass, looking for a sight of his hair, perhaps his open eyes. But he was nowhere there.

When we met Saliba, her face frightened me, it was so quiet, like a dead woman's. She would not speak at first.

"We are too late?" I said, asking gently, not to show her my disappointment.

"No," she said. "He is still at the stones, himself alone."

"We have been there," I said. "He is gone."

"I shall show you," she said, very still, "where to find him."

At the stones one would be alone truly, more alone than any man chooses to be. I wondered that he was not afraid. In the moon that came and went the stones that those people had moved to make a circle for the machine shone pale and had the look of waiting. And I thought: What if they should come, what if Metusela knows? But I did not believe that, that he knew; though I thought and I think now that some day they may come, and then I shall be ready.

Outside the circle they had built their house, their shed, for the cargo. It was still not finished. By daylight they would finish it, that is what they would be thinking; all of them, the women too, working at the shed, to have it ready for the next night. Only she and I, looking out from the bush at the bare slope and the half-thatched frame of the house that those men had put together in such excitement, knew that when they came again there would be nothing there but ashes.

"Where?" I asked her.

"In the shadow of the house," she said. She was unmoved, she was stern, with thoughts that she had not spoken to me. "I will go now, I will sleep."

"No, wait," I said. "Come with me." And she followed, saying nothing, to the shadow of the madmen's cargo-shed.

He was lying on his back in that darkness. I supposed that he was sleeping, and did not like to think of what had made him tired. But a reflection of moonlight from a stone shone on the whites of his eyes.

"I could not," she said. "I could not do what you asked of me, what he wanted. I told him that if we came here, alone, I would make him happy. But I could not."

She had driven the sword through his throat, and downwards into his chest and belly. The handle forced his head back. I could see on it the mark of the King of France, which Misa Kodo told me was a flower.

IV
TROPPO

DALWOOD

Because of the weather the *Igau* couldn't anchor off the Government station, and we had to go by truck to the northern tip of Osiwa island, through the dark and the driving rain. I'd never seen a night so black, so threatening, but we took Sayam's word for it that it was possible to get to Kailuana. After all the hullabaloo of canoes and dinghy and Tilley lamps and torches, and the loading of the ridiculous amount of stuff we have to cart with us, Misa Kodo wrapped himself up in the red trade-store blanket and went to bed, it looked like.

When the storm hit us, I was standing beside Sayam at the wheel. By the dim blue light I saw his old wooden face get grimmer and grimmer, and I felt the fear.

Not that there was panic. But a lot of rushing around, for a long time. For two hours, I think, and all that while there was not a thing to be seen but the black sky and the black sea and the bared teeth of foam.

I saw the big veins on Sayam's hands, gripping the wheel. At least he had something to hang on to, till the end.

I don't scare easily. Or maybe my brothers made me scared to admit it to myself. What I felt wasn't the same thing as being afraid. I was excited, and, in a funny way, randy. Not that I was thinking of anyone on earth, least of all her, but it was like that. And I stood there by Sayam, gripping whatever handhold was near, and thought I could understand things I'd read about people in wars and plagues going wild.

Of course I was remembering, as everyone else was, the *Munu-wata*, that disappeared off the face of the sea a few months ago. And

169

it was just when I thought we were going that it seemed that the only thing that mattered was to live, to fuck.

But in a small corner of my mind I was thinking about my family, and about the people who had put us out there in a boat designed for calm rivers: a boat like the little ferry that used to take us, when we were kids, from Perth to South Perth, to the Zoo.

And in the same small corner I was mourning. Mourning the enormous waste, the waste of myself.

Then I thought of him, the waste of him. So I left Sayam and went to where he lay cocooned in his red blanket. It was because he spoke my language.

I said: "Are you fit?"

By the dregs of blue light from over Sayam's head his face looked like something from a POW camp. But he sort of grinned, and said: "You can guess."

I sat down by him, and on some stupid impulse lifted his head and slid my thigh under it, like a pillow. It wasn't for his benefit, really, and it probably irritated him. It was because I wanted to tell Saint Peter: I was a good mate to someone.

"Is that any better?" I asked him.

"No," he said.

His face, upside down, was like a sweating skull.

"You ought to get that dog," he said.

"I'm sorry, Alistair," I said. "About everything. About the rows. And my being so tactless."

"You don't know what a row is," he said. "You're sort of sweet. Or wet."

Literally speaking, that was true. And he was soaked, too, and shivering inside the sodden blanket.

"I just wanted to say that," I explained.

"Save it for the next time," he said. "My gut is an infallible instrument. I know when we nearly went down, and just then that was what I wanted. But we're coming out of this."

I did feel that he might be right, because the pitching and wallowing seemed a little less, and I began to worry not so much about being seasick, for the first time in my life, in front of all those half-panicky people. And then suddenly the moon came out, and there was a tremendous shout.

"Hey, look," I said, shaking his shoulder.

He sat up beside me and stared, down the black and white wake, towards the low full moon, with tattered clouds racing across it, and the low dark hump of an island in silhouette.

"Kailuana, taubada," Osana called out at us. I didn't need to look at him to know how scared he'd been.

"Sayam was all at sea," I said to Alistair. "How far back would you say it was?"

"I can't judge," he said. "Funny, though. Our first landfall, if we'd ever made one, would have been my native heath."

"You'll have to spell it out," I said. "Where *is* your native heath?"

"Guadalcanal," he said. "I was born there."

Sayam was beginning to put about. I thought how little I knew about anything, even geography, and of those stones which, some people say, young blokes used to study before setting out to visit islands all over the Solomon Sea that they'd never seen before.

MACDONNELL

When Naibusi woke me it was about eleven o'clock, and I came out in no very sweet temper to where the two of them were standing, soaked to the skin, by the Tilley lamp which Naibusi had put on the table, and at which Cawdor seemed to be trying to warm himself.

"Funny time of night to turn up," I said. "And you didn't hurry."

"Weather, Mak," Cawdor said. "Also bureaucracy. Some Health and Agriculture people from headquarters had the boat."

He was very subdued, and shivering. "Well," I said, "before you turn in, a drop of rum and hot water wouldn't do you any harm."

"No, thanks, " he said. "We had a rough trip. If you don't mind, I'll just go and crash."

"Please yourself, old man," I said. "You know where your bed is." And he nodded at us and went, and we heard the door in the passage close.

I said to Dalwood, whose clothes were gummed to his skin: "You'd better do the same."

"Yes," he said. "We're both a bit shaken up."

"Cawdor certainly looks it," I said. "He's very quiet."

"Mak," the boy said, "I might as well tell you. When we got back to Osiwa last time, there was a telegram to say his father had died. I think he felt that more than he expected."

171

I said: "Very sorry to hear it. He can't have been very old."

"He was fifty-two," Dalwood said, and I clicked my tongue. It hadn't occurred to me that I was old enough to be Cawdor's grandfather.

"What sort of man was he?" I asked.

"He had been a missionary," Dalwood said, "in the Solomons. When he died he was holding down some sort of religious desk-job in Sydney. I don't think there was ever much contact between them. Alistair was raised in boarding schools. Still, it would rock you a bit, I can imagine."

"And no mother?" I asked.

"Not that I ever heard of," the boy said. "But I don't know much. He told me tonight, for the first time, that he was born on Guadalcanal. Why are you looking like that?"

"Just thinking," I said. "When the Japs arrived in the Solomons, I've heard that some missionaries went missing. Perhaps some missionaries' wives too."

"I don't know," the young fellow said. "He's never mentioned anything like that."

He picked up a sponge-bag from the table, the only luggage he had with him. "I'll take your advice about bed."

"Good idea," I said. "By the way, something you can pass on to Cawdor. If I've ever spoken my mind about Benoni in front of you two, I take it all back."

"He's in control, then?" the boy said.

"I'm very impressed," I said, "very impressed indeed. If he lives long enough, he could be the first native District Commissioner, that young chap."

"That's good news," Dalwood said, turning away. "It will be a load off his mind. Off Alistair's, I mean. Mak, it can't last much longer."

"No," I said. "I'm very sorry for both of you, but it can't. I saw that in his eyes."

BENONI

I met Misa Kodo and Misa Dolu'udi at the end of the path from Rotten Wood, and I walked with them around the villages of Olumata and Obomatu, where all the men, and women too, were working on the new houses and yam-houses, and at planting new palms and fruit-trees. Now and again Misa Kodo would say: "Very good, Benoni," and nod to me, though he did not seem to notice as much as I thought he would notice.

He was very silent, but I did not pay much attention to that, as he was usually silent. And besides, Misa Dolu'udi was talking a great deal, and saying to me, through Osana, very kind things.

But when we went to the resthouse, and Misa Kodo had all the people in front of him on the grass, and started his questions, then I began to see the change.

At first the questions were about the fight on the path near Olumata, then about the damage at Olumata. He wanted to know and write down what damage every single man had done, so that if he had chopped down a tree or broken a cooking-pot he would replant it or buy a new one for the person who owned it.

In the beginning we thought that it was only our heads which were going round with all these questions. But we soon saw that Misa Kodo himself was more confused than anyone.

Then he began about the boy Teava, who was burned to death at Olumata while he was lying unconscious. Misa Kodo wanted to know how Teava was wounded, and as soon as the people said that he was hurt with a shotgun, Misa Kodo became very excited. It was a long time before we could make him understand that Teava had not been shot, only hit on the head with the iron part of an old shotgun, and that there were three like that on the island.

Then from talking about Teava he went on, with no kind of sense that we could follow, to ask about Metusela, about where he had gone. And nobody could say, of course, because not even Saliba knows. The only people who know are I and Tobeba'i, who took the pieces away in his canoe and threw them to the fish.

But I was frightened for a moment because Boulata, one of my uncle's wives, said that Metusela had told her, when he left the church, that he was going to the stones. And I thought that he might have made some joke, as would have been natural in such a miserable little creature, about going to meet Saliba. But no, Boulata had heard nothing of that.

For a long while Misa Kodo wrote away in his book. Then he told all the people that he was arresting Boitoku, the VC, and taking him on the *Igau* to the calaboose at Osiwa for the time being. At that Boitoku's old wife cried out, but Boitoku himself was quiet.

Then Misa Dolu'udi, who was always hungry, wanted to eat. But Misa Kodo said: "No, first let us talk with Dipapa."

173

When we came to my uncle's house, all the Government men and the prisoner, Boitoku, and some of the men who were with me, my uncle was alone on his covered platform. He was not asleep and did not even pretend to be, but raised himself and looked at Misa Kodo with his eyes that were bright and cloudy.

"I am looking for Metusela," said Misa Kodo.

My uncle sat as if he were thinking, moving his mouth as he so often did, and said: "I know nothing about Metusela."

"Then he has vanished?" said Misa Kodo.

"I think so," said my uncle. "Yes, he has vanished."

"Dipapa," said Misa Kodo, "there is very great trouble. Trouble, I believe, for you."

My uncle simply lay back again, with his neck on his head-rest, and said: "You say."

"You understand me?" asked Misa Kodo.

"I understand," said my uncle. "But Misa Kodo, who are you? A young man of no importance. And I command Kailuana, and have spoken with the Queen's husband."

"True, Dipapa," said Misa Kodo. "I am a young man of no importance. But I should be sorry to see an old man like you, an important man like you, die in the calaboose."

"What is your mind?" asked my uncle.

"That I think," said Misa Kodo, "that Metusela is dead. That I think you killed him."

My uncle said: "I am an old man, you have already said it. Do you believe I kill people?"

"With your own hands," Misa Kodo said, "no. But I ask you another time. Where is Metusela?"

"I have heard," my uncle said, "that he went to the stones. The machine had been there before. Perhaps it came again."

"Dipapa," Misa Kodo said, "do not forget the calaboose."

My uncle sat up once more, and only looked. And I was afraid for Misa Kodo. I came to stand near him, so that when my uncle looked at Misa Kodo he would have to see me beside him, with the bushknife in my hand.

While we three were like that, Osana had been gossiping, in whispers, with Boitoku and a few other men. Suddenly some of them hissed, and some others laughed in an uneasy way, as if Osana had said something of which he should have been ashamed.

174

I did not hear what Osana said, and nothing he said would interest me. But Misa Kodo, who was nearer, had understood, or thought that he had.

Misa Kodo seized the bushknife from my hand, and rushed at Osana. And Osana was terrified. Misa Kodo meant to cut off his head, as Tudava did to Dokonikan.

"Say it another time," Misa Kodo said to Osana.

"Say what?" Osana cried out. He was trembling, but not more than Misa Kodo.

"What you have said already," said Misa Kodo.

"Taubada, you did not understand," Osana was gabbling. "You do not understand everything. There are words you do not know."

That was so true that we felt a little sorry for Osana. Nevertheless, Misa Kodo was going to cut off his head.

But Misa Dolu'udi came behind Misa Kodo and closed his hand around Misa Kodo's wrist. They did not struggle, or even speak, but my bushknife fell to the ground, and Misa Kodo turned and went away towards the resthouse.

Some of the men would have followed him, but Misa Dolu'udi called in a deep voice, in the language: "You stay here." And he was so stern, and so different, that they did not move.

Misa Dolu'udi said a few words in English to Osana, and later Osana translated a speech of Misa Dolu'udi's. Misa Dolu'udi said: "The older taubada is ill. This time we cannot stay long in Kailuana. In the meantime, I shall manage matters and hear your talk. And I shall come again before long."

The people were so interested in Misa Dolu'udi, who was suddenly so changed, that they almost forgot Misa Kodo. I saw my uncle watching, sucking his lips and the inside of his cheeks in the way that he had. I saw his thoughts in his face. He was thinking: This is a taubada of the sort I understand. He was pleased with Misa Dolu'udi. That was one more reason for him to want Misa Kodo dead.

DALWOOD

After leaving Dipapa I took Osana and the policemen with me, and we went round the villages again, to the church and to the stones, while I put together as much information as I could collect. Osana was pretty cast down, which was good to see; but in any case,

175

I soon found I hadn't much need of Osana. Because Benoni started trying his Pidgin on me, and though I don't speak it, I had learned enough from a book, while I was still expecting a posting on the New Guinea side, to be able to follow and answer. That way I was able to get a very good picture of what had happened, and what Benoni had done about it afterwards, and it gave me quite a respect for him, as well as just a skerrick of sympathy for Dipapa, because it was certainly checkmate there.

It was twilight when I came back to the resthouse, and there wasn't a light, so I shouted out for Biyu to attend to that. While he was dealing with the Tilley lamp on the veranda, I went into the room where we slept. Alistair was lying, wrapped in the red blanket with the tiger on it, on one of the hard bunks lashed with vines that Benoni had had built for us the first time we came. But he had been busy, apparently, because his day-book was lying open on the other bunk, mine, covered with writing which I would see at a glance was about the Metusela business.

He wasn't asleep, though, and when I only sat on my bunk without saying anything he felt he had to say: "Well?"

"Alistair," I said, "I've taken over, you realize that."

"Have you?" he said.

"I don't know what the rules are," I said. "Perhaps, if it came to it, I have the right to arrest you for what happened today. Anyway, I'm stronger than you are, and we don't want public trouble."

He showed hardly any reaction. All he asked was: "What will you tell them here?"

"I have told them," I said. "That you're sick. That I have to get you back to Osiwa tomorrow, to the doctor. Thank God we've got one at last. We'll take Boitoku and some of the witnesses, say Tobeba'i and Saliba. But we'll have to leave this half-finished for the time being. Benoni can handle it, I'm sure of that."

In the dim light I had been able to make out his face, more or less, but just then Biyu got the lamp going properly, and the glare coming over the half-wall made a shadow in which I lost him.

"Sorry," I said.

176

"It's all right," he said. Then he gave a sort of laugh, like a sob. "Am I to consider myself under arrest now?"

"No," I said. "On sick leave."

"Fine," he said, and rolled over and pulled the flimsy blanket around his head.

BENONI

When I wanted to see Misa Kodo, first Kailusa tried to stop me, than Misa Dolu'udi did. But I kept saying, in Pidgin, that I knew that Masta Alistair was sick, and knew why, and would do something to help him. And at last he let me go into the room where they slept.

Misa Kodo must have been listening to us, because when I came in he turned on the bed and said, very quietly: "O, Benoni."

"Taubada," I said, "I want to talk."

"Talk, then," he said.

"Taubada, I want you to come and sleep in my house. It is not safe here."

"Why is it not safe?" he asked.

"It is built off the ground, taubada. Look at the cracks between the floorboards. And the walls do not meet the roof, and there is no door."

"E," he murmured. "So you fear sorcery for me?"

"Yes, taubada. Very much. In my house you would be safe. I will not sleep with you if you do not want, though it would be better. But I will be watching."

"You are kind," he said. "But I think I shall live as long as Dipapa. I am a Dimdim, Beni. I laugh at sorcery."

"My friend," I said, "do you laugh at my fear?"

"No, my friend," he said. "But I want to be alone now. You know I have a fever. In the morning perhaps I shall be better."

I knew how it would be. But I only said: "Well, then, I am going." And he said: "Sleep peacefully."

DALWOOD

At first, waking and finding him gone, I made nothing of it, thinking that he had wandered out to the small-house, or perhaps was on the veranda having a solitary session with the rum-bottle, as he used to do before he changed so much. But I couldn't sleep again, thinking of that blanket lying there uninhabited, opposite, and at last got up and went out, just as I was, in bare feet and underpants, to look for him.

As I was taking the path towards the small-house, Benoni suddenly appeared beside me, and asked in Pidgin: "Masta Tim, you like to find Masta Alistair?"

"Do you know where he is?" I said.

"Yes," he said, "we know. We are watching, many of us. He is all right."

"Take me to him," I said; and he walked on, telling me with a jerk of his head to follow.

He spoke the truth about there being many of them. As we went along the beach-path, people kept popping out of the bushes. Most of the younger men on the island must have been out of bed that night. Nobody said much, there were just a few mutters meaning that there was no news.

In the moonlight the place where the stones were looked more desolate even than when I saw it first. In burning the cargo storehouse, as they called it, Benoni's men had started other fires in the scrub, and whatever wasn't barren rock was charred. Behind the biggest of the stones, one that Metusela's crowd could never have moved, Kailusa was keeping guard over his boss.

With all that shadowy activity around him, Alistair thought he was alone. He was sitting on one of the rectangular stones, staring at the ground.

The coral-rock tore at my feet as I went towards him, and at one point I stopped with a bit of a yelp, and he looked up, startled.

"You," he said, as if he'd forgotten that there was such a person.

"Alistair," I said, "this isn't doing you any good. Come back to the resthouse. You're keeping a lot of people awake."

Still he didn't seem to realize how many eyes were watching. All he had to say was: "Aren't you cold?" He was fully dressed himself, but shivering.

"No, I'm not," I said. "Come on, there's that nice blanket waiting for you, and if you like you can have my mosquito-net on top of it. D'you hear me, Batman? This is your boy-apprentice reasoning with you."

He put back his head as if to take one last look at the stars, and seemed to fix in that position, and keep gazing.

"Come on," I said again. "You know I'm quite capable of carrying you, if I have to."

I heard him take a sudden deep breath, then he muttered to himself: "It won't come to that."

CAWDOR

The space-craft was seen over Boianai for two nights in late June. From here, Boianai is about 125 miles S.W. Coming from there to here it would have passed over Vaimuna: specifically, over Kaulagu village.

The first sighting at Boianai was on 26th June. It may be possible, with the co-operation of the Kailuana people and Mr MacDonnell, to establish the dates of the sightings at Wayouyo.

Check the date of the disappearance at sea of the Munuwata. *It was near the end of June, beginning of July. No trace was found. At that time I was at Vaimuna and heard of it. On Vaimuna there is no wireless, no radio, and no one speaks English anyway. The abandoned church in Kaulagu village has been restored and strangely decorated. Most of the objects hanging from the rafters are based on a rather vague notion of aircraft.*

It will pretty certainly never be possible to date the disappearance of the three men from Budibudi island, but the fact was known on Kailuana in late October.

There is also the disappearance of Metusela. Is the idea of murder too simple?

SALIBA

At midday we all came back to Rotten Wood, the Government people and Boitoku and my aunt's husband and I. I went straight into the cookhouse and began helping Naibusi, as if I had never been away. I wanted to be alone with her, but the other girls were coming and going, and calling out that Saliba was being taken to Osiwa, that she was being sent to the calaboose. And at that Naibusi grew angry, and told them they lied, that I and my aunt's husband were only going to help the Government, to tell about the painted men.

On the veranda there was much talk and movement, and Naibusi came back from there to say that Sayam would not sail until nearly dark, because there was bad weather coming, and if the *Igau* left then, it would not be able to anchor at the Government's village.

179

She said that Misa Kodo was shut up in the room where he slept, and that Misa Makadoneli was in a bad temper with the other Dimdims and was reading a book, and that Misa Dolu'udi was angry.

He is angry today. No, not angry, but sad and hard. He never notices me. Benoni calls him: "Masta Tim," but when I was talking to the ADO and called him: "Timi," he looked surprised and then ashamed.

Is Benoni ashamed? O, my mind is very heavy. He is so beautiful, he is so noble now. Does he want to forget everything he said to me on the night of the painted men?

DALWOOD

It is because of that radio that we are here.

Old Mak was fed up about having us hanging around all afternoon, and left me to entertain myself. So most of the time I sat at the table on the veranda, watching the canoes go out to the *Igau* with all our stupid gear: the patrol-table, the chairs, the typewriter, the patrol-boxes, all the Government's signs of rank.

Later, Mak came out to be sociable, carrying the radio. He said: "Something for you to do, old man. It's kaput again."

I took the back off, saw what a simple thing it was, and fixed it. I gave him a blast to prove that, then killed it.

Presently Naibusi came out of the cookhouse with the tray and the rum and the lemon, and we were ready, a bit early, for the sundowner ritual.

She asked Mak some question about "Alistea", as she had taken to calling him, and after he had muttered something she went into the main part of the house and I heard her knock on the door in the passage.

When Alistair came out to join us his clothes were crumpled and damp with sweat. He stood leaning on the rotten veranda-rail, looking down on the *Igau*, and said after a while: "I thought we'd have been off by now."

"Any minute," I said. "Sayam will send a boat-boy to tell us."

"Here's your rum," Mak said, "young Alistair." It was probably the first time in half a century that he'd called a grown man by his Christian name.

But Alistair just shook his head and said: "No, thanks, Mak," still with his eyes on the boat.

Mak looked at his watch, then clicked on the radio. "Might as well hear the news," he said.

So we listened, Mak and I. I didn't think that Alistair even heard it. It started with a local story, pretty grim, about sharks. Then it whipped quickly round the rest of the world. There was something happening in France, and something else in America. One of Harold Macmillan's men was saying something important about independence somewhere, and the South Pacific Commission was saying or doing something not so important. Whatever it was, it sounded like progress, and so Mak switched off.

"Sad, that," I said. "I mean, about the fellow at Vuna."

"Sad," Mak said, "but always, I can't help thinking, a bit fishy. At least, people will say so, and think so. The clothes left on the beach — we've all heard that one before. Sad, anyway, for his wife. Of course he can't be presumed dead for seven years."

I wondered whether Alistair had heard it, and whether it had given him any more crazy ideas about flying saucers. But he still had his back to us, at the rail.

"When I said fishy," Mak said, "I meant, why should a chap go for a swim alone at night?"

Alistair said, not looking round: "He'd probably had a row with Sheila, and stormed out of the house for a while."

"What was that, old man?" Mak said. "I say. Did you know him?"

Then I realized why the name Manson had rung a bell. It was the only friend he'd ever spoken of. That day in the resthouse at Vilakota he had said that he might go and stay with them, because Mrs Manson was a good cook.

"It's the watch I can't get over," Alistair said. "The watch ticking away on the beach, when Jack was — all in bits."

He went away so fast that we couldn't see his face. We heard the door slam, on that sweating, musty room that looks like a cage.

"Don't go after him," Mak said to me. "He won't want to talk. If he does, he'll talk to Naibusi."

I couldn't have talked to him, anyway. Those words of his, "all in bits", had hit me too hard. I was seeing what he saw: the real sea, flowering with a real man's blood.

MACDONNELL

Well, we're coming to the end of it. Browne promises to read us a draft of his report, to put us all in the picture. Just in case we should be blaming ourselves. Very civil of him, too.

I shan't be sorry to see the stern of the *Igau* this time. Then I can call my house my own. I don't care if these are the last white men I ever meet. White men are more trouble than they're worth.

Saliba looks peaky. Something is wrong there. I think it's Benoni.

Amazing, the change in that young fellow. That is my idea of a chief.

I'm not so happy about the change in Dalwood. Our puppyish man-mountain is turning into something rather formidable. I preferred him before.

Yes, I heard you. When the boat-boy came to fetch them I called for Naibusi to go and tell Cawdor. They came out of the passage together, and stood talking for a few minutes at the far end of the veranda. She was crying, and he put a hand on each of her shoulders and looked into her eyes, before coming to join us at the top of the steps.

I held out my hand to him. "Safe journey," I said. "Get fit, and come back soon."

I knew I should never see him again. You had only to look at his face to know that he had died already.

OSANA

Long before we reached the strait between Vaimuna and the south of Osiwa the rain was falling hard and the sea growing rougher. And Sayam called to me, and asked me to tell Mister Cawdor that we could not anchor at the Government station that night. He said that we should go ashore at Vilakota, and he would take the *Igau* around the tip of Vaimuna into the lagoon.

We both knew that Mister Cawdor was too sick to be in charge, but we did not wish to discuss important matters with a boy like Mister Dalwood.

Mister Cawdor was lying, wrapped in his red blanket, on the bench. He was holding a book in front of him, but I do not think he was looking at it.

When I told him what Sayam had said, he sat up and was thoughtful. After a moment, he said: "Very well, we shall sleep at Vilakota."

I went back to Sayam, but kept watching Mister Cawdor. Presently he took a blue pencil out of his pocket and wrote something in the front of the book. Then he stood up, and went to one of the patrol-boxes, and opened it. He put the book inside, and before he closed the lid I saw him take something from the box and drop it into the pocket of his shirt.

Afterwards, when he was sitting on the bench again, he was looking at his arms.

The last time I spoke to Mister Cawdor was when he was getting into Keroni's canoe to go ashore at Vilakota. I leaned out from the *Igau* and said, almost into his ear: "Very bad, taubada." But he pretended not to hear.

DALWOOD

From Keroni's canoe we went straight to the resthouse, through the rain. The palms were thrashing overhead, and one nut just missed me. In the resthouse, Alistair wandered off without a word into the sleeping-room. All he had with him was that stupid blanket.

Not that I had much more, for once. Just my sponge-bag, two tins and a tin-opener, and it felt good to be without all the usual Government clutter. We were going to sleep on mats on the bare boards, and if the *Igau* had gone down overnight with the typewriter there would have been mixed feelings in me.

At first Keroni and I squatted on the veranda by the blaze of a torch, which flickered wildly in the growing wind, and exchanged polite mutters, from which I gathered that he was peeved about being ignored in that way by his friend Misa Kodo. But I explained: "Misa Kodo is sick," which was a word I had good reason to know by then, and he got all concerned and said a lot of things in which I picked out several times the words "my wife". Remembering his wife and her teapot, I could imagine a banquet suddenly arriving, so it was a relief when Kailusa came ashore with the Tilley lamp and started explaining something about how things were.

I opened the two tins, one of sausages and one of beans, and went into the room. I said: "Are you still not eating?"

183

"No, thanks," he said, from his mat on the floor. On that last patrol I don't remember seeing him eat or drink at all, and he'd almost given up his foul tobacco. I had noticed that if he did smoke, the shaking of his hands got worse.

"I won't be long," I said. "When I've got rid of the locals and finished with the lamp, you can have a good night's sleep."

"Thanks," he said.

But it took quite a while to lose them all, and even afterwards it was hardly peaceful. There was a lot of running around in the dark, and muttering and whispering, and the sound of the storm was growing tremendous.

So as not to disturb him, I turned out the lamp on the veranda, and groped my way through the dark to my mat in the room which was roaring with wind. That night even I felt cool, and lay down with all my clothes on.

Just before I went to sleep, he said: "Tim."

"What ?" I said.

"I can't go out," he said. "They're watching. Osana is watching. I'm sorry, Tim."

I didn't know what he meant, and was too sleepy to wonder. I thought perhaps he was going to take a leak through a crack in the floor boards, which was hardly the sort of thing to bother me.

"I'm sorry," he said again. "You won't forget?"

"No," I said, just before falling asleep. "I won't forget."

SALIBA

That night I slept in the house with Keroni's wife, because you never know about those mainland policemen, and I felt that I was Benoni's woman. I say I slept, but there were so many noises that we two women both lay awake, and sometimes smoked and sometimes chewed. I do not know where Keroni was, but I could hear men moving about outside and talking, or calling quietly to each other.

The sound of the storm was very great, because two seas meet at Vilakota, and there is so little land between the sea and the cliffs that the palms are planted very thickly, like a Dimdim plantation. All night the nuts were thudding around us, and the branches crashing, and the two seas thundering together.

When the screaming began, I was wide awake, and ran immediately out of the house, and was one of the first people to see Kailusa.

He was just outside, lit up by the fire of Keroni's torch. He was shining in the light. He was shining with blood.

"O my taubada," he kept screaming. "I was sleeping underneath his house. O my taubada. His house is bleeding."

DALWOOD

I can't.

Anyway, you don't need me to tell you what it looked like. You saw for yourself.

My first thought, when Keroni's torch burst into the room, was that it had been done in frenzy, with exultation. I thought that it must have been with a sort of joy that he did it.

He had started on his wrists, and worked up to the big veins, arteries, whichever they are, inside his elbows. And then, I suppose because that wasn't quick enough, he had done his throat. But his hands by then must have been nearly useless, which was why it took so long.

Through all the commotion of getting him to the *Igau*, getting everyone else to the *Igau*, he was still alive. In Keroni's canoe he was even conscious for a moment, and whispered to me, in a high feeble voice: "Tim, don't hurry." Or perhaps it was: "Don't worry."

I didn't answer. I was angry with him, furiously angry.

When we were well out on the lagoon, I was standing at his head, and old Boitoku came and looked at his throat. Boitoku said to himself in a wondering way: "*Makawala lekoleko*," and I understood that. He meant like a chicken, one that had had its head cut off with a bushknife.

The last time he was conscious he said to me, in that falsetto whisper: "I saw. Timi, I saw. Down the tunnel. My body. Atoms. Stars."

I bent over to look at his black face. His eyes were closed, but his mouth was open. There was blood even on his teeth. In his paralysed right hand the razor-blade was still gripped between thumb and forefinger, glued there with blood. I couldn't bring myself to touch him, not even his forehead, because his hair was soaked with blood.

He reached out his useless left hand and laid it on my arm. He said: "I can never die." Then he died.

I left him to Kailusa and Biyu. I saw them hide him away, under the red blanket with the almost obliterated tiger.

I went up to the bow, and watched the boat butt its way over the rough, milky-green lagoon. I thought: I will be different now. See nothing by accident. Hear nothing by accident. Say nothing by accident. Move through the villages like royalty, like a wooden figurehead.

I remembered his asking, when I stood in that place, what did I think I was, the boat's figurehead? I lifted my arm to my eyes, and saw on my skin the marks of his four fingers, stamped in his dead blood.

BROWNE

I am now in a position to submit a brief preliminary report on the recent events at Kailuana, in the resthouse at Vilakota and on board the Government work-boat *Eagle*. The enquiry was held on Kailuana, at Wayouyo village and in Mr MacDonnell's house, most of the witnesses being natives of the island, and Mr MacDonnell feeling unable to make the journey to Osiwa. [You in Samarai will be sorry to hear that "King Mak" has become rather frail.]

Because of my colleague's death, I have been obliged to depend more than I should have wished on the Government Interpreter OSANA. He is, however, increasingly indispensable.

Through OSANA, I have collected much direct testimony, and more rumours, concerning the events leading up to the rioting.

It now seems clear that the instigator of all the trouble was DIPAPA, the former chief. The man METUSELA, who was almost certainly insane, was merely a cats'-paw. DIPAPA saw in METUSELA's embryo cargo-cult a chance to destroy the institution of the chieftainship itself. In this he was motivated by spite against his heir, the present chief, BENONI.

Rumours that METUSELA was removed by a "flying saucer" will probably persist for a long time, as DIPAPA, their originator, intended. I myself have little doubt that METUSELA was murdered, either by DIPAPA himself or by people acting on his behalf.

DIPAPA died on November 17th, 1959, three days after Mr Cawdor, and there is a strong suspicion that he was poisoned by his youngest wife, SENUBETA, using part of a well-known local fish. However, out of respect for local sensitivities, I have cancelled plans for a post-mortem. This would almost certainly be inconclusive, given the limited facilities at our disposal and the likely state of the body, which was interred 12 hours after death.

Though the woman SENUBETA was once the mistress of the new chief, BENONI, there is no suggestion from any quarter that BENONI was implicated in his uncle's removal. I have the highest hopes of this young man, who is personally and intellectually impressive. Under his leadership much of the damage caused by the rioting has been repaired, and though not himself a Christian, he has sent messengers by canoe to both the Methodist and Roman Catholic Missions at Osiwa, with a view to restoring the church used by METUSELA to its original purpose.

The illness and death of Mr Alistair Cawdor, PO Osiwa, has distressed people throughout the islands. Though his irrational mental state in the last weeks of his life has contributed to our difficulties, we remember him as a tireless worker, and a remarkable diplomat. It could perhaps be said that he came on the scene a little too early in the Territory's history.

According to Dr Johannes Buchmann, MO Osiwa, Mr Cawdor would have been unlikely to survive this form of malaria, and had probably already suffered brain damage. The injuries inflicted were appalling, at least to the eye of a layman like myself. I saw the body on board the *Eagle* as soon as she arrived at Osiwa. It was so covered with dried blood that it was unrecognizable as the body of a European. The effect was best summed up by SAYAM, native skipper of the *Eagle*, who said to me: "Now he is a black man true."

Arrangements are being made through Konedobu for the transfer of Mr T. A. Dalwood, CPO Osiwa, to a posting in the Southern Highlands. He had coped admirably with this crisis, and is in every way one of the most promising young officers I have known.

A sad sequel to the event at Vilakota was the death of Mr Cawdor's houseboy, KAILUSA, who committed suicide by leaping from a coconut-palm on November 16th. He was deformed, and his exact age is given by the Methodist Mission as 37. According to OSANA, such a man could never have had any kind of sexual experience in his life, and his devotion to Mr Cawdor, and previously to Mr Cawdor's estranged wife, reflected this.

Prayers were said for the repose of the souls of Mr Cawdor and KAILUSA at both Missions. At the request of Mrs Alison Cawdor they were buried in the same grave, near the house formerly occupied by Mr and Mrs Cawdor, and beside the young American anthropologist who died of blackwater fever. The funeral, among this naturally demonstrative people, was very moving.

It is an indication of Mr Cawdor's confusion of mind that his last note, scribbled on the fly-leaf of Prescott's *Conquest of Mexico*, was written in the local language, though addressed to Mr Dalwood, who does not speak it. As translated by OSANA, it reads:
"Timi, my younger brother Timi:
Do not be sorry. Everything will be good, yes,
everything will be good, yes, every kind of
thing will be good."
Father Galagher believes that this note contains a quotation from English. When the exact words have been ascertained, they will be inscribed on the stone which Mrs Cawdor proposes to erect.

[I can guess what impression you in Samarai must have of Alistair. I only ask you to consider that it could have happened to you.]

OSANA

Who spoke to the people about the star-machine and the *Mina-uluwa*?
Mister Cawdor.
Who caused the destruction of Olumata and Obomatu?
Mister Cawdor.
Who caused the death of the boy Teava at Olumata?
Mister Cawdor.
Who caused somebody to murder Metusela?
Mister Cawdor.
Who caused Senubeta to poison Dipapa?
Naibusi, because of Mister Cawdor.
Who killed Kailusa?
Mister Cawdor.
What caused Mister Cawdor?

NAIBUSI

Alistea i lukwegu, tuta ka sisu o veranda, i livala: "O Naibus', nanogu sena mwau." I livala: "A katoulo." I livala: "A doki ba kaliga. Magigu ba kaliga. Gala magigu ba nagowa. . .

OSANA

The old woman say: Alistair said to me, when we were on the veranda, he said: "O Naibusi, my mind is very heavy." He said: "I am sick." He said: "I think I am going to die. I want to die. I do not want to be mad. I am mad now, Naibusi, and I will not be better. It is like somebody inside me, like a visitor. It is like my body is a house, and some visitor has come, and attacked the person who lived there." He said: "O Naibus'. O my mother. My house is echoing with the footsteps of the visitor, and the person who lived there before is dying. That person is bleeding. My house is bleeding to death."